# Texas
# Rose
*always*

Jennifer,
Thanks for joining
The Katis. I hope
you will Texas Rose
Always. Happy reading,
Katherine
Garbera

# ALSO BY KATIE GRAYKOWSKI

## The Marilyns
*Place Your Betts*

*Getting Lucky*

## The Lone Stars
*Perfect Summer*

*Saving Grace*

*Changing Lanes*

*The Debra Dilemma*

## PTO Murder Club Mystery
*Rest in Pieces*

*Blown To Pieces*

## Texas Rose Ranch
*Texas Rose Forever*

A TEXAS ROSE
RANCH NOVEL

# Texas
# Rose
# *always*

## Katie
## Graykowski

Montlake
Romance

Published by Montlake Romance, Seattle

www.apub.com

Amazon, the Amazon logo, and Montlake Romance are trademarks of Amazon.com, Inc., or its affiliates.

ISBN-13: 9781503950733
ISBN-10: 1503950735

Cover design by Damonza

Printed in the United States of America

*For Aunt Virginia—lover of Big Red, dark pink
lipstick, hair spray, and French fried potatoes.
Give Uncle Virgil a kiss from me.*

# PROLOGUE

*Burning Man—The Playa*

Black Rock City, Nevada, which was also known as the Playa to Burning Man festival participants, was beautiful in its arid desolation. With the mountains in the distance and miles upon miles of open, flat desert, it was a land of possibility . . . as long as you provided your own electricity, ingenuity, and water.

Once a year, Rowdy Rose traded in his Hugo Boss suits and Gucci loafers for Birkenstocks and cutoffs and became a Burner to embrace the radical self-expression that was Burning Man. Here, he was Houston—his actual first name—and that's it. No last name, no commitments, no timetables, and no regrets.

Except one.

Every year he left Daisy—his Burner Only girlfriend and his heart—in Black Rock City while he counted the days until he could see her again. For one week a year, Daisy was his soul mate. Anything longer would equal a commitment, and he wasn't sure that either of them was ready for that.

But commitment wasn't the only issue. He didn't think Daisy would still love him if she knew the person he pretended to be when he wasn't at Burning Man. He was the second-oldest son of the Rose family, which owned the Texas Rose Ranch, one of the largest ranches in Texas, and he didn't fit the rugged country lifestyle he'd grown up with.

Where his family was practical, he was creative. Where they ranched cattle, he made wine. Where they wore boots and jeans, he preferred tailored designer suits and Gucci loafers. He hid his artistic side from them because he didn't feel like they'd understand it. In fact, the idea of actually sharing his paintings with them, the most vulnerable part of himself, made him feel physically ill.

Daisy was the only person in the world with whom he shared his creative self, and if it was all the same, he'd like to keep it that way. It wasn't that his family wasn't understanding, it was just that he couldn't bear the thought of them realizing that he wasn't like them. He'd always felt like a fish swimming in a herd of cattle—different, apart, alone. Burning Man was the only place Houston truly felt that he could be himself.

"So you're taking one last crack at the effigy before he burns tonight?" Daisy handed him a cold bottle of water, and he took a moment to drink her in. With her long blond hair and green eyes, she was the most beautiful woman he'd ever seen. She was a natural beauty who never wore makeup of any sort, and her skin's healthy glow and ready smile were among her best features. The first time he'd seen her, she'd been handing out daisies. Their eyes met, and he just knew that she was his and he was hers. Still, he'd managed to walk by her several times before he'd half teasingly asked her to marry him. He always wondered what would have happened if she'd said yes.

Rowdy put his watercolor palette down on a stool and downed the bottle of water. He wanted to finish painting the wooden man before the Burning Man effigy was reduced to ashes. He was almost there. He set the empty bottle down next to the stool and the two bottles of wine that he and Daisy had sipped their way through all day.

Maybe wine wasn't the best drink choice under the hot desert sun, but it certainly made spending the day way more fun.

This was their last night together—tomorrow he'd kiss Daisy good-bye, return the RV, and catch a flight back to normalcy. The future weighed heavily on his shoulders. He'd go back to a life that he liked but didn't love.

Every single year, it got harder and harder to leave her. Since they were Burning Man Only, he knew little of her life outside of the festival, and she knew even less about his. All they knew of each other was what they had shared over the five years they'd been coming to Burning Man.

"Why don't you ever paint yourself into the picture?" She leaned in to get a better view.

"I don't know. I guess when it comes to Burning Man, I only see you."

"One day, I hope you actually paint both of us." She kissed him on the cheek. "Now, I think you need a little Towanda."

"I still don't know what that even means." But he really didn't care. "Towanda" was the battle cry she used right before she did something crazy like shuck off all of her clothes so they could make love under the effigy, which was exactly what she was doing at this moment.

God, he loved this woman, but she sure as hell wouldn't fit into his everyday life. She was wild and crazy and wore her heart on her sleeve. She was everything he wanted to be but wouldn't dare let himself. He couldn't afford to be that vulnerable.

An hour later, after they'd properly christened the effigy, they lay side by side, staring up at the intricately built wooden flying saucer that served as the base of this year's effigy. Dust swirled around them in little dirt devils. On the Playa, dust was part of the experience. It coated everything and tended to invade uncovered orifices.

"Ever thought about meeting in real life?" Daisy asked matter-of-factly.

"No . . . and yes." He didn't want to risk what they had. So many times he'd been on the verge of giving her his contact info, but he knew part of their magic was seeing each other only once a year. Here, their love was perfect. Here, he didn't analyze it for flaws or worry that things wouldn't work out. Here, he let his guard down so she could see the side of him he couldn't share with anyone else. "I'm not sure that our relationship would work outside of Burning Man."

That was the understatement of the century.

She propped her chin on her fist and watched him. "I don't agree. One day, I'd like a family, and since I'm in love with you, I feel like it should be with you."

"Um . . . well . . . uhhhhh. A family." He truly had no idea what he was supposed to say.

She quirked an eyebrow up. "You're doing that thing that you do when you're trying to figure out what I want to hear."

God, she knew him so well.

"The truth, please." She wasn't going to give up. One of the things he loved most about her was the fact that she was always honest. It was also one of the things he liked least about her. Honest people tended to tell the truth . . . all of the time, even when it hurt others.

"Okay, I don't see myself as a family man." He hated to burst her bubble, but she wanted the truth. "I don't want kids, in fact, it's kind of a deal breaker for me. Kids are messy and clingy and always sick. I'd make a terrible father and an even worse husband."

"Why do you say that?" She didn't sound angry, just curious. "Did you have a hard childhood?"

"No, not at all. I love my parents, it's just . . ." It wasn't that his childhood had been difficult, it was more that he'd been a difficult child. He'd been artistic and whimsical in a family that didn't understand artistic and whimsical.

"What?" Now she was getting upset. "Why do I have to pull information out of you? I know you like to live in the moment, but I'd like to know more about you."

"I'm an artist who makes wine. I'm in love with you. What more do you need to know?" Now he was getting upset. Everything between them was perfect. Why was she trying to rock the boat?

She sat up and slipped her T-shirt on over her head. "I get that we're Burning Man Only. I understand that. It's just that I'd like to be able to text or email you sometimes. I think of you every single day, and I guess I just want to know that you do too."

She stood and looked around . . . probably for her shorts. He took her hand and gently pulled her down on top of him.

"You are my first thought in the morning and my last thought in the evening. I count the days and sometimes the hours and minutes until I can see you again. If you need more than Burning Man . . ." He shifted her so that she was straddling him. "That's all I can give you right now, but I do love you."

---

Daisy grinned so hard that she almost ground her teeth to dust. After a week with him, she'd finally worked up the courage to tell Houston that he was a father to a beautiful three-month-old son, but he'd shut her down . . . cold . . . practically slammed the door in her face.

What was she supposed to do now? Somehow, presenting him with the "World's Best Dad" mug she'd stuffed in her suitcase didn't feel like the best idea.

Houston didn't want children . . . he didn't want his son. She knew what it felt like to be unwanted, and she would not let that happen to her son. She already loved him enough for two parents. This week, Hugh was staying with her father and stepmother, who absolutely adored him. Maybe that was all the family her son would know.

She actually felt her heart break. Houston's rejection wasn't like in the movies where the heroine drops to the ground, overcome with sadness. No, it was more of a tiny tearing deep in her soul. There would be no happily ever after. She wouldn't get to spend the next eighty or so years with the love of her life, surrounded by their children and grandchildren.

She should end things with Houston, right here and now, but she'd couldn't get the words to come out of her mouth.

Tears burned her eyes. She needed to get out of here . . . she needed some alone time.

She pointed to the watercolor he'd been working on before she'd Towanda-ed him. "Why don't you finish up and then meet me back at the RV? I'm going to, um . . ." Her voice wobbled. "Finish packing."

He scrutinized her face for any sign of distress, so she stapled on her I'm-fine smile. He kissed her cheek and returned to his painting. "Okay, I'll only be an hour or so."

Holding in her tears made her chest hurt, but she made it all the way back to the motor home that they shared. She pulled open the door, made it up the two steps, closed the door, and sank onto the beige banquette seat that horseshoed the small kitchen table. Reaching under the table, she pulled out her old brown leather tote. She unzipped the bag and pulled out the small photo album she'd carefully put together for him.

It seemed ridiculous now—all the time she'd spent combing through the gazillions of photos she'd taken of their son. She'd been so worried about picking just the right ones to show to Houston. Never in a million years had she ever thought they wouldn't end up together.

Warm tears slid down her cheeks. She'd made a mess of things, and now her son would never know his father.

# CHAPTER 1

*Seven years later*

Justus Jacobi loved the country . . . in theory. Being a landscape designer, she appreciated Mother Nature's style, but the lack of pizza delivery and not-so-close proximity to a grocery store could make life complicated. Or so she imagined. She'd never lived anywhere but downtown Austin.

She sighed long and hard and looked over at her seven-year-old son, Hugh. She'd given up one life in return for another, and it was fulfilling and wonderful, but it had cost her the man she loved.

On purpose, she'd started a new job today to take her mind off the fact that Burning Man was this week, and this was her first year missing the festival. It was the right thing to do. She was leaving the past in the past and making a future with her son. She was done wanting what she couldn't have.

No doubt, right now, Houston was looking for her. How long would it take before he realized she wasn't coming?

She rolled her eyes and wanted to slap herself out of all of this self-pity, but taking the high road was so far out of the way.

Would she ever find a man that she loved as much as she loved Houston?

Doing the right thing didn't make her heart less broken. Last year, she'd broached the subject of having a family with him for the last time. Since their first discussion all those years ago, he hadn't changed his mind . . . nope, not one little bit.

Her baby boy was getting older and starting to ask questions about his father, and sneaking away to see a man who didn't want her for more than a week felt wrong. She needed more, and that realization had set her on a path that ended at the Texas Rose Ranch.

She glanced over at Hugh, sitting on the truck's bench seat next to her.

Hugh had his father's eyes and hair color and a quest for knowledge that came from who knows where. He had her nose and that was pretty much it. Nine months of pregnancy and forty hours of labor, and all she got was a nose. If he wasn't the cutest thing in the world, she'd be offended.

"Turn right here, baby," Elvis Presley's voice crooned from the Garmin GPS she'd velcroed to the dash of her 1952 Chevy work truck. What the truck lacked in modern convenience it certainly made up for in style. The only addition, besides the Garmin, were seat belts. Safety first.

"Mommy, did you know that in Kentucky it's illegal to carry ice cream in your back pockets?" Hugh laughed. Her son loved him some facts. Ever since he'd started reading, he couldn't get enough of them.

"Seems kind of messy." She took her eyes off the road only long enough to check out what he was reading. *The Book of Useless Information.* "If we ever go to Kentucky, remind me not to store my ice cream in my back pockets."

She turned as Elvis instructed.

"In Paris it's against the law to stare at the mayor." Hugh's round, tortoiseshell glasses magnified his serious, aqua-blue eyes.

She was doing the right thing. Houston was in the past. Her little boy was the only future she needed. Maybe if she said it a bazillion times, she'd actually believe it? Kind of like Dorothy and the ruby slippers. If she said, "I don't love Houston," three times and clicked her heels, it would come true. She really needed some ruby slippers. She had some red Converses, would those work?

Her gaze went back to the two-track road that she'd been told the family used instead of the grand entrance for tourists. Five minutes later, she pulled in front of a giant white limestone four-story house that looked like a gothic Alamo, complete with turrets. The pictures she'd been sent didn't do the house justice.

Elvis announced, "We're here. Until we meet again, may God bless you as he has blessed me."

She put the truck in park, turned off the engine, and opened the door. She needed to get a three-sixty view. She'd received photos and measurements, but now that she saw the surrounding grounds, she mentally adjusted the drawings she'd done of the proposed landscaping to account for the scale of the house.

"Wait for me." Hugh unclicked his seat belt, opened his own door, and hopped down. She would love to have helped him, but he'd announced three months ago, on his seventh birthday, that he was old enough to do some things by himself and that hand-holding was strictly forbidden. "In Texas, it's illegal to put graffiti on someone else's cow."

"I'll have to tell that to my husband and sons in case they take up tagging the neighbor's cows."

Justus turned around to find a woman close to her height of five foot two with large, aqua-blue eyes and a no-nonsense blond bob. The lady held out her hand. "I'm Lucy Rose."

Justus shook her hand. The woman's handshake was firm but not bone crushing. "I'm Justus Jacobi. Nice to meet you. So you're the birthday girl."

Justus had been hired by the Rose sons to landscape the main house and surrounding areas as a present for their mother's birthday.

"My birthday is next month, and I'm too old be called a girl." The older woman squatted down in front of Hugh and held out her hand. "You must be Hugh. Nice to meet you."

Hugh nodded once and shook her hand. "Nice to meet you too. Did you know that in Arizona it's illegal to hunt camels?"

"I did not. That's good to know. If I ever take up camel hunting, I'll remember to stay clear of Arizona." The older woman grinned, and her eyes took in every detail of his face. "You look familiar, have we met?"

Hugh scrunched up his face and thought about it. "No ma'am. I don't think so."

Justus ruffled her son's blond hair. They'd been working on manners, and clearly he'd paid attention. Not even a year ago, he'd have hidden behind her legs and peeked out at a new acquaintance. Now, he was seven going on forty.

Mrs. Rose straightened. "Mrs. Jacobi—"

"Call me Justus." She didn't like to interrupt people, but her stepmother was the only Mrs. Jacobi in the family. God knew her mother, aka the egg donor, hadn't kept that title any longer than she'd had to.

"Call me Lucy." She grinned as she looped her arm through Justus's and held her hand out for Hugh. He took it.

"Why don't you come in? I was about to sit down to lunch, and I'd love it if you two join me. I'm sure you're hungry after your long ride from Austin. After lunch, I'll show you to the cottage where you'll be staying, and you can unpack." Lucy led them up the front porch steps to the front door.

"If you live in Michigan, it's illegal to put a skunk in your boss's desk." Hugh looked up at Lucy to make sure she was listening. "I'm learning facts about every state in the US."

"Good for you. Wait until you meet my husband. He loves random facts. The two of you can go at it for hours." Lucy glanced at Justus and nodded at Hugh. "He's just about the cutest thing I've ever seen."

"I know . . . right? I have the best kid in the world." Justus couldn't help but like this woman, who was obviously an excellent judge of kids. Heck, she'd raised five sons, so the woman practically had a PhD in little boy. "He's so much fun."

"In California, it's illegal to eat oranges in the bathtub." Lucy waggled her eyebrows at Hugh. "My husband laid that fact on me on our first date. To this day, I can't figure out how they regulate it. The last time I went to California, I ate three oranges while taking a bath. Nothing happened. It was disappointing."

"Fresno, California, is the raisin capital of the world." His tone suggested that he was throwing out that fact by way of consolation. "I don't like raisins."

"Me either. If you're going to eat a grape, you should eat it before it gets all dried up." Lucy turned a huge iron doorknob and the right side of the double front doors swung open. "I don't mind them in oatmeal raisin cookies."

"My mom makes the best oatmeal cookies. She leaves the raisins out for me." Hugh looked around and glanced up at Lucy. "You live here all by yourself?"

"No, my husband and our housekeeper live here too. I have five sons, but they all live in their own houses now." She followed his eyes. "I know it's a big house. It's been in my husband's family for generations. I'm hoping your mom can make the outside look good."

In the living room there were groupings of overstuffed brown leather furniture, colorful knickknacks, and off-white throw rugs. Very Pottery Barn.

Justus eyed the many houseplants. The woman liked greenery. In her experience, that was a sign of good people. To date, she'd never heard of a serial killer who liked houseplants. Maybe it was the exchange of carbon dioxide to oxygen that plants provided. Highly oxygenated people tended to be happier, so they didn't grab an ax and go all Lizzie

Borden on the world around them. "Did you have a chance to review the drawings I sent?"

"Yes, they are fantastic. I like how you make everything look like it belongs here. I hate landscaping that doesn't fit the natural flow of the land. It should look like it was always here."

"I agree. I try to use native plants. Don't get me wrong, I like a pop of color here and there, but I think the beauty of the land should show through." Relief relaxed the tense muscles at the back of her neck. Although Justus prided herself on playing to the strengths of whatever environment she was working with, she'd had more than one client who'd wanted a tricked-out English garden in hot and dry central Texas. The flowers they insisted on died about ten seconds after she planted them under the hot southern sun.

"I think we're going to get along just fine." Lucy nodded. "Oh, I'm supposed to tell you that CanDee really wanted to be here, but unfortunately, she is out of town."

"Yes, in New York, hashing out the details of her publishing contract. She texted me. I'm so happy for her. I can't wait to meet Cinco." Her best friend had come to the Texas Rose Ranch a few months ago to write the family history and had met Mr. Right in Cinco Rose, the oldest of the Rose sons. She was about to become CanDee Rose.

"Aunt CanDee is coming home next week." Hugh looked around like he was taking mental notes on the house. Her little boy could be so intense at times, which never ceased to make her smile.

Lucy led them to a sunny room with windows on three walls. It was filled with potted ficus and rubber trees, bromeliads, violets, and several varieties of orchids. In the middle of the room was a beautiful and dainty dining set of whitewashed wrought iron table and chairs. Without a doubt this was the most charming room Justus had ever seen. "This is fantastic."

She noticed that the table was set for three. So lunch had been planned. It was sweet that a woman she'd just met had thought of her and her son.

"I thought you might like this room. It's my favorite, except for one thing." She dropped Justus's arm and pointed to the back wall of windows. "My view is about as exciting as a moonscape."

Even in the sunshine of the September morning, the only thing appealing about the side yard was a huge old pecan tree that was begging for a tire swing. Her palms itched to dig in the dirt. She pulled at the pale green cotton dress she was wearing. It was way too clean. She needed to get her hands in some good, honest mud.

"I was hoping we could add a few more jobs." Lucy smiled nervously. "Can you stay longer?"

Justus evaluated the side yard and imagined one long, meandering crushed granite path that went from the house to the pecan tree. Or maybe not crushed granite . . . mortared limestone or fieldstone. She changed gears and pulled up her mental calendar. She was scheduled to be here two months and didn't have anything pressing after. "I'm happy to stay."

The Roses were paying her top dollar. More work here would go a long way toward a down payment for a house. With the rents in Austin skyrocketing, it was time for her to buy something of her own, plus they'd outgrown their one-bedroom apartment. Her baby boy needed his own bedroom, and they both needed a little privacy.

A squawking noise from over her left shoulder drew her attention. Justus turned around to find a large, bright red macaw sitting on the perch inside a huge wrought iron cage located in the corner of the room. "Maybe I didn't love you quite as often as I should have."

"I wish I had an Oscar Meyer wiener." This from a second bird . . . possibly a cockatiel . . . in a matching cage next to it.

"Don't mind them. That's Coke and Dr. Pepper. They belong to my twin sons and have picked up some bad manners and interesting sayings over the years." She shook her head. "I'm still not sure why they live with me instead of my sons."

"Have a Coke and a smile." It was the cockatiel.

"I love you like a fat kid loves cake," the macaw shot back.

"Oh good, now Dr. Pepper is quoting 50 Cent." Lucy rolled her eyes. "You never get used to it."

So Lucy Rose knew who 50 Cent was? For some reason, that made Justus like her even more.

"Cool." Hugh went straight to the cages and looked up, transfixed.

Dr. Pepper jerked his head like he was nodding. "Save a horse, ride a cowboy."

"Bounty, the quicker picker upper." Coke used his beak to climb down off his perch so he could be closer to Hugh.

Hugh held his index finger out and looked like he was about to stick it between the bars of the cage.

"No, baby. Don't stick your hand in the cage." Justus rushed to her son.

Hugh turned around and shot her a look with one eyebrow up. She was strictly forbidden to call him "baby," even in private. Now that she thought about it, he'd been so much cuter before he'd turned seven.

"It's fine. They won't bite." Lucy walked up behind them. "Watch this."

She opened Coke's cage and patted her left forearm. Coke flew over to her and landed on her forearm. "Can you open that bottle of water on the table, pour some into the cap, and lay the cap on the floor?"

Justus rushed over and filled the cap. She set it on the floor and stepped back.

"Coke, do you want to stretch your legs?" Lucy bent over and put him on the floor, and then she turned her back on him.

"Taste the rainbow." The bird looked back at Lucy and then the cap of water and then back at Lucy. Once he was satisfied that she wasn't watching, he ran over to the cap, used his beak to pick it up, and downed the water.

Lucy turned around. "Who drank my water?"

Coke used his left foot to push the cap behind him and refused to make eye contact.

"Coke, did you drink my water?" Lucy folded her arms.

His head bobbed up and down, and then he hung his head as he shuffled back to the cage.

Justus had never seen anything like it. She clapped.

"Wow. Does the other bird do tricks?" Hugh pushed his glasses back up.

"Make a gun with your hand and shoot Dr. Pepper. Say 'bang' when you shoot him." Lucy patted her right shoulder and Coke flew to it.

Hugh stuck out his index finger and cocked his thumb. "Bang."

Dr. Pepper stumbled around on his perch and then listed to the side, twitched, and closed his eyes.

Lucy walked over to his cage and said, "Oops, gun wasn't loaded."

Dr. Pepper popped up. "Don't let your babies grow up to be cowboys."

Justus and Hugh clapped.

Hugh watched Dr. Pepper. "How did you teach them that?"

"I didn't. My sons did." She put Coke back in his cage. "I'll introduce them to you at dinner tonight." She looked over at Justus. "That is, if you'll come to dinner tonight."

"We would love to." Justus liked Lucy Rose and couldn't wait to build her the garden of her dreams.

# CHAPTER 2

Later that afternoon, Justus stared at the contents of her suitcase. What was she supposed to wear for dinner at the main house? She hadn't brought any dressy clothes, but then again, she really didn't see Lucy Rose as a dressy person. She pulled out a white cotton dress and some red wedges.

She slipped on the dress and then walked into the tiny bathroom of the one-room cottage where she and Hugh were staying and used the mirror above the sink to make sure that she looked presentable. The bathroom was a simple affair with walls painted a light blue that contrasted nicely with the claw-foot tub, which was original to the hundred-year-old house.

After smoothing on some red-tinted lip gloss and a little mascara, she was pretty much ready.

Hugh was sitting in one of the old, dark brown leather chairs that surrounded a huge round wood-burning fireplace in the middle of the cottage. He was reading his fact book. Her son had gone more casual in a pair of jeans, black Converses, and his favorite Minions T-shirt. As a finishing touch, he'd added a red Superman cape. Since her little boy had wanted independence, which involved picking out his clothes and dressing himself, she didn't judge. His outfits were often hilarious, so she chose to laugh with him instead of micromanaging his wardrobe.

"Ready, buddy?" She walked to him and fought the urge to hold out her hand.

"I think so." He looked down at the page so he could memorize the page number, a trick her father had taught him, and then closed the book.

"How do I look?" She did a runway twirl.

He shrugged. "You look very . . ." He pushed his glasses up. "Clean."

"You do wonders for my self-esteem." She ruffled his hair.

They walked across the field that separated the cottage from the main house and knocked on the front door.

A man, more than six foot tall in his late twenties with dark brown hair and baby-blue eyes, opened the door. He grinned, and matching dimples popped out on his cheeks. He held out his hand. "I'm Dallas Rose, you must be Justus."

She shook his hand.

"Come in." He stepped aside and then bent down. "You must be Hugh. My brother Worth and I have been waiting to meet you."

Hugh pushed his glasses up and then held out his hand. "Nice to meet you."

Dallas's grin got wider. "My brother and I are having the checker world championships tonight and we need someone to play the winner. Think you could help us out?"

Hugh looked up at his mother for approval.

Justus nodded.

"Yes." Hugh nodded vigorously.

"Whew." Dallas made a big show of wiping his brow. "That's a load off of my mind. I thought we were going to have to ask my dad to play the winner, and he's terrible at checkers." He arched an eyebrow. "You look like a checkers champion."

"Did he say yes?" A man who looked exactly like Dallas walked down the hall toward them.

"Yep. I talked him into it." Dallas held out his hand for Hugh, who took it.

So everyone else was welcome to hold her little boy's hand but her?

"Justus and Hugh, this is my twin brother, Worth, short for Fort Worth." They walked down the hall to the dining room.

"Dallas and Fort Worth, those are interesting names." Justus liked the men, and they seemed to really want to hang out with her son. She'd fretted about bringing him and not having child care, but the Rose family seemed to like children. Still, these men were strangers, so she'd go to the checker match just to watch.

"Our parents named us after the cities where they think we were conceived. Apparently it was a very fun weekend, because they couldn't decide if we were created in Dallas or Fort Worth."

"What's conswived mean?" Hugh glanced at his mother.

"Made." She winked at him. They'd had the sex talk and were continuing to have it, but thank God he didn't put two and two together and come up with "conceived" equals "making babies."

Hugh looked up at Dallas. "Did you know that some forest fires are started by lightning?"

"Actually, I did know that. We had a really big fire here like a hundred years ago that was started by lightning." Dallas leaned down and stage-whispered, "Maybe we can talk your mom into letting us take you to the watchtower. It's super high in the sky and they used it to watch for fire. Now we just have cameras everywhere to monitor the ranch."

"Can I?" Hugh turned excited eyes on his mother.

"As long as it's safe, I'm good with it." Plus, she would go with them. She caught Dallas's eye. "Thanks in advance."

"It will be fun. I need someone else around who appreciates adventure." Dallas huffed out a breath dramatically. "Worth over there is about as exciting as watching paint dry."

"Hey, I'm right here. I can hear you." Worth rolled his eyes and turned to Justus. "Dallas may be chatty, but I got the brains. I definitely got the better end of the deal."

"There you are." Lucy walked toward them. "I hope Dallas didn't talk your ear off."

"See." Worth threw up his hands. "Chatty."

"Your jealousy is noted. Just because everybody likes me doesn't mean that you have to be rude." Dallas put a hand over his heart. "It's a burden to be so popular, no matter what all of those mean girl movies say. It's hard work."

"That's it. No more *Glee* episodes for you. I'm cutting you off. You're going cold turkey. It will be hard, but you can do it." Worth clapped his brother on the back.

"It's good to get in touch with your inner mean girl. If I ever get into a girl fight, I've got to be able to defend myself." Dallas walked Hugh over to Lucy. "Mom, make him stop being mean to me."

"Mean? You think this is mean?" Worth put his twin in a headlock and noogied his hair.

"Don't make me get out my stun gun, because I will, and I'll sort of feel bad after using it . . . sort of." Lucy let out a long, exasperated breath and slipped her arm through Justus's. "Let me introduce you to my husband." There was pride in the older woman's voice.

Stun gun? Maybe she should supervise all of her son's adventures with the Rose family. Only, she really liked Lucy and her family. They were open and loving and really seemed to enjoy each other's company. But . . . stun gun?

"This is Kendall Lehman Rose the Fourth, but we call him Bear." Lucy led her to a huge, burly man with kind blue eyes and dark hair.

"It's so nice to meet you." Justus stuck out her hand and he shook it. She expected his grip to be bone crushing, but it was firm yet gentle. She got the impression that he was a firm yet gentle person.

"It's good to meet you." Bear's eyes flickered to Hugh. "I hear you have a son who likes facts as much as I do."

Hugh and Dallas came to stand next to her.

Bear took a knee. "Did you know that the chocolate chip cookie was invented in 1937?"

Hugh's large eyes went huge. "No, I didn't. Did you know that ketchup was invented in China?"

Bear shook his head. "Good to know. Fortune cookies don't come from China, they come from San Francisco."

"Really?" Hugh had found a kindred spirit. "San Francisco once had a law that said that ugly people couldn't show their faces in public."

"You made that up." Bear grinned down at Hugh.

"Did not. It's in my fact book back at the cottage." Hugh looked back at Justus. "Can I go get it and show him?"

"After dinner." She nodded. "We'll walk back over and you can get it."

"Did you know that caterpillars have four thousand muscles? That's a lot." Hugh would not be outfacted.

"A large swarm of locusts can eat two-hundred-thousand tons of food in a day." Bear Rose could hold his own.

Lucy led her to the table. "Those two will be at it for a while. Let me introduce you to Mary, our housekeeper."

She led Justus through the large dining room.

"I'm not sure I should leave him. I mean, he doesn't really know anyone here." She hoped that didn't sound like she didn't trust the Rose family.

"He's fine. Bear loves kids. That's why we had so many. He kept saying, 'just one more.'" Lucy shook her head. "Hooked me every time."

They stepped into a bright, cheerful lemon-yellow kitchen that was big enough to feed a small hotel.

"Justus, this is Mary, our keeper of house and order." Lucy grinned up at Mary. "Mary this is Justus, she and her son, Hugh, will be staying with us for a while. She's going to make the outside of my house as pretty as the inside."

"Now, Dr. Rose, we talked about this. When company comes over, you're supposed to ring the bell, and then I come out and serve the food. You're not supposed to bring the guests back here." Mary had to be almost six foot tall with wiry gray hair that was scraped into tight curls at her scalp. Her black maid's dress and crisp white apron were straight out of *The Brady Bunch*. Justus judged her to be about sixty-five.

"Dr. Rose?" Crapola, Justus had no idea Lucy was a doctor. Thank goodness the woman didn't stand on ceremony.

"I'm chief of surgery at Roseville Hospital, but I prefer Lucy. Only Mary refuses to call me that."

Mary shook her head. "It just isn't proper. Mrs. Rose is probably rolling in her grave right now."

"Mrs. Rose was my mother-in-law and Mary's first employer. She died over two decades ago, and Mary runs the house now." Lucy leaned up on her tippy-toes and kissed the old woman on the cheek. "She's the glue that keeps this family together."

Mary flushed. "Now, Dr. Rose, that's not true."

Clearly Mary loved this family as much as the family loved her.

"Okay, we'll get out of your hair. I just wanted to introduce Justus to the family." Lucy led her back into the dining room.

"In Cleveland, it used to be against the law to catch mice without a hunting license." Bear now held Hugh propped on his hip.

Okay, Bear Rose was definitely a kid lover. He grinned from ear to ear and seemed as delighted with her son as her son was with him.

"In Oklahoma it used to be against the law to hunt whales." Hugh grinned. Her little boy loved having the last word.

"In Kansas, it's against the law to catch fish with your hands." Bear showed no signs of stopping.

"I'm sorry that I can't introduce you to my other three sons, but Cinco—Kendall Lehman Rose the Fifth, is off with CanDee. San

Antonio—T-Bone—is at Texas A&M getting his PhD, and Rowdy, who you've been corresponding with online, is out of town."

"Yes, but doing what?" Dallas grinned at his mother.

"One week a year, Rowdy goes on a mysterious vacation. He's been doing it for over a decade, and he won't tell us where he goes." Lucy shrugged. "The family and the ranch hands all have different theories."

Dallas made sure Hugh was out of earshot. He whispered, "I think he's having an affair with a married woman . . . well, Worth and I both do. This woman must only be able to get away one week a year."

She appreciated that he'd thought of Hugh and hadn't blurted that out.

"Mom thinks he's gay and so in the closet that he only allows himself to be who he really is once a year." Dallas heaved a dramatic sigh that would have made the Disney Channel proud. "That makes me sad."

"We just want him to be happy." Worth nodded. He was completely serious.

"Our baby brother, T-Bone, thinks he's a spy—"

"He ain't no spy. He's a cat burglar."

Justus turned around to find a stooped, craggy-faced old man with an eye patch over his right eye. Was that a rhinestone butterfly on the eye patch?

Lucy put her arm around the old man. "This is Lefty. He's in charge of everything with an engine on the ranch."

Lefty's one keen eye landed on Justus. "I hope you ain't gonna be as much trouble as your friend CanDee." His words might have been harsh, but his tone wasn't.

"I'll be on my best behavior." She stuck out her hand. "I'm Justus."

He pumped it once. "Is that your '52 Chevy parked at the cottage?" His face softened. "If you ever need any help with her, you let me know. My daddy had one of them. I remember riding in it."

CanDee had told her that Lefty was a bit hard to get along with, but maybe his interest in vintage trucks would give them common ground.

"Why don't you take her out for a spin? I don't have the keys with me now, but drop by anytime and I'll hand them over."

His whole face lit up and slowly he nodded his head. "I'd like that." He slapped her lightly on the shoulder. "Tell you what I'm gonna do in return. I'm gonna fast-track your golf cart application so you can use it around the ranch. I'd hate for . . . what's your truck's name?"

"Imogene." How could she not love this old man? The thought of driving her truck made him look like a little boy on Christmas morning.

"Imogene." He thought about it for a second. "You know, she looks like an Imogene. Anyway, I'd hate for her to take all of them bumps on them dirt roads we got around here, so I'm going to issue you a golf cart. You ain't gotta take the driving test on account of your great taste in trucks."

"Thank you. I'd appreciate that." She smiled at him. "So you're thinking that Rowdy is a cat burglar?"

"Yes ma'am. He's gone the first week of September every single year." Lefty's butterfly twinkled in the light. "Every year I check to see if something expensive shows up stolen on the news." He shook his head. "Rowdy must be really good at it, because I ain't heard about no big-ticket items coming up missing."

"Cinco thinks he's a serial killer and that one week a year he's out hunting for his next victim." Dallas didn't sound like he believed it.

Was her son safe with Rowdy? She'd need to steer clear of him.

"Don't scare her." Lucy patted Justus on the shoulder. "He's not a serial killer."

"Hold on a minute. You said that he takes off the first week of September every year?" The family was way off. "He's a Burner."

"What?" Lucy's brow screwed up.

"He's a Burner. He goes to the Burning Man festival." That's what she would be doing right now if she hadn't decided to leave her past in the dust.

"No, not Rowdy." Lucy shook her head. "Of all of my sons, he's the most buttoned-up. Burning Man's a little too messy for him."

"If you say so." Justus pressed her lips together to keep from smiling. She'd met lots of buttoned-up people at Burning Man.

She couldn't wait to meet Rowdy Rose.

# CHAPTER 3

Houston was either about to make the biggest mistake of his life or possibly achieve total happiness—it was too early to tell.

He'd had eleven whole months to prepare for this morning, but as he stepped out into the stifling September heat and onto the Playa, he felt like he was going to have a panic attack. Not that he'd ever had one, but if there was ever a time to have a panic attack, it was right now.

Over the last year, he'd created a carefully calculated plan to break his eleventh commandment: thou shalt not commit. A ring was too conventional for his Daisy, so he'd had a necklace made. The charm was a tiny, delicate daisy with emeralds for the stem and white diamonds for the petals and a yellow diamond in the center. His Daisy . . . would she take it? Would she agree to be his always? He was ready to commit to her in whatever way she would let him. Whatever commitment looked like to her—whether it was a legal ceremony or a simple promise—he was willing to do it.

He wanted nothing but love between them.

While they'd been in their Burning Man cocoon, he hadn't actually lied about who he was, but he had omitted giant chunks of his life. Now he was ready to come clean. He was going legit and hopefully taking her with him. They would be together . . . always.

He closed the front door of his rented RV and went to find her. He glanced at his watch. Usually she was here by now.

Nerves ping-ponged in his stomach.

This was it. This was going to be the moment when his life really started. By sundown, he would be with Daisy.

The next morning, sunrise came and went, and she still wasn't there.

He waited outside the RV, but there was no sign of her. That didn't mean a thing. She was running late . . . that was all. But every minute that ticked by ate away at the hope in his heart. That night, he made dinner for two because he knew she'd be there.

By day three, Rowdy's heart had shriveled up to the size of a muscadine grape. As he watched a seventy-foot-tall, neon-lighted rainbow dragon roll by, followed by an equally tall Aztec pyramid made out of elbow macaroni, he finally understood that it was over. She wasn't coming. He would never see her again. She had moved on.

Disappointment cut so deep his mind shut down. His heart didn't break so much as die. The longing for her filled every molecule of his soul. She was gone. He would never see her again or smell the coconut scent of her hair or feel her calloused hands rubbing up and down his back. Her golden hair would never fan out on his pillow; he'd never watch her eyes crinkle in the corners when she read something funny or hear her teasing laugh or any of the other eight different but distinct laughs he'd come to love.

She was gone.

All he had of her were memories and his paintings.

She was gone.

He'd blown it. When she'd wanted commitment, he'd pushed her away. It was over.

She was gone.

The fog of loss bear-hugged him. He knew he should get up, walk around, and talk to people, but he didn't have the will or the brainpower to pull it off. So he sat outside of his RV in a folding chair watching the

Burning Man world pass him by and tried not to search the crowd for her face. Why hadn't she come? Had something happened to her? Was she sick? Had she had an accident?

He touched the phone in his back pocket, thinking that he'd call the police and report her as a missing person. He dropped his hand. He didn't even know her real name. All she'd ever been to him was Daisy.

He wanted to wring his own neck for not taking her up on her offer of exchanging email addresses. She brought it up every single year, and he'd always declined. Why had he been so stupid?

He pulled out the necklace that he'd hope she would take and tossed it as hard as he could into what passed for a street in front of him.

He put a hand over his heart in an effort to hold in the pain. All around him the world kept turning, but he wasn't sure he'd ever see things the same again. Daisy was gone. There was no happily ever after for him.

# CHAPTER 4

Five days later, Justus was outside and about to start demolition of the land around the main house. The last four days had been devoted to mapping out plans for six new landscaping projects and putting her life in Austin on hold. She and Hugh would be here for a minimum of six months, if not longer.

Maeve, her stepmother, and her father had packed up Justus's apartment, moved all of her and Hugh's things into storage, and turned in Justus's keys the day before they left for the Alaskan cruise they'd saved up ten years to pay for. Justus's landlord had been more than happy to break the lease because he could get double what she'd paid in rent. With a minimum of six months here and very few expenses, she'd have more than enough for a down payment for a house. By this time next year, she'd be a homeowner.

She did a mental happy dance.

She grabbed a can of orange spray paint, shook it, and clicked it into the marking wand she'd use to outline the beds.

"Hey, Mom, I finished my homework, is it okay if I go with Mr. Bear to do some man stuff?" Because her schedule often took her out of town, she'd always homeschooled him. Hugh ran down the front porch steps of the main house. Since being here, Hugh had charmed everyone on the ranch, especially the matriarch and patriarch. Lucy and Bear Rose seemed starved for grandchildren, and what kid couldn't use some extra grandparents, even if they were stand-ins? Justus had been a little leery at first about having her son hang out with strangers, but the more she got to know the family, the more she liked them.

Plus, Hugh was at the age when every new experience was an adventure. He gladly mucked out horse stalls, fed the chickens, helped stack hay, and was ready to help with any task. He loved the ranch and the Rose family, and all of the ranch hands seemed to like having him around.

Life here was turning out to be wonderful.

"Man stuff? That sounds like fun. You can go, but make sure to help out in any way that you can." She set the marking wand down, squatted down, and opened her arms wide. "Hug."

Hugh wrapped his arms around her neck and hugged her with his whole body. She stood and he dangled around her neck like a bib. She swung him from side to side, and his snorting giggles made her heart smile. He let go and slid down her body, and his cowboy-booted feet hit the ground. She loved how kids did everything at 100 percent. They laughed, loved, and lived at full speed ahead. Adults could learn a thing or two from them.

Lucy had pulled several slightly worn pairs of cowboy boots down from her attic that had belonged to her sons and had given them to Hugh. He had proudly told her that real cowboys only wore cowboy boots and he was a cowboy in training. Today's ensemble included a flame-retardant Batman costume with the pant legs shoved into a pair of dark brown Tony Lamas. His cape fluttered in the breeze.

The front door opened and Bear stepped out. "Ready, Batman?"

"Yes sir." Hugh put his arms out in front of him and "flew" over. "Be back later," he called over his shoulder.

"I'll see you at lunch." She waved. He was getting so big. Just yesterday he was a tiny baby. Tears filled her eyes and she did her best to blink them away. She'd never really thought of herself as a crier, but she was still emotionally raw over Houston, so maybe that was why she teared up at the drop of a hat.

"Hey there, Miss Justus," a husky male voice called from behind her.

She swiped at her tears, turned around, and shaded her eyes from the sun. "Hey there, Lefty."

"I come to test out Imogene." He grinned at Justus's work truck. "You said I could."

"I'll trade you Imogene for a golf cart." She reached into the back pocket of her cutoffs, pulled out a key ring with a single key, and handed it to him.

He took it gingerly, like it was the crown jewels. He nodded to the golf cart parked under an oak tree about fifty yards away. "Number seven is all gassed up and the key's in her." He couldn't keep his eyes off the truck. "I'll be real careful and safe." He looked like a teenaged boy who'd come to take her daughter out on a date. "Is it okay if I take her into town? I'd like to get a feel for her on the open road."

"Knock yourself out." She grinned at him. "Her clutch is a little sluggish from first to second, but other than that, she purrs like a kitten."

"I'll be back real soon. Need anything from town?" He opened Imogene's driver-side door.

"Nope, I'm good." She unrolled the plans for the main house and laid them on the bottom step. She grabbed a couple of small rocks and used them to hold down the sides of the paper.

Lefty waved as he drove off down the dirt two-track that led to the highway.

Using the plans, she began outlining the flower beds and the placement of pipe for the sprinkler system. One hour melted into the next and then the next.

Sweat trickled down her forehead and stung her eyes. She wiped it away with the hem of her tank top. She glanced up at the sun. Based on the fact that it was at its highest point, it had to be close to one. She picked up her forty-ounce purple Hydro Flask and downed the rest of her water.

Hugh was nowhere to be found. They must be doing some really fun "man stuff," because he was late for lunch. She stretched to loosen up her back. Hunching over the plans was wearing on her. It was finally time to start digging. There was nothing better than getting her hands dirty. She'd use the Bobcat for building the actual beds, but she needed to shovel out a path for the main water line. Yesterday, Lefty had showed her the amazing array of machinery parked in the barn closest to the cottage. The Rose family liked them some farm machines, and she couldn't wait to get behind the wheel of the brand-new Bobcat that had just been delivered last week.

Two hours later, she'd found and turned off the main water line to the house and then tied into it. She'd turned the water back on, and the small diverter pipe she'd installed was holding water and not leaking, which was a miracle considering that the pipe she'd tapped into had to be at least ninety years old. Thank God it was copper and not galvanized iron or worse, lead.

She climbed out of the three-foot-deep hole she'd dug to the water-line and glanced down at herself. Her work boots and pretty much her legs all the way to her thighs were covered in orangey-brown mud, her denim cutoffs were splattered with assorted muck, and her tank was wet-T-shirted to her body with sweat. There was nothing like some good, honest mud to show for her good, honest day's work.

A brown-and-white basset hound lumbered over to her.

She sat cross-legged and patted the ground next to her. "Come on, Elvis. Come on, boy. Come play in the mud with me."

Elvis picked up his pace slightly, or that might have been wishful thinking. Elvis didn't ever seem to be in a hurry. A man in a dark brown three-piece suit walked just as leisurely a hundred or so yards behind the dog. It had to be over a hundred degrees, and the man was wearing a suit. That must be Rowdy Rose, Elvis's human. According to his family, the man wore a suit no matter what.

She attempted to brush some of the mud off of her thighs, but all she managed to do was spread the stuff around. Not the best way to meet a member of the family and technically one of her bosses, but at least he'd know she was a hard worker. She rolled onto her heels and stood. She wiped her hands on her back pockets in preparation for the business handshake, but that only made things worse. Blades of grass stuck to the mud drying on her hands. Using her shirt, she got most of the mud off of her right hand as Elvis sat in front of her and watched her with his tail thumping like a metronome against the ground.

She picked up a stick and threw it.

Elvis looked up at her like it was great she could throw a stick, but what did that have to do with him?

"We really need to work on your fetching skills." She squatted down and with her cleanest hand, scratched behind his ears.

He melted and rolled over for a belly rub. She gave him a vigorous belly scratch.

"I've been trying to teach him to fetch for the past five years, but he's really more into laying on the sofa and watching Animal Planet." His owner waved at her.

She knew that voice.

But it couldn't be. No, it absolutely couldn't be.

As she stood, she shaded her eyes from the blistering sun. Not five yards away from her, Houston stopped and stared at her. "Houston?"

He blinked twice and then looked her up and down.

Recognition dawned and his jaw practically bounced off the ground.

"Daisy?" His voiced cracked, so he cleared his throat. "Daisy?"

She pulled off her floppy straw hat and nodded. What was he doing here? She glanced down at Elvis and the neurons finally fired in her brain. "You're Rowdy Rose?"

Her heart pounded in her chest. This was amazing and terrible and wonderful and awful and too surreal for words. Fate was a cheeky bitch, and Justus could almost hear the Universe laughing at her.

"You're Justus Jacobi?" The astonishment cracked on his face, making way for a watermelon slice of a smile. He swept her up in his arms, mud and all, and kissed the breath out of her.

She gave herself over to this moment, this perfect moment. She kissed him back with all of the love she'd kept bottled up inside. He pressed her to him and she wrapped her legs around his waist.

This was the moment she'd both dreamed of and feared. Houston was here and they could finally be together.

"Why are you kissing my mother?" Hugh said from behind her.

Houston's body tensed as Hugh's words sank in. "Mother?"

His arms loosened, and she slid down his body like a stripper working the pole. Her feet touched the ground, but it felt like it was tilting more than a little to the left. Finally she got her balance.

"Um?" She couldn't seem to make words come out of her mouth. How exactly was she supposed to introduce the man she loved to the son he didn't know he had? She'd always planned on telling Hugh about his father when he got older . . . like fifty . . . or possibly never. True, he'd asked questions over the years, but that wasn't the same as meeting his father face-to-face.

She looked down at her little boy. There was more than just question in his eyes, there was dawning animosity. His short arms folded over his chest as he glared up at her. He was too young to fully understand about his father.

She glanced at Houston. He was full-on animosity as he crossed his arms and glared down at her. Standing side by side, Hugh was a tiny version of Houston. Two worlds that she'd never thought would collide were crashing down around her.

If she told either one of them now, they weren't going to hug it out and start planning their first family vacation. Years of purposely avoiding the truth coiled around her like a rope hobbling a horse.

This was wrong . . . all wrong.

"I take it that you two know each other."

Justus looked up to find Lucy standing next to Hugh and watching her very carefully.

"Yes, we've known each other for years." Houston's gaze locked on to his mother. "At least I thought I knew her."

"We met eleven years ago at Bur—"

"We haven't seen each other in a year." Houston looked anywhere but at Justus.

Lucy looked from her son and then to Hugh and back to her son. The older woman's eyes turned the size of mason jar lids and her mouth fell open. "Oh, my God. Rowdy, you have a—" It was both accusation and question.

"Lucy, would you mind um . . . you know . . . um . . . Hugh, are you hungry?" Justus's eyes silently pleaded with Lucy to take Hugh away. Lucy opened her mouth like she was going to speak and then closed it again. Justus had a feeling that Lucy wasn't going to blithely accept having just found out that she had a grandson. There would most certainly be questions. Justus only hoped that now wouldn't be the time the older woman would want to discuss it.

Lucy nodded once and glanced down at Hugh. "I'll race you to the kitchen. I'll bet Mary is frantic because we're so late for lunch."

Hugh just stood there with his little arms folded, glaring at Houston as his Batman cape fluttered in the breeze.

"Come on, we need to let your pare . . . um . . . your mom talk to Rowdy." Lucy tugged gently on Hugh's hand, and he finally followed her into the main house.

It was Rowdy's turn to look dumbstruck, only she'd never known Houston . . . er . . . Rowdy to ever be dumbstruck.

"Son?" His eyes nailed Justus to the spot where she was standing. There was something very caged-animal about his expression. "So that's why you kept bringing it up?"

"Yes." Justus's voice was a choked whisper. She needed to explain, but she couldn't get the words out.

"A son? I have a son?" He'd moved past the shocked phase and into something that sounded like anger. "Wait a minute . . . I'm not the father. I can't be. We used protection every single time."

He concentrated on his shoes, and it looked like he was sifting through memories to confirm his argument. "Oh . . . that night we went stargazing on the Playa." He took a deep breath and let it out slowly. It was like the weight of fatherhood sucked all of the air out of his lungs. "How could you not tell me I have a son?"

Because she'd been afraid of exactly this reaction, but she was done hiding the truth. "I didn't tell you because I know how you feel about children. You don't want them." The last words were ground out more than spoken.

He scrubbed his face with his hands. "That's not the same and you know it. Don't you think you should have mentioned it at least once in the last seven years?"

"Houst—"

"My name is Rowdy." His eyes narrowed to reptilian slits. It seemed that the five stages of finding out he had a seven-year-old son were not unlike the five stages of grief. Would they ever get to the acceptance part?

Rowdy and not Houston . . . right. "I won't have my son hurt."

And knowing that his father didn't want him would definitely hurt. "You didn't want children . . . you were firm on that."

"Son? I have a son?" Rowdy tunneled his fingers through his hair. Then his whole body relaxed, and a maniacal grin twisted his face into a hopeful kind of horror. "Sure . . . right, I have a son."

Clearly he was waiting for a punch line that didn't exist.

He looked down and seemed to notice for the first time that he was covered in mud.

"This is a mistake." She turned on her heel. "We're going. You can go back to the happy life you refused to share with me."

He put a hand on her shoulder. "Talk about not sharing your life, hello . . . you gave birth to my son. Shouldn't that have rated a mention at some point in the last seven years?"

This was going nowhere fast. She shrugged off his hand and stomped in the direction of the cottage. They were leaving. There was nothing else to be done.

"I missed you last week," he said through gritted teeth.

She didn't turn back.

"I was in love with you." His voice was low and controlled.

Her heart stopped beating and she stopped dead in her tracks, but she didn't turn around. She couldn't help but notice that he'd used the past tense.

"It's complicated." That was the understatement of the century.

"No, it's actually very simple. You lied to me—"

"I never lied." She turned around and pointed her right index finger like a gun aimed at his chest. "You were very clear on what was a deal breaker for you."

"You should have given me a chance, but you decided for me." His jaw was so tight she could have bounced a quarter off of it. "Go ahead . . . run away, just like you always do."

He turned on his heel and headed back in the direction he'd come from.

Now he was the one running, well, walking away.

Elvis looked up at her like he was really sorry that his master was an asshole but there wasn't a whole lot he could do about it, and then turned around and lumbered after Rowdy.

In the space of five minutes, she'd gone from total happiness to utter despair, and then reality settled its cold, hard arms around her.

There was no way to make this right. She'd chosen her son over the man she loved. This was the year she'd finally given up on the possibility of a life with Houston. And while her mind knew that she'd made the right decision, her heart broke nonetheless.

# CHAPTER 5

In his heart, Rowdy knew that life wasn't black-and-white, and the more he tried to paint it that way, the grayer it got.

What had he been thinking? She didn't belong here. She only knew the person he was at Burning Man. Why had he ever thought that he could merge his two worlds?

And he had a son. A son. He HAD a son.

Christ, what was he supposed to do now?

With every step he took away from Daisy, the more his heart broke. Fate had practically dumped her on his doorstep and then in a cruel twist had turned her into someone he didn't know. She wasn't Daisy, she was Justus . . . not Daisy . . . Justus.

The same person but not.

Just like the color red had a million shades, so did Daisy. Which shade was the real Daisy . . . um . . . Justus?

She had his child and forgot to mention it every year at Burning Man. Who did that?

They'd used protection every time . . . except for one. Logically he knew that it only took one time, but damn . . . it wasn't fair.

Beside him, Elvis stopped walking and looked up. The dog nodded once in support of "life ain't fair."

"Two levels of protection. Condoms and the pill." Wait a minute . . . she was supposed to be on the pill. Come to think of it, how did birth control pills actually work, or in this case not work? As soon as he got home, he was googling it.

Elvis sighed heavily and shot him a look that said that Rowdy needed to pick up the pace because they were missing a *River Monsters* marathon on Animal Planet.

"Don't look at me like that. We both know you watch too much TV. Exercise is good for you." Elvis wasn't into the outdoors. He preferred a life that involved air-conditioning, a big-screen TV, and a human who was at his bark and call.

Rowdy slid his arms underneath Elvis and lifted him up. "Crap, you weigh a ton. We need to discuss some portion control when it comes to your fettuccini Alfredo addiction. And those breakfast tacos aren't doing you any favors."

Elvis arched an eyebrow.

"Don't look at me in that tone of voice." Rowdy needed to practice some tough love. "It's diet dog food from now on."

Elvis drew in a startled breath. Rowdy knew it wasn't the diet part that Elvis objected to, it was the dog food. Elvis preferred caviar to kibble and Evian to tap water.

It was time for Elvis to face the music. "You do realize that you're a dog, right?"

Elvis raised his lip and growled.

"Don't take that tone with me or you'll be hoofing it all the way back to the sofa. You are in fact a dog, and you need to come to grips with that. I wonder if there's a crotch-sniffing, toilet-drinking class you can take."

In protest, Elvis went completely boneless, which made him feel like he actually weighed more.

Rowdy shifted him to a better position. "You completely defy the laws of physics. How do those stumpy little legs of yours actually hold you up?"

Elvis refused to dignify that with an answer.

The rumble of a truck came from over Rowdy's right shoulder. He turned around to find his older brother, Cinco, behind the wheel of his Chevy truck, bounding down the dirt two-track.

His brother pulled up alongside of him, and the passenger's-side window glided down. "I've never seen a dog walk a human before. Isn't it supposed to be the other way around?"

"Don't start." Rowdy one-armed Elvis as he opened the back passenger's door and laid the dog on the bench seat. He closed the door and opened the front door and slid into Cinco's truck.

"Where's CanDee?" His brother and his fiancée, CanDee, had been in New York City, and based on the luggage in the truck bed, they were on their way home from the San Antonio airport.

"I dropped her off at the main house. She wanted to see Justus." Cinco eyed his brother. "What exactly did you do to make you persona non grata? CanDee talked Mom out of coming here and murdering you. Personally, I say it's a free country, and if Mom wants to murder you, that's between her and Jesus."

Rowdy shot him the bird.

"Wow, fatherhood." Cinco glanced his way. "You know what . . . it suits you."

"No, it doesn't." Rowdy could do with a little less family right about now. "I don't want to talk about it." He wasn't in the mood to be rational or to see Justus's side of anything. He just wanted to be mad and wounded. He needed to take some time and work things out in his mind.

"Burning Man?" Cinco put the truck in drive and eased down the road.

Damn, Justus and her big mouth. Then again, she had no idea that he'd hidden that from his family. Again, he really wasn't in the mood to be rational.

"Yes. The mysterious one week a year that I take off, I go to Burning Man." There it was. His family would know exactly how much he didn't fit in.

Cinco took his time mulling it over. "Damn, none of us saw that coming." He looked over at Rowdy. "You were so much more interesting when I thought you were a serial killer. Now you're just alternative." He shook his head. "Are you sure you're really not a serial killer? I mean way down deep, there's bound to be someone you want to kill and keep their right pinkie finger as a trophy."

"No one but you." Rowdy made a big show of leaning over and inspecting Cinco's right pinkie finger. "That would make an excellent ornament for my Christmas tree . . . or maybe I could string a bunch of them together and make a nice wreath for my front door."

"See." Cinco threw up an index finger and pointed it at him. "There's a serial killer down deep just waiting to come out."

"Always the optimist." Rowdy glanced back at Elvis, who was sleeping contently away on the backseat.

Christ, he was a father. Hell, he'd been taking care of a high-maintenance canine kid for years, how much harder could a human kid be?

"I'm just a little ray of sunshine," Cinco singsonged in the same tone he'd know-you-are-but-what-am-I-ed Rowdy to death with when they were kids. "CanDee is always telling me that."

"We both know that CanDee only agreed to marry you because she felt sorry for you. The unloved older brother. I'm so sorry that Mom and Dad tried to sell you on eBay, but no one bid."

"That's where you're wrong. A couple in China was looking to adopt an American baby, only PayPal couldn't handle a bazillion-dollar transaction. I was the bazillion-dollar baby." Cinco eased down on the gas.

"You drive like a little old lady." Rowdy sat back and eyed his brother. "Do you do anything fast?"

"Nope." Cinco grinned. "Just ask CanDee, and she'll tell you that I always take my time."

CanDee was good for Cinco. His first wife, Naomi, screwed her way through half the guys in Gillespie County and broke Cinco's heart. Now he smiled all of the time instead of retreating inward. Thanks to CanDee, his older brother was back to being the man he'd grown up with instead of a brooding stranger.

His brother continued driving in slow motion. "I want to go to Burning Man. Can I come with you next year?"

If Cinco had expressed a wish to dress up as Queen Elizabeth, Rowdy couldn't have been more flabbergasted. Cinco was the newly elected state representative of Gillespie County. He couldn't be any more of a WASP if he sprouted wings and flew around stinging people. "Okay."

No matter how supportive his older brother thought he was being, Burning Man really wasn't his kind of thing. His family had been trying to understand him for as long as he could remember. But he knew the truth: if they saw the real Rowdy, they might not like what they saw. Ranch life had almost sucked the art right out of him.

"I'm ready to embrace decommodification." Cinco's eyes glanced briefly his way, and then they were back on the road ahead. "As soon as I figure out what that means."

Decommodification? Wow, he'd actually researched Burning Man.

"Yeah, I'm not so sure about that one either. I just like the art aspect of it. There are some super creative people." Last week, after he'd given up on Daisy, he'd thrown himself into his art. Four paintings later, he still hadn't gotten it totally out of his system. His art was personal. No one in his family knew or understood his need for a creative outlet. Wine making used to be enough, but now it was more about the business and less about the actual art of wine making. Yes, he tested new blends, but the joy of creation just wasn't the same as with painting. There was an art to wine making, but there was a lot of chemistry too.

Nothing stirred his soul like painting. It was the life calling he let go to voice mail.

"You know, I thought about Burning Man a couple of years ago. Researched it. From what I remember, the sex is supposed to be crazy good." Cinco shot his brother an overly dramatic wink. He really didn't do subtlety. "Now that I have CanDee, I have crazy good sex all of the time." His older brother's head bobbed up and down like a bobblehead.

"I hate you so much." Rowdy hadn't had sex in over a year. "As far as the crazy Burning Man sex—it is. There are orgy tents." But he'd never been inside one. On his first day of being a Burning Man virgin, he'd met Daisy, and that was it for him. She was all he saw . . . all he wanted. It had been her smile. True, she had a killer body, but her smile had gone straight to his soul and planted itself there.

"So . . . what did you do to make Justus cry?" Cinco wasn't a beat-around-the-busher, he was more of a mow-down-the-bush-and-keep-on-going-er.

Jesus, he'd made her cry. Of course he'd made her cry. Crap. Daisy . . . Justus wasn't a crier. He'd never seen her shed a single tear. Part of him was tempted to kick his own ass, and then the part of him that felt betrayed wanted to kick that other part's ass. Either way he looked at it, it felt like he needed an ass kicking.

He gritted his teeth to try and keep the words in, but it wasn't enough. "How upset is she?"

"She looked pretty bad." His brother kept his eyes on the road and his hands at ten and two. Always the rule follower . . . except when it came to CanDee. She lit a fire under him and brought him out of himself. His brother had finally found the love of his life, and so had Rowdy . . . he'd thought.

"Is she okay?" He hated the weakness in him that needed to know, and he hated the fact that he wanted to rush to her and beg for forgiveness, even though he hadn't done anything wrong.

"She'll be fine. Mom and CanDee have declared that men over the age of seven are no longer allowed at the cottage. Since CanDee talked Mom out of killing you, I volunteered to beat the crap out of you." Cinco checked the rearview mirror and the side mirrors just like Coach Conners had showed them in driver's ed all those years ago. "It's a thankless job, if you ask me. I mean, I do get to beat on you, which is kinda fun, but I'm probably going to bruise my knuckles and break a sweat."

"You're such a humanitarian." He almost wished that his brother would take a swing at him. Some hand-to-hand combat would feel pretty good about now.

Cinco passed the turnoff to Rowdy's house. "Where are we going?"

"The bunkhouse. The twins and I are getting you stinkin' drunk. While the women are talking about their feelings, we'll be watching a Terminator marathon and killing a couple bottles of Don Julio. If you ask me, tequila is way better than talking about your feelings. Hell, after a couple of shots, who even remembers they have feelings?"

"I'm surrounded by Neanderthals." More tequila than was good for him sounded like and excellent plan. "We all have our crosses to bear."

"Look at you . . . turning the other cheek. Buck up, little camper, your girlfriend only hates you with the fire of a thousand suns . . . her words, not mine." His cautious brother spared him a brief glance. "You'll probably get over it in a hundred or so years." He shrugged. "Then again, you're shallow, so maybe it will only take you five minutes. In fact you look like you're already over it."

"Self-involvement has its privileges." Two lifetimes wouldn't be enough to get over Justus. If only he were shallow, then he'd be able to get over the whole betrayal, had-his-son-and-forgot-to-tell-him thing. He had so much to hold against her that he almost forgot that he was in love with her . . . almost.

"Hey, I almost forgot. Congrats, Dad. Too bad the little rug rat is too big to fit into one of those backpack things. I could stand to see you wearing one strapped to your chest." He brother's eyes flicked his way and then back to the road. "Want to talk about it?"

"Nope. I thought we were down with Plan Tequila." He didn't feel like talking. In fact, he didn't feel like thinking. Tequila was a good idea. He'd hate himself in the morning, but tonight he needed a vacation from his life.

"Just making sure you hadn't turned into a girl while I was out of town." Cinco checked his mirrors again.

"You were only gone two weeks. I'm pretty sure sexual reassignment surgery takes longer to plan, but I don't know for sure. I can ask around if you secretly want me to find out. CanDee's going to be pretty pissed if you decide on an equipment change. Honestly, I'm not sure I can take her, so make sure she knows that it wasn't my idea." He certainly could use some male bonding right about now. "Oh, can we stop by my house and drop off Elvis? He's got a date with the sofa and Animal Planet."

Cinco flipped a *U*. "You do realize that he's a dog . . . right?"

"Shhh. Don't say that too loud," Rowdy whispered. "It makes him angry."

# CHAPTER 6

Justus knew that she should be packing, but she couldn't wrap her mind around that right now. Tears stung her eyes and burned the inside of her nose. She wasn't a delicate crier, racking sobs were more her style. Warm tears slipped past her eyelashes and ran down her cheeks. She didn't even bother to wipe them away.

She sat on the end of the bed in the small, cozy one-room cottage. In the short time she'd been here, it had become home. The cottage had a small kitchen complete with an oven, a bookshelf-divided area with a queen-size bed, and she'd been looking forward to winter so she could build a huge fire, sit back in one of the chairs around the fireplace, and just watch the flames. Now, that wasn't going to happen . . . nothing had turned out the way she'd planned. She no longer had a place to live, her son wouldn't ever know his father, she would have to leave a very lucrative job that would have finally allowed her some financial freedom, and the love of her life would never, ever look at her again with that twinkle in his eye that always filled her heart.

After her hard day's work, she was bone tired and her heart and mind were exhausted. She should get up, take a shower, and pack up. She glanced at the windows by the front door. It had to be five thirty.

It wouldn't be fully dark until nine. If she hurried, she and Hugh could be back in Austin before sunset.

She couldn't muster the energy to stand up, much less pack. Maybe Lucy and Bear would let them stay the night and then leave in the morning? They would be mad, and rightfully so. She'd never considered that Hugh should know his father's family. In her defense, she hadn't known that Houston was a Rose.

She would miss the Rose family. It was funny that Bear and Lucy treated Hugh like a grandson before they knew he was family. Surely they'd still want to see Hugh. Justus would work out some sort of visitation. Since Rowdy didn't want to have anything to do with her or her son, Bear and Lucy would have to come to Austin to see Hugh. Hopefully that wouldn't be a problem for them.

It was nice that Hugh would have a relationship with his father's family. Maybe when he got older, she'd tell him that they really were his grandparents, but for now it didn't seem like a good idea.

She'd made a mess of things.

Tears came faster and harder as snot poured out of her nose. Looking around, she didn't see anything handy with which to wipe her face, so she grabbed the corner of the patchwork quilt she was sitting on and mopped her cheeks.

"Knock, knock," Lucy called as she opened the front door. Her head peeked around the door and then her body followed. "Anyone home?"

Justus found a dry patch of quilt and dried her face as best she could.

She took a deep breath and called, "Over here."

"CanDee's back and went to her house to change clothes and get some chocolate. I have a feeling that we're going to need some serious chocolate." Lucy's eyes found her and the grin froze on her face. "Are you okay?"

"Why are you being so nice? You have every right to be angry with me. I didn't come here looking for something from the Rose family. I didn't even know Hous—Rowdy was a Rose." She hated that her voice was pleading. The only other time she'd remembered pleading with anyone was when she pleaded with her mother to love her. And that hadn't turned out well.

Lucy tilted her head to the left and ducked her chin. "Yes, I have questions, but I don't see you or Hugh as anything but a godsend." Lucy's voiced cracked, and she watched the older woman swipe at her own tears like they were annoying bees buzzing around her cheeks. "Now I know why y'all felt like family from the very start."

The woman was showing her nothing but kindness. It was funny. Rowdy had never spoken directly about his family, but she'd always gotten the impression that they didn't approve of lifestyle choices that he'd made. That didn't fit with the actual family. They were warm and open and understanding—the exact opposite of what she'd pictured.

She should be packing and told her legs to stand, but they refused to listen. "I'm sorry to impose, but could we stay another night? Hugh and I'll be gone in the morning."

And then go where? She'd given up her apartment. Maybe it wasn't rented yet and she could move back in? Home ownership would have to wait.

"You can't leave. Rowdy will come around. He's just blindsided right now. He likes to take his time and plot things out." Lucy came over to the bed, sat down beside Justus, and brushed a lock of Justus's hair behind her ear. "You and Hugh are welcome here for as long as you'd like to stay." She noticed that the older woman and Rowdy had the same nose and mouth. "I'm tempted to throw my second-to-oldest son off the ranch. As it is, it's taking all the restraint I have not to get my stun gun, march over to his house, and zap him a good one. Hell, just for fun, I might wake him up and zap him again."

Again, not the person that Rowdy made his mother out to be.

"I'm sure it was a huge shock to find out he has a son." Crapola, now she was defending Rowdy? Even her subconscious knew she was in the wrong. Unfortunately, Rowdy wasn't likely to give her a second chance to explain.

"Hugh is Houston's . . . right?" The older woman sounded so hopeful. "I mean, I guessed it, but I just want to double-check."

The muscles at the back of Justus's neck bunched up, so she massaged them. She took a long, deep breath and let it out slowly. "Yes."

Lucy let out a long breath, and her shoulders relaxed. "That's good to hear, because my Bear has a big heart, and once I tell him the truth about Hugh, he's going to fall hard for the kid." Lucy's chest shook with laughter. "What am I saying, he's already fallen hard for Hugh."

Lucy pulled her into a hug. For such a small woman, she was remarkably strong. "If you feel comfortable telling me about it, I'd love to know how you met my son."

Where did she start? Justus couldn't explain why she hadn't told Rowdy about his son to a woman who couldn't possibly understand. Even the mere idea that Hugh wouldn't be wanted had her balling her fists in defense of her child. Rowdy hadn't wanted kids, but how did she go about telling that to his mother? Justus had always assumed that the reason Rowdy hadn't wanted children was because of his parents, but they were wonderful. What was she missing?

At least she owed Lucy an explanation, so she laid her head on Lucy's shoulder and allowed herself to be comforted.

"We met at the Center City Café. It's kind of a pop-up restaurant in the middle of the Playa. We were both Burner virgins—it was our first year. I was handing out daisies." When she talked about Burning Man to someone who'd never been, it seemed so silly. "I was handing out flowers, and he walked right up to me, introduced himself, and asked me to marry him. I thought he was hilarious."

Lucy stiffened and released Justus. "My son walked up to you and asked you to marry him . . . without knowing you?" She sounded like she didn't believe it. "My son, Rowdy . . . who plans everything down to the minutia, walked up to someone he didn't know and asked you to marry him."

"Yes. Rowdy, well, Houston, that was the name he went by, is a very different person at Burning Man than the one who lives here." At least he seemed different. She used the quilt to wipe her face again.

"Houston is his real name, but he goes by Rowdy. And what do you mean he's different here?" Lucy looked like she was trying to understand the situation.

"I've never seen him wear anything but cutoffs and Birks. He seems so serious here. The Houston I know is always open and laughs at everything." She didn't remember seeing any of his work in the great house. Lucy loved her children and seemed like the type that would hang their art and achievements everywhere. "Why don't you have any of his art hanging anywhere?"

"What art?" Lucy's brow scrunched up. "What are you talking about?"

"Houston, er, Rowdy is a wonderful artist. He did this watercolor of me on the Playa at dusk, and several art gallery owners offered to buy it, and some even offered to sponsor a show for him." She snort-laughed at the absurdity of him actually needing a sponsor. He was probably worth millions.

"Watercolor?" Lucy sat back, stunned. "He was very artistic as a child, but to my knowledge he hasn't done anything but make wine his whole adult life."

"When I met him, he told me he was a painter who made wine." She really didn't know Rowdy at all. "I assumed that wine making was something he did in his spare time." Finally, the tears had stopped flowing, and she swiped a hand over her puffy eyes. "I guess it's the other way around."

"Painting?" Lucy looked like she was having a hard time imagining her son as anything but the person she knew. Apparently her version of Rowdy wasn't anything like Justus's version of Houston. "The only thing I've ever seen him paint was the old barn, and that was only as a punishment for having a huge party at our house while we were out of town. That was his senior year in high school."

"Wait a minute . . . hang on. I think I have a photo of the painting." Justus worked her smartphone out of her back pocket and pulled up her pictures. She scrolled and scrolled and scrolled. She definitely needed to thin these out. Finally the set of photos she was looking for popped up. She clicked on the one of the painting and handed the phone to Lucy.

The older woman's mouth dropped open. "He painted this?"

"He gave this to me our second year at Burning Man." She pointed to the sunset. "Sunset on the Playa is one of my most favorite things, so he painted me watching it go down."

"My son, Rowdy, painted this?" Lucy looked like a child who wasn't buying the whole birds-and-the-bees talk and was sticking with the stork version.

Justus nodded. "Yes, I mean I didn't see him paint it, but it's definitely his style."

"He has a style?" She studied the picture on the phone. "It's so vivid. It's like I can see the wind ruffling the sand. Wow."

"Let me show you the others." Gently, Justus took the phone and scrolled to some of the paintings that Rowdy had done while at Burning Man. There was even a photo of him standing alone with his easel, painting the mountains at dawn.

"It really is him." Lucy's voice cracked and silent tears rolled down her cheeks. "It's not that I didn't believe you, it was more that I have no frame of reference for his talent. How could I have missed this?" She held the phone up. "What did I do or say that made him hide this from me?"

Justus shook her head. "I can't believe you didn't know." It was her turn to offer comfort. "If it helps, I know he loves you all very much." Sort of . . . it's not that Rowdy had been unkind about his family, it was more that he'd said that they didn't understand him. She pulled Lucy in for a tight hug. "Maybe he wasn't hiding, maybe it's just so personal that he didn't want to share it."

"He shared it with you." She swiped at the tears like they were more nuisance than emotion.

"That's different. I'm . . . well . . . was"—the word choked in her mouth—"his Burner Only girlfriend. If I didn't like his art, he only had to live with me one week a year."

"Still, I feel like a failure as a parent because I had no idea that Rowdy was so talented." She swiped away more tears. "I must have done something to make him hide this. I know I'm not the best mother in the world. I missed a lot of my sons' childhood because I was working. I hope I didn't do this to him."

Lucy was honestly upset. If she were in Lucy's shoes, she'd be upset too. If Hugh hid a big part of his life from her . . . it would hurt . . . a lot. Lucy seemed like a good mother . . . unlike Justus's own biological mother, who put herself first, second, and third. All others were relegated to the cheap seats at the back of the bus.

Still, Justus couldn't let Lucy wallow. "I've seen bad parenting, and you're not it."

"But you talk about your father and stepmother so fondly." Lucy looked up at her with sad eyes.

"My father and stepmother are wonderful, but my bio mom is a train wreck. When I was a sophomore in college, I worked at a jewelry store. We got this gold and diamond watch in as a trade. As soon as I saw it, I thought of her. It was just the perfect gift for her. Back then I thought I still needed her love and approval, so I worked extra hours, ate nothing but peanut butter and crackers for an entire month so I could buy her that watch. I mailed it to her on her birthday. The day she got it, she called the store and asked if she could return it for the cash value because she didn't want some used piece of trash. She had no idea I was the one on the other end of the phone. Come to think of it, even if she had known, I don't think it would have mattered." Justus had never told anyone that story. It was strange, the simple act of sharing it had taken away some of the sting.

"What a bitch. I've never met her and I want to kill her." Lucy tapped her right index finger against her pursed lips, and then a confident smile inched its way across her face. "I could make it look like an accident. We could bury her in the peach orchard. No one would ever know."

"Know what?" CanDee stood in the open front doorway. Her arms were loaded down with several packages of Double Stuf Oreos, two giant yellow Peanut M&M's bags, and three bags of Reese's Peanut Butter Cups Miniatures. "The door was cracked open, so I let myself in."

Justus rushed to grab a couple of packs of Oreos before they fell to the ground. She helped CanDee carry her chocolate burden to the small, round kitchen table.

"That's a lot of chocolate." Justus leaned up on her tippy-toes and hugged her friend.

She hadn't seen her good friend in close to five months. That was the longest they'd been apart since meeting freshman year of college.

"Me too. New York was fun, but there's nothing like home." CanDee was six feet in her bare feet, had long, coppery hair, and didn't take crap from anyone. Well, now she didn't take crap from anyone.

CanDee released her and stepped back. "So what did I walk in on? No one would ever know what?"

"If we killed her biological mother." Lucy arched an eyebrow. "Want in?"

"Hell yes." She ripped open a Double Stuf Oreo bag and grabbed a handful. "But if you're serious, we really should include Maeve. I have a feeling that she's put up with more shit from the first Mrs. Jacobi than she lets on. If we're planning on using a baseball bat, I say first swing goes to Justus, second to Maeve, third to me, and Lucy, you bring up the rear. We can continue in that order until the job is done. According to Cinco, the best way to get rid of a body is to throw it in the wood chipper and then feed it to the pigs." She put her hand over her heart. "I don't know that for sure, but I'm willing to give it a try."

Lucy nodded in agreement. "Wood chipper. That's way better than burying her in the peach orchard. With the wood chipper, there are no dental records." She looked like she was filing that little tidbit away for future reference.

Justus laughed it off. She was reasonably sure they weren't serious.

"Just so that I'm completely caught up, have we discussed Rowdy's murder? I thought we were mad at him." CanDee plopped down on the bed next to Lucy and shoved the handful of Oreos in her mouth.

"No, he gets to live . . . for now." Lucy picked up the hem of the quilt and mopped her face. "Did you know that Rowdy is Hugh's father?"

CanDee's mouth fell open and chunky Oreo goo threatened to spill out, so Lucy leaned over and gently pushed her jaw closed. CanDee chewed and chewed and finally swallowed.

"No way." Her eyes screwed up in concentration. "Houston is Hugh's dad's real name. Still, he's not an artist."

"That's what I've been saying." Lucy threw up her hands. "Apparently our Rowdy is very different from her Houston."

"Now I know where I know him from. All the pictures you have of him. Why didn't I put that together earlier?" CanDee shook her head. "Did he really paint that picture of you at sunset?"

"Yes." Justus seemed to be the only one who'd ever seen the artistic side of Rowdy.

CanDee and Lucy shared a look.

"It's not that we don't believe you, it's just that Rowdy is the exact opposite of creative. He's more tax attorney or stockbroker than painter."

CanDee pointed to the pile of chocolate on the table. "Friends don't let friends eat chocolate alone."

Lucy stood, stretched her back, and grabbed a pounder of Peanut M&Ms. "This is unconfirmed, but I'm fairly certain that Rowdy and Elvis get weekly mani-pedis." She tore open the bag and grabbed a handful.

Yep, their version of Hugh's father was very different from hers. The Rowdy she knew didn't care about his cuticles or would have thought the whole mani-pedi process was frivolous. Which was the real Rowdy? Was there any way to reconcile the two?

# CHAPTER 7

Rowdy hadn't done nearly enough drinking to drown out his need to make sure Justus was okay. True, he had been wronged, but he'd made her cry, and that actually made him sick to his stomach. Or it might be the uneven ground he was attempting to walk on to get to the cottage.

It was funny, he didn't remember the horizon veering so far to the left.

"Son, you been drinkin'?" Lefty came out of nowhere and appeared right in front of him. That was a neat trick. Maybe Lefty would teach him how to teleport places. That was certainly more convenient than walking. Heck, Elvis would be all over the not-having-to-walk idea.

"Maybe, just a little." He held his index finger and thumb close together, showing Lefty just how little he'd been drinking.

"Christ, son, I can smell the tequila from here." Lefty threw an arm around his shoulders. "How about we get you back to your house so you can sleep it off?"

"Nope." He shook off Lefty's arm and continued his left-leaning walk. "I'm on my way to see Justus. She's mad at me."

"Fine, keep on going, but I'd like to make a suggestion." Lefty stepped back and crossed his arms. His one eye crinkled in the corner.

"Okay, shoot." No one was talking him out of going to the cottage. He just needed to see her. No idea what he would say when he did, but seeing her sounded like a wonderful idea. Maybe he'd peek into the window and then go home. That way words weren't necessary. Yep, Peeping-Tom-ing her was an excellent plan.

"You might try walking in a straight line. You've been walking in a giant circle for the last ten minutes." Lefty held out his smartphone. "I've been filming you, and I just uploaded the video to that YouTube channel CanDee fixed up for me." He glanced down at the phone. "Already got twelve hits. Looks like you're a popular man."

Rowdy made a swipe for the phone, but Lefty was a quick one and the phone stayed with the old man. "You have a YouTube channel? Why?"

He pulled his battered straw hat off his head and held it over his heart. "I'm what they call a cowboy poet. Want to hear my latest piece? I'm up to eighteen followers on the Twitter, and it's only been a month and a half."

"Not especially." Lefty was a poet and Rowdy was a father. It was like Revelations in the Bible. Pretty soon locusts and apocalyptic horsemen were going to pour down from the sky and wine was going to turn into blood.

Damn, maybe he should go tap a few barrels of the Riesling he was about to bring to market and make sure it didn't have a clotting factor.

"Fine, be that way." Lefty shoved his hat back down on his head and stepped back. "You can find your own way to the cottage. Here's some free advice, I mean I ain't got no fancy college education like you, but it seems to me that walking in a circle ain't the easiest way to get from point A to point B."

"Huh?" He wasn't walking in a circle. The ground was off. "I am walking in a straight line, but the ground is tilted to the left."

Lefty caught up to him, leaned up on the balls of his feet, and put a hand on either side of Rowdy's jaw, gently pushing Rowdy's head upright. Miraculously, the horizon righted itself.

"That is so much better, thank you." He pulled the stooped old man into a hug. The scents of Old Spice, cow manure, and sweat mingled into something that was all Lefty. "You're such a good friend."

"Son, I love you too, but you're squashing the life out of me." Lefty patted him on the back like an indulgent grandfather.

Rowdy let go and stepped back. "Sorry."

"It's good that you want to check on Justus, but I don't think you're in any shape to see her right now." Lefty nodded in the direction of the cottage, which was a good quarter mile down the dirt road. "How about if I go check on her for you and then report back? That way you won't have to walk as far."

"You're so smart. I'm always saying that." He smiled down at Lefty. This man had been his grandfather's friend and had taken over the job of grandfather when his own paternal granddad had passed away. "I love you."

"Uh-huh." He clamped an arm around Rowdy's waist. "You're a lot heavier than you look. Where in Sam Hill are your brothers?"

"The twins are having an Xbox dance off, Cinco wandered back to his house an hour ago, and T-Bone is in College Station working on his PhD—"

"I know T-Bone's at College Station." Lefty's tone suggested an eye roll, but the sun had gone down so he couldn't tell for sure. "I was hopin' one of them would help me haul your butt home. Looks like I'm on my own. I'm taking you to my house, 'cause yours is too far and I ain't about to drive you home on account of the last time I drove you home when you'd had too much to drink, you puked all over my truck." He shook his head. "Poor Esther was never the same after that."

Rowdy stopped and stared down at Lefty. "Poor Esther? What about poor me? You made me clean her out, and then when I was super hungover, you made me paint the barn and mow all of the grass around the houses. I puked all the next day."

"And here you are making the same mistake over again. I thought that would have taught you a thing or two about overindulging, but no, here we are again."

"Did I mention that you're my most favorite person in the world?" Rowdy knew charm wouldn't work on the old man, but it was worth a shot.

"Nope, and I'd heard that Justus was your most favorite person in the world." Lefty guided him toward the barn, where Lefty lived on the second floor.

"No, she is no longer my most favorite person." Rowdy leaned down and stage-whispered, "She has a son and I'm his father."

Lefty stumbled and then righted himself. "Hugh's your boy?" His head pumped up and down. "Now that you mention it, he is the spittin' image of you."

"She had my son and didn't tell me for seven whole years. That's a long time to keep a secret." See, he could hold a grudge just as good as the next man.

"From what I hear, you got some secrets of your own, and you kept them from the family for a heck of a lot longer than seven years." Lefty practically dragged him all the way to the barn.

"That's different." There was no comparison between Burning Man and a secret kid. Hello, there were big secrets and little secrets, and his was definitely of the little variety.

"How's it different? A secret is a secret. We all have them, but sometimes keeping them does us more harm than good. We all got our reasons for not telling, so maybe you should think about hers." Lefty propped Rowdy up against the side of the barn while he opened the huge sliding barn door.

"What possible motivation could she have for keeping that from me?" His shoulders bounced up and down. "I got nothing." His mad was returning. No one had ever accused him of being a mean drunk—not that he drank liquor all that much—but he could see how easily it would be to descend into rage. But no, he wouldn't give her the satisfaction of watching him fall apart.

"Stop all that deep thinking. You look like you're trying to figure out the meaning of life." Lefty gathered him up and helped him stumble over to the elevator. "Everybody knows there ain't no meaning to life."

Now that Rowdy thought about it, he'd never heard of another barn with an elevator—well, it was more of a giant dumbwaiter with a hand crank, but it still qualified as an elevator.

"Son, I could use a hand here." Lefty nodded to the hand crank as he lounged against the back of the wooden box and folded his arms. "Put your back into it."

"Why do I have to do all of the work?" Fair was fair. Lefty was riding in the elevator too, it was time he pulled his weight.

"I'm old and you ain't. I could throw my back out or break a hip. I already hauled your sorry ass halfway acrossed this ranch. Now you want me to do the heavy lifting too?" Lefty shook his head. "Ungrateful whelp."

"We both know you're stronger than me and my brothers put together. Didn't I see you jackhammering out some limestone a couple of weeks ago?" Rowdy grabbed the hand crank with both hands and turned. "Jackhammering's a young man's game."

"That's besides the point. Son, you sure are whiny." He crossed one dusty, brown booted foot over the other. "You was always tough so I guess it's the liquor. Maybe you should give up the bottle on account of it's making you wimpy. You need to sack up and crank that handle for all you're worth."

"I'm going as fast as I can." But his voice was very whiny. "I'm just tired and you and this old, crappy elevator weigh like a million pounds."

"Son, bend your knees and use your back. Crank that handle like you got hair on your peaches."

The elevator finally made it to the second floor, and Lefty rolled the wooden door open onto his apartment, which spanned the whole length of the barn. The giant open room had to be at least two thousand square feet that housed one full-size bed, two beaten-up black leather Barcaloungers, and the old brown leather sofa that used to be in his parents' living room, a giant seventy-inch TV, and a small kitchenette complete with a little kitchen table. "Why haven't you ever fixed this place up?"

Lefty looked around. "What do you mean?"

"There's a lot of open space that needs to be filled. You could add some bookshelves and some rugs."

"Do I look like an interior decorator to you?" Lefty's eye turned antagonistic. "Besides, I got myself one of them fancy Keurig coffee-makers, a nice truck, and a giant color TV. What else does a man need?"

If only Rowdy's life were that simple.

Lefty helped him to the sofa. "Want me to go check on Justus now?"

"Yes. Make sure she's okay, but don't tell her I sent you or that I'm sorry, because I'm not." Rowdy yawned as he slid down to the sofa. He hadn't realized how tired he was until now. He closed his eyes and a wave of warm slid around him as Lefty covered him with a blanket.

"Okeydokey." Lefty's boots tapped on the sturdy wooden floor as he made his way to the door. "Sleep it off."

The warmth of the blanket and the softness of the couch cushions settled around him, and he drifted off.

When he woke hours later, happy morning sunshine assaulted his eyes from between the dark wooden slats striping the windows. He could swear his eyes were on the verge of bleeding. The smell of coffee brewing and fatty bacon frying made his stomach roll and churn, threatening to send its contents back up for a second appearance.

"Good, you're awake." Lefty set a plate of scrambled eggs and bacon on the coffee table in front of him, and then he set down two bottles of water. "No coffee for you until after you've drank the water and eaten the food. Having something in your stomach will help to settle it. I should know. Over twenty years of hard drinking, I've had my share of hangovers."

Lefty had been an alcoholic when Rowdy's grandfather had picked him up, brushed him off, and given him a job at the ranch. Lefty hadn't touched a drop of alcohol since. Maybe Rowdy should think about doing the same. It's wasn't like the tequila had actually helped get Justus off his mind, and he felt like he'd been run over by an eighteen wheeler.

He had to ask, he couldn't wait any longer. "How's Justus?"

"Okay. She, your momma, and CanDee had a slumber party. They talked her out of leaving the ranch—"

"Leave." He sprang up and his head nearly toppled off his shoulders and rolled around the living room like a wayward bowling ball. She couldn't leave, he needed to see her. His stomach lurched, and he clamped a hand over his mouth in a vain effort to keep the bile down. He ran for the bathroom and dry heaved into the toilet.

Lefty followed him into the small bathroom with a bottle of water and the plate of food. "You need to eat so's your stomach'll stop rolling." The old man grabbed a piece of bacon and practically shoved it in Rowdy's face.

It took everything he had to take the bacon and bite down on it. It felt like salty tree bark rolling around his mouth, but he managed to swallow it. He took the water and downed half the bottle. Slowly the nausea began to pass. He stood, took the plate, and headed back to the sofa.

"So she's not leaving? How did she look?" He hated that he wanted to know so damn bad.

"She looked like Justus." The older man hunched his shoulders. "She looked good, I guess. You can look at her yourself tonight. She's coming over to your house for dinner."

Rowdy froze. "What?"

"I took the liberty of inviting her to dinner for you." Lefty's mouth gathered in the corners with a mischievous grin. "You should have dinner ready at seven."

"But? I didn't tell you to do that." Sure, he wanted her to be okay, but he certainly wasn't ready to cook her dinner.

"I know. You ain't gotta thank me." Lefty picked up the other bottle of water and handed it to Rowdy. "Don't forget to drink this."

"Thank you. Thank you?" Right now, he was more likely to wring the old man's neck. "I don't want to have dinner with her . . . alone."

He guessed she'd bring the kid . . . um, Hugh, so they wouldn't exactly be alone. He should probably get to know the boy. That was the sensible thing to do.

"First you want to see her and now you don't. Son, make up your damn mind." Lefty sat down next to him. "Let me tell you something about relationships. None of them is perfect. It takes work, or at least that what my fourth wife, Joan, was always saying. Then again, she was a damn chatterbox, and that's why I divorced her."

"I thought Fancy was your fourth wife." Depending on the day, Lefty'd had anywhere from three to six ex-wives.

"Fancy was wife number three. Try and keep up." He stood, stretched, and grabbed his own plate of food off the kitchen table. He headed back to the sofa.

So she was coming over for dinner tonight. Why did that thought both annoy and excite him?

# CHAPTER 8

Justus felt like shit. Her crying-jag-turned-girls'-night had meant that she'd stayed up too late, had drunk too much wine, and laughed herself hoarse. She might not have resolved anything, but she'd forgotten—for a while—that she had anything that needed resolving.

As she stood in the hole she'd dug yesterday, she was willing to admit to herself that she was more than a little nervous about having dinner with Rowdy tonight. This morning Dallas or Worth, she still couldn't tell them apart, had insisted that Hugh had to spend the night with them tonight because they were having a movie marathon that included Hugh getting to eat his weight in popcorn.

Hugh was excited at the possibility of gorging on popcorn, and she hadn't had the heart to say no. Now—she squared her shoulders—she'd be stuck having dinner alone with Rowdy.

Had Rowdy asked his brothers to take Hugh for the night? Did he really not want to get to know his son? Her mood went from bad to worse. They couldn't stay here if all Rowdy was going to do was ignore his son. She didn't want that for Hugh or Rowdy or herself.

Tonight, would it be like old times? Part of her warmed to the idea and another part of her feared that it would be just as they had been at Burning Man. Every year at Burning Man, the moment she'd seen him, she'd lost herself in him. She couldn't do that anymore. Hugh was and always needed to be her first priority. Rowdy would have to come second.

A nagging voice in the back of her head asked, "If your child and your man come first, where do you fit in?"

It didn't matter where she fit in. Mothers always put themselves last. She snorted. Well, except for her bio mom. She'd chosen herself and what she wanted over everything else.

Justus stopped shoveling the dirt and rocks out of the hole and leaned on the shovel. Being self-absorbed . . . was that her fear?

Was she afraid that she'd choose what she wanted over what was best for her child? That's what her dear old bio mom had done.

Christ, she was just like Katarina Smythe-Herringdale.

She sat down hard on the hole's ledge. It was so clear to her now. She'd left her baby boy with his grandparents and gone off with her lover without a care in the world. All her life she'd wondered what was wrong with her, and now she knew.

Warm tears burned a path down her grimy cheeks. How could she have put herself first? Her little boy was her life, but she sure as hell packed up and left him for a week a year.

Footsteps crunched the dried grass behind her.

"Ms. Justus, I brought you them keys back. Your Imogene is one hell of a good ride." It was Lefty.

She swiped at the tears, planted a smile on her face, and turned around.

Lefty stopped dead in his tracks and his whole body flinched. "You're cryin'." He took a step back like she had malaria or pinkeye or snakes for hair. "Oh, God, you're cryin'."

"It's okay." She choked on her words. "I'm okay."

She was as far from okay as was humanly possible. She'd put herself before her son. She'd felt the sting of rejection, and she'd passed that on to her son. She remembered the all-consuming need for her mother's love, and she never wanted to see the love dim in his eyes.

"Um . . ." He flipped back his straw cowboy hat and scratched his forehead. "Um . . . let me go get . . ." It looked like he was vetting possible candidates in his head. "Somebody else . . . you know . . . like a girl or somethin'." Lefty's eye turned downright feral, as he must have come to the conclusion that there were no other women on the ranch this morning. He checked his watch like he was about to come up with some urgent appointment that he'd forgotten about.

This tough cowboy seemed completely undone when it came to tears, which was funny, so she smiled for real. "It's okay. I'm fine. Why don't you leave the keys on the ground over there and we can both get back to work?"

"Um . . . okay . . . if you're sure." He dropped the keys like they were burning a hole in his palm. Cautiously, he edged closer to her, pulled a crumpled red bandana out of his back pocket, and tossed it in her general direction. She got the impression that if he'd had a metal pole, he'd have tied the bandana to it and extended it so he could stay as far away from her as possible.

She used the bandana to mop her face and then shoved it in her front left shorts pocket. It needed a good wash after she'd muddied it up.

"So, um, that golf cart treating you okay?" He studied a limestone rock on the ground. He must have seen something she couldn't, because his eyes were glued to it.

"Yes, it's wonderful. Everything's fine." More tears leaked from her eyes. She pulled out the dirt-spattered bandana and patted at her eyes.

"I'm going to go fill up Imogene's wiper fluid." He clamped his hands behind his back and finally moved his gaze off the limestone and up to the sky. Today's eye patch had a unicorn that twinkled in the sunlight. "You never know when a storm's gonna pop up."

"Thanks." She did her best to suck back the tears, but it was like unringing a bell.

He turned so fast, it was a wonder that his head didn't pop back.

Justus wiped her cheeks again. It was ridiculous that a few tears could send a tough old cowboy running in the opposite direction.

A horn honked off in the distance over her right shoulder, and Justus turned around. CanDee pulled into the main house's crushed granite driveway and waved out the driver's-side window. She pulled right up to Justus. Her friend's face twisted in horror—she must have seen the tears.

Justus had never realized how much damage saline leaking from her eyeballs could cause. It was so much more fun to cry in private and way less complicated.

"What happened?" CanDee did a three-sixty. "Was Rowdy here? Did he upset you again?"

"No, I was just having one of those crap-I'm-a-terrible-mother moments." Justus took a deep yoga breath and let it out slowly. "It's just another wonderful facet of motherhood."

"Stop. You're the best mother I've ever seen." Since CanDee's mother had died when she was little, Justus didn't want to point out that her friend didn't actually know that many mothers. "Was that Lefty I just saw?"

"Yes, he was here and gave me this." She held up the damp bandana.

"Let me guess, he hightailed it out of here ASAP." CanDee squatted down so that she was on the same level as Justus. "It's the tears. He freaks when he sees a woman cry. A couple of weeks ago he caught me PMSing over having bought the wrong shampoo. He shoved a bandana at me and then went to fill up my windshield wiper fluid."

"He's topping off Imogene as we speak." Justus climbed out of the hole. She shoved the bandana back into her pocket. "No more tears. I'm done."

"Good, because we're going shopping. You have a moral imperative to look stunning tonight so that Rowdy will stumble all over himself. He made you cry; therefore, you must make him bleed with want."

CanDee heaved a what-can-you-do shrug. "It's the way of the world, I don't make the rules."

"I can't. I'm meeting Hugh for lunch and then we're hitting his math hard." Work was one thing, but Hugh had to keep up with his schoolwork. And she needed to tell him the truth about his father. She hadn't done it yesterday because Bear had taken Hugh fishing and then they'd had an all-men's sleepover at the main house. He needed to know the truth, but she was taking the coward's way out and delaying until the last possible moment. It's not that she didn't want to tell him, it was more like she wanted to see how he and Rowdy got on before upending Hugh's whole world.

"I'll text Cinco to hit the math with him. Cinco stole Hugh from Bear, and they are in the saddle, working cows—whatever that means—this afternoon. He's so excited to have a nephew—"

"Please tell him not to say anything." She would have to tell Hugh soon, because the whole family had caught little-boy fever.

"Mum's the word until you're ready. Lucy laid down the law yesterday, and no one defies her. For someone so tiny, she sure does command respect. You'd think that Bear—being enormous—would be the one everyone fears, but Lucy can calm a brotherly riot with the arch of an eyebrow. It's pretty spectacular to watch. She's promised to teach me how she does it."

"That is impressive. Maybe she'll teach me too." Justus would like to have more children someday, so knowing how to stop a riot sounded like a great idea. Now, if she could only get Rowdy to see that kids were wonderful instead of awful, they could go ahead with making some more. Who was she kidding? She'd have more luck making the blind see—oh, wait, that's exactly what she needed to do with Rowdy.

"Load up, we're going shopping." Shopping implied that she had extra money, which she didn't, but when CanDee was in one of her I'm-going-to-cheer-you-up-whether-you-like-it-or-not moods, there was no point in turning her down. Because if she was rejected, she'd just peppy-cheerleader you to death. Besides, shopping was so much more pleasant than someone following Justus around spouting positive motivational messages.

"Okay." She pulled at her filthy Justus Flor-All T-shirt. "Give me ten minutes to change." She looked down at her shorts. "Make that fifteen. I need a shower."

"Want a ride back to the cottage?" CanDee nodded toward the enormous truck she'd driven up in. "Today, I have the truck. Cinco took my Escalade to Fredericksburg."

Her friend didn't seem like the Escalade type, in fact, she was definitely more of a beat-up ten-year-old Toyota Corolla type, which was what she'd had until her fiancé insisted that her car was missing most, if not all, of the safety features necessary to keep her alive, so he'd bought her a huge tank of a car. He wanted her surrounded by metal, airbags, and luxury. It wasn't candy and roses, but it was sort of romantic.

Would Rowdy ever feel the need to keep her safe? She was pretty sure he was feeling the need to wring her neck right about now.

"I'll ride in the back." Justus pointed to the bed of the pickup.

"No, up front. Most of the mud on you is dry." CanDee started the engine. "Cinco won't care. It was his idea to take you shopping. He lives for making his brother uncomfortable. It's how they bond. Well, not just them, all of the brothers. Since we're both only children, trust me, you can't imagine how much trouble siblings came be. I now have four brothers who all try to coddle me. Thank God Lucy didn't have any daughters or the Rose men would have used the first poor boy who showed up to take her out as target practice."

Justus opened the door and a running board rolled down from under the truck's underbelly. She stepped up on it and sat down in the softest leather she'd ever felt. "Nice."

"This is the Texas Rose edition. Cinco supplies the leather to Chevy." CanDee's proud smile spoke volumes about her love for Cinco.

Justus felt the same pride about Rowdy's art. "Those are self-deploying running boards."

"It sounds like they're going off to war." Justus fastened her seat belt.

A little over three hours later, the best friends were deep into a game of twenty-buck dare. Twenty-buck dare had started when they were college roommates. They went to Goodwill with a twenty-dollar budget. Whoever put together the cutest outfit wouldn't have to do the dishes for two weeks. These days, the winner just got bragging rights.

The dressing room they shared was littered with castoffs.

"Loser has to hang all of this stuff back up." Justus slipped on a pair of clear, plastic Stuart Weitzmans she'd found under one of the rolling racks. Silly people. If they'd wanted to hide them away so someone wouldn't buy them, they should have done better than under a clothes rack.

"Someone's a little cocky over some slightly used Stuart Weitzmans." CanDee slipped a golden silk sheath dress over her head. It fell to her midthigh. It was the exactly color of her golden eyes.

"I hate you so much right now. I'm the one who's supposed to look hot tonight and all I've found is a decent pair of shoes." Justus picked up an off-white dress with ruffled sleeves. The color was good, but the ruffles made her look like a matador.

"Personally, I think you should just wear the shoes and nothing else. The shoes speak for themselves." CanDee cupped an ear and leaned down to shoes. "Right now, they're saying, 'I'm a slut, take me on the kitchen table.'"

"Oh, please. I haven't had sex in so long that my lady parts ran away and joined a convent because they've given up all hope of an orgasm." Justus glanced down at the heels on her feet. "They are pretty spectacular."

CanDee blew an errant red curl out of her eyes. "I can't believe I'm going to do this, but . . ." She dug around in the pile of clothes on the metal folding chair that served as a seat and handed it to Justus. "Here, it's perfect for you. I'm handing you the win because I feel really sorry for your ovaries."

The grass-green cotton dress was strapless, fitted to the waist, and then flared out into a full skirt. It was simple and elegant, and Justus prayed that it fit. She practically ripped the zipper down and threw it over her head.

"That color looks wonderful against your tanned arms." CanDee zipped her up.

"It fits perfectly." Justus turned left and then right, getting the whole picture.

CanDee sighed dramatically. "I'll start hanging all of this crap back up."

"I'll help. We're calling this one a tie. You did just throw the game." Justus turned this way and that, admiring herself in the mirror. "What do you think? Is this hot enough?"

A slow smile dawned on CanDee's expressive face. "He's going to beg for forgiveness."

That sounded good, only he really hadn't done anything that needed to be forgiven. She was at fault, and hopefully he'd give her another chance to explain.

# CHAPTER 9

That afternoon, Rowdy sat at the desk in his office above the wine-tasting room and gift shop. He had a mountain of invoices that needed paying, supplies to order, and at least a dozen emails from wine-club members asking for wine recommendations. And then there was the Riesling launch in a couple of weeks.

Now that his wines were garnering worldwide attention, the preorders for his new Riesling were coming in fast and furious. The fact that no one outside of family and friends had tried it didn't seem to matter. At this rate, he would be lucky to have enough to serve at the launch.

He needed to talk with Ernesto, his foreman, about planting fifty more acres and expanding the barrel room. His once-tiny winery was experiencing some growing pains. He had five blog interviews to do and he needed to put the finishing touches on the social media campaign for the Riesling launch.

Unfortunately, all he could do was sit here and stare out the bay window that faced his parents' house. It was too far away for him to see Justus, who was no doubt deep in mud, but that didn't stop his mind from wandering in her direction.

Justus was coming to dinner. How was that going to work?

His stomach rolled, and he couldn't tell if it was from a hangover or nervous anticipation. Justus was here and not even a mile away. She hadn't left and he would get to see her tonight. She wasn't out of his life forever. He couldn't shake the mad, but something deep down inside of him had to make sure she was okay. It didn't make sense. He was hurt and confused, but her well-being meant more to him than his own. He glanced at the clock on his iMac. It was two forty-one and she was coming over at seven. A little over four hours to wait.

How could he be angry and happy at the same time?

What should he make for her? At Burning Man, he'd told her that like she, he was a vegetarian. Holy crap, he'd actually given up meat for her. Love was so weird.

Steak would be a surefire way of showing her that he wasn't a vegetarian. He'd picked up a tub of baby spinach in Fredericksburg on his way home from the airport. So, he'd throw together a salad. He also had a decent crème brûlée recipe that he was pretty sure he could pull off.

Oh, God. He scraped his hands over his face. God help him, he was looking forward to seeing her. She'd omitted the truth of them having a son together, and he was looking forward to seeing her.

What was he going to do? What was there to do? Hugh was his son. The way he saw it, he only had two choices. He could get to know the little guy and make the best of things, and if that failed, he would make sure Hugh and Justus were provided for. He'd buy them a house—something nice and close by—so he could still see Justus, and he'd pay child support. Hell, he could afford it. He made good money with the winery, and then there was his trust fund. He hit the space bar, and his iMac lit up and stood to attention, ready to do his bidding. He fired off an email to his attorney, outlining his idea for the house and child support.

The more he thought about it, the more he liked the idea of having Justus close. Maybe they could even build something for her and Hugh on the ranch. That way they could have their space and Rowdy could have his. It was the best thing for everyone.

Light knocking sounded at his closed office door. He couldn't have stopped his lip snarl if he'd wanted to. Couldn't a man have a personal crisis in peace? For the love of God, he and his family lived on eight hundred thousand acres. With all of that open country, whoever was at the door should be able to find something to do other than bother him.

The knocking got louder.

"What." He wasn't shouting exactly, he was merely using his loud voice. Now that he had the Hugh situation handled, he moved on to the Riesling launch. Two weeks wasn't that far away, and he still had so many things to do. Because of the success of his Hill Country Sparkling Wine, what he'd thought was going to be a small affair was turning into something huge and unwieldy. Everyone he'd invited was planning on coming and needed a place to stay and food and a private tour. He was a details man, but things were getting out of hand.

The door opened and his mother popped her head in. "Somebody woke up on the wrong side of the bed this morning."

He loved his mother dearly, but this morning he would have preferred to love her from a distance. His foul mood and not much sleep would probably make him say some things that he'd need to apologize for later.

She stepped into the room, closed the door, and leaned on it. Her eyes went to his neck, which was absent his usual necktie. "Or is it because you woke up alone?"

"I'll have you know that I didn't wake up alone. Lefty was standing over me. And I'm not discussing my sex life with you." He couldn't help but wonder if any other man in the history of mankind had ever uttered that sentence to his mother before now. He hoped to never say it again.

"What sex life?" She folded her arms and took on the tone she used with her unruliest of patients. There were times that he loved his mother's open-mindedness and times that he wished she weren't a doctor and was a prude.

"Oh, God, you're not going to lecture me on female orgasms and how achieving those are the mark of a good lover again are you? We covered that in nauseating detail back in puberty. I remember because it actually made me nauseated. It's a wonder I ever had sex after that." It was tough having a mother who saw the human body as nothing more than a machine and was embarrassed by nothing.

"Not unless you have questions, but based on the smile on Jenny What's-her-face who snuck out of your window in high school, I'm pretty sure you have the basics down."

"You knew about that?" He knew his eyes were so big they were in danger of falling out of his head.

"I am all knowing. Think of me as God, only closer and less forgiving." She shot him her infamous I-know-what-you-did-so-go-ahead-and-confess-it look. "Don't you have something you'd like to tell me?"

Crap. What had he done? He searched his mind for something that needed confessing, but he couldn't think of anything. Was he supposed to make something up? She wasn't about to leave without some sort of confession.

"Burning Man?" she prompted. "That was your big secret? On second thought, I guess I'm not all knowing."

Damn, Justus strikes again. Of course she'd outed him to his mother. Hell, his brothers knew. Now he not only felt betrayed by her, but embarrassed as well. It was a terrible thing to be embarrassed in front of his parents. By now his father would know, because his parents never kept secrets from each other.

Going to Burning Man was not a productive way to spend his time. He hunkered down, waiting for the lecture she'd once given him on responsibilities. She was all about work before play, and Burning Man was nothing but play. This was going to be just like the time in college when he'd skipped work for a boys' weekend in San Antonio. The fact that he hadn't bothered to call and tell them he wasn't coming in had prompted a welfare check from the sheriff's office.

"You thought I wouldn't understand?" His mother looked wounded.

"It's not that I didn't think you'd understand . . ." He rubbed the tense muscles at the back of his neck. Well, that wasn't quite the truth. Not only would they not understand, but they would figure out that he was different.

"You're a terrible liar." She sighed heavily. "You rub your neck when you lie." Her intense stare never left him. "Why would you think that I wouldn't understand?"

Because he didn't feel like he fit in to his own family. He liked fine wine and opera and reality TV and Gucci loafers while everyone else with his DNA loved beer and football and killing innocent animals. If he looked up "cowboy" on Dictionary.com, there'd be a picture of the other Rose men, but he didn't fit in. He could hold his own on the ranch, but his passion was wine instead of livestock. Sure, he liked the way meat tasted, but analyzing how the meat went from cow to plate made him physically ill.

"We all live so close to one another that not much is private. I guess I wanted something just for me." That was partly true. He'd worked so hard and so long to fit in that he couldn't stand for anyone to think less of him because he didn't share the same beliefs or hobbies or interests as the rest of his family. Hell, in the last presidential election, he'd voted Democrat. In his family, associating himself with the D-word was akin to confessing that he was an ax murderer or a domestic terrorist or a vegan.

He'd always been on the outside looking in, so to protect himself, he never let them know who he really was. It felt like he'd been pretending his whole life. A memory niggled at the back of his mind. A picture that he wanted to share with his mother. She'd been pregnant—maybe with T-Bone—and on her way to the hospital to work her shift. He had to have been about five. He'd been so proud to show her his drawing of a horse. She'd barely looked at it before rushing out the door. The next morning, he'd found the picture in the trash.

It was odd to find that it still hurt.

"I guess I can buy that." She looked like she didn't buy it at all. "And the art?"

The image of the crumpled picture he'd pulled from the big kitchen trash can popped into his head.

"What art?" Blood pounded in his ears, but outwardly, he shrugged one shoulder dramatically to drive home the idea that he didn't know what she was talking about. They both knew he was lying.

She gave him her one-eyebrow-up, yeah-right look.

What else had Justus outed him on?

"I paint just for me. The only person I've shared it with is Justus. My art is personal, and I'm not ready to share it with the family." Just talking about it felt like someone was slowly squeezing all of the air out of his lungs.

"I can understand that. You father has his mosaics and I have my *People* magazine. Sorry, gossip mags are how I relax."

"What?" If she'd sprouted two heads and started speaking Russian, he couldn't have been more surprised. His mother who read only medical journals also read *People* magazine? It seemed that he didn't know his family as well as he thought he did.

"What can I say, I love me some celebrity gossip." She grinned.

"Wait a minute. Dad does mosaics? I don't understand." His father could barely draw a stick figure. Rowdy remembered so clearly his father telling him that art was nothing but a waste of time.

"After he retired this last time, he took a class at the junior college." She nodded. "He's very talented. I think he was a little embarrassed to tell the rest of the family, but I'm truly in awe of his talent. He and Hugh are working on a piece for the hospital's healing garden. You should stop by and check it out. It's incredible. Almost as good as your watercolors." She shot him a tell-your-mother-everything look.

He should have known that Justus would have showed his mother pictures of his paintings. This felt like another layer of betrayal. The trouble with someone who's as open as Justus was, was that she's open with everyone . . . except apparently with him as it related to her having given birth to his son.

His dad was an artist. It didn't fit, but at the same time he could totally see it. Was that where he got it from? Why had he never seen his father do anything remotely artistic?

Since Rowdy wasn't forthcoming on the watercolor info, she moved on. "Now, what did you do you plan on doing to make up with Justus?"

"Don't you think it should be the other way around?" He liked the view from his high horse. "She's the one who neglected to mention that we have a son."

"Yes . . . you're right, but why didn't she tell you?" His mother had that all-knowing mom tone going on. "I know that you're hurt and angry, but so is Justus. You have every right to your feelings, and yes, she does need to explain . . . but she doesn't strike me as a person who would purposefully hurt anyone. But you know her better than I do."

No, she wasn't, but he wasn't willing to admit that out loud.

"She's hurting too." His mother was too reasonable for her own good.

That should give him some sense of pleasure, but he loved her. Hurting Justus made him feel like a giant asshole.

Hold on . . . he still loved her? He tunneled his fingers through his hair. Of course he still loved her. He always knew that when he fell in love, he'd fall hard and forever. And he had fallen hard the very moment he'd seen her. He needed to sit down . . . wait, he was sitting down.

"Is it Hugh?" His mother watched him like a hawk.

"It's complicated." The "stay out of it" was implied, because if he'd actually said it out loud, he'd have to make it up to two women that he loved.

"Uncomplicate it." She stood and walked to his desk. "Hugh's the cutest kid I've ever met, and that includes all five of my sons."

"Come on. I'm cute." His whininess seemed to have showed up at the same time as Justus. So love made a man whiny?

"Why don't you get to know Hugh before passing judgment on him and his mother?" It wasn't a request. When Dr. Lucy Rose issued an order, she expected that it would be followed to the letter with no questions asked.

He knew it was pretty good advice, but he had a plan. "I've been giving that some thought."

"Good." Her eyes drew together and three lines dented her forehead. Uh-oh. He knew that look. It was the one she used when she finally figured out the hardest, most obscure word in the *New York Times* crossword puzzle. "Does this have something to do with you always saying that you don't like children?"

Maybe. "No."

Actually, he didn't know that many . . . or for that matter, any children.

His mother walked around the desk, leaned down, and kissed him on the top of the head. "It's different when they are your own kids. Look at me, I wasn't that into kids until I had one. Trust me, kids can be fun. Don't get me wrong, it's hard work, but so worth it."

"I'm pretty sure you weren't thinking that when I broke your grandmother's crystal vase. You certainly didn't look like you were having fun then." In fact, he remembered her looking like she wanted to banish him to China.

"You were playing football in the house." Even all these years later, she didn't look mildly amused.

"It was winter and cold outside. Where exactly was I supposed to practice? Everyone in Texas knows that you could freeze to death if you go outside when it's below forty degrees." He put his hand over his chest. "We Texans are a warm-blooded species more acclimated to a hundred and eight degrees, I am merely a product of my environment."

"Yeah, that argument didn't work when you were in high school, and it's not any better now." She mussed his hair. "See if you and Justus can find some common ground. That's where you need to start."

Besides Burning Man and the son he just found out about, the only other common ground he shared with Justus was sex. It seemed to work for them at Burning Man. It wasn't a forever, but it was a start.

# CHAPTER 10

Rowdy took the steaks out of the fridge and set them on the counter.

He gritted his teeth. They had a son.

Finding out about Hugh had been a punch straight to the heart. He could understand her forgetting to tell him that she had a dog or a ton of credit-card debt or even—his hands fisted—a lover, but a child? They'd been together for over a decade, and over half of that time, she'd neglected to mention they had a son. He ground a mountain of salt on one steak, so he brushed off a good bit. She'd had a little bitty baby who'd turned into a not-so-little boy . . . all by herself.

Why did he feel cheated? He'd missed a lot of her life and his son's.

Rowdy had a son. Besides Justus bringing up children at Burning Man, he'd never really given fatherhood much thought—well, there was that one scare in college when his girlfriend's period was late. Back then, fatherhood had gotten him in a choke hold for two long weeks, and he'd almost lost his mind.

He was a father. The title didn't sit easily on his shoulders. He didn't have all that much to offer a child. Yes, he was successful and financially stable, but emotionally, he didn't have much to give. He poured everything he had into his wine. Between his business and his family responsibilities, he didn't have time for a child. Everyone he knew who had a child always said that after a kid, their life had changed. He didn't want his life to change. He liked his life just fine.

Which was why he'd wanted to change it by marrying Justus. Still, children were messy and clingy and needy. He didn't have time for that.

It always seemed that he had the good fortune to sit by the parents who sipped calmly on their margaritas as their kids Tarzaned off tables and swung from the chandeliers. Surely there were good kids too.

Shouldn't there have been some sort of genetic recognition when he first laid eyes on Hugh? He rolled his eyes. What the hell was genetic recognition?

Christ, he had a family . . . him . . . the confirmed bachelor who made exceptional wine and lived a neat, color-inside-the-lines life. Days ago, when he'd been about to propose to Daisy . . . well, Justus, he hadn't figured a kid into the plan. If he was being honest, he really hadn't had a plan so much as a desire to spend the rest of his life with her in whatever capacity she'd let him. That was Burner-self talking . . . no thinking, just doing. That worked at Burning Man, but not so much in his real life.

Now things had changed.

Or had they?

What if she had told him that she was pregnant? Not that she could have since they were Burning Man Only. What would he have done?

Seven years ago, he'd barely gotten the winery off the ground and was about to release his first cabernet sauvignon. He worked sixty-, seventy-hour workweeks.

After the cab was released, Rowdy had traveled across the country, harassing possible distributors into carrying his wine. His life had been hectic and frantic and no place for a pregnant wife and then a baby.

He would have had to divide his time between his business and personal lives . . . both would have suffered. If he looked at it objectively, he probably wouldn't have gotten the Texas Rose Winery off the ground. His life had been a hectic mess until last year, when he'd finally hired a seasoned vintner from California, a warehouse foreman, and a general manager.

His dream of having a successful winery would have been nothing more than a dream if he'd had a family to support. Hell, the wine only started turning a profit two years ago. If it weren't for his trust fund, he'd have been working cattle like everyone else. It's not that he didn't like working on the ranch, it just didn't suit him like making wine did. In the beginning, he'd done everything himself, including creating the wine labels. He'd worked hard, and it had taken some fast-talking to convince his father that making wine was more than just a hobby. He'd worked twice as hard as his brothers because he'd had twice as much to prove.

He was doing exactly what he wanted to do, and people were paying top dollar for him to do it.

Certainly, it would have taken him longer to establish his winery if he hadn't been able to pour all of his time into the endeavor. Having a family wouldn't have necessarily wiped out the winery, but it would have taken many more years.

Deep down, he knew that he'd have resented Justus and maybe even Hugh. He didn't like other people to make decisions for him. But that was the thing. Even if Justus had told him about Hugh, she wouldn't have wanted or expected anything from him.

Outside of his mother, Justus was the most fiercely independent woman he'd ever met. She didn't ask for help—not because she was afraid of appearing weak, but because she didn't need it. He grinned. Damn, he liked that about her. There didn't seem to be anything she couldn't do. Self-sufficiency was an understatement.

He would have insisted that they get married because his family would have expected it, and if he was being honest, he would have expected it. He'd always admired his parents' relationship. They genuinely loved each other. They hadn't had a shotgun marriage.

He grabbed a bottle of 2009 Rancho Red from the floor-to-ceiling wine rack that covered an entire wall of his kitchen, popped the cork, and set it out to breathe on the counter.

Justus as a mother. That would be interesting to see. She was probably a good one because she liked taking care of other people. At Burning Man, she'd always taken care of complete strangers. If someone was sick, she had a purse full of medicine, if they needed a shoulder to lean on, she was there propping them up, if someone was carrying something heavy, she was there to lend a hand. She noticed when others were in need, and she acted.

Rowdy picked up the bag of baby spinach, opened it, and dumped it into a colander. Sure, the bag said that it was triple washed, but he liked to make sure. He rinsed again and set it in the sink to drain. A week ago if someone had told him that he would be fixing dinner for Justus, he would have told them they were crazy.

Nerves ping-ponged around in his stomach. He absolutely couldn't wait to see her and didn't want to see her at the same time.

He assumed that Justus would bring Hugh to dinner. How awkward was that going to be?

He'd pulled out three steaks. Was Hugh a vegetarian too? Could little kids be vegetarians? For that matter, could he eat an entire steak? Maybe he should put back one of the steaks. He hesitated. No, he'd cook it along with the others and if no one ate it, he'd have it over a salad tomorrow for lunch.

At the sound of the doorbell, his stomach dropped to his knees. He had a feeling that this evening was going to be a disaster.

Rowdy smoothed his white button-down and made sure that it was tucked into his dark brown Armani trousers. In Justus's eyes, this would be a different look for him. She was used to seeing him in cutoffs and Birks, but this was how he normally dressed. Here, he felt more at ease in a tailored suit than he did in a T-shirt.

He opened the huge reclaimed-oak, cantilevered front door.

Justus stood there, holding a pie. He looked around for Hugh, but the little guy was nowhere to be found.

Was it bad that he felt a little relieved?

"Hugh?" He stepped aside to let her in. It was surreal having her in his house.

"Dallas and Worth invited him to an Avengers movie night at Dallas's house. Hugh wanted to come tonight, but they promised him that he could eat his weight in popcorn and that's hard to pass up." She held the pie out to him. "I made a coconut cream pie."

"My favorite." He took the pie from her. "Thanks."

Silence settled in like early-morning fog over a lake. Awkward didn't begin to cover it.

"Look, this is weird. I feel like things shouldn't be so strange between us." Her green eyes were the same color as the Autumncrisp grapes that were just ripening on his vines. The dress she wore hugged her curves and was a shade or two darker than her eyes. Her long, golden-blond hair was a straight curtain down to the middle of her back, and her sun-bronzed shoulders were bare. She smelled like vanilla and coconut. He shoved his hands in his pockets to keep from touching her.

"It does seem odd having you here." He just stood there, holding the pie and staring at her. "You know, odd, but not in a bad way."

Five seconds in her presence and he'd already lost the ability to form coherent sentences. No one clouded his head like Justus.

"This is stupid. We know each other so well, but I guess we need to start again." She held out her hand. "Hello, my name is Justus Jacobi, nice to meet you."

He shifted the pie in his grip and shook her hand. "I'm Rowdy Rose, it's nice to meet you too." Considering everything that had happened in the last two days, it was stupid to feel this happy just being near her. Now was as good of a time as any to make a confession. "Just so you know, I'm not a vegetarian."

She grinned, and he noticed that one of her top teeth was slightly crooked. He'd forgotten that. "Me either." Her eyebrows bounced off of her hairline. "Cows taste good."

It occurred to him that he could happily spend the rest of his life standing right here and just staring at her. She was here . . . at his house. Would he always be gobsmacked by the depth of feeling she brought out in him? Or several years from now, would he get used to having her around and take her for granted? God, he hoped not. Every time he saw her, he fell a little bit more in love.

Considering their recent past, he didn't know why her not being a vegetarian came as such a shock to him. "So that soy bacon?"

"Nasty stuff. Choked it down because I wanted to impress you." She slipped her arm through his. "Kept my stash of beef jerky in my tampon box."

"I always wondered why you insisted on bringing the world's largest box of tampons every year. Seriously, it looked like you had enough for half the female population of Black Rock City." Joking with her was comfortable ground. This was how it had been at Burning Man.

"If you want to hide something from men, disguise it as feminine hygiene products. Works every time. So." She looked up at him. "Show me to the kitchen so we can put that pie down, and then I want to see the rest of the house."

He'd forgotten how wonderful it was just to be near her. Only she'd had his son and didn't tell him. The longer he stared at her, the less it seemed to matter.

"I'm guessing you're not going to be into the black bean burgers I have planned." He shot her a grin. "I bought the best veganaise I could find."

She blanched. "I hope you're kidding, because I'm not above running back to the cottage and getting the tampon box. I will if I have to, but fair warning, I'm not sharing. A girl's beef jerky is a private thing and shouldn't be shared with other fake vegetarians."

God he wanted to kiss her. He could just back her up against the wall and set his mouth on her. But they were getting reacquainted—meeting their non-Burner selves—and he wanted so much more from her than sex. Instead, he led her to his kitchen.

"Wow, this is huge." She looked around, taking it all in. She liked to cook and to bake—he'd forgotten that.

"It's one of my favorite rooms." He loved the miles and miles of beige-, black-, and maroon-flecked granite countertops. He'd painted the walls a warm taupe that contrasted well with the dark maple cabinets and the bronze barrel ceiling that ran the entire length of the kitchen and living room. One entire wall was floor-to-ceiling windows. There were three islands, four ovens, two stoves, and a wood-burning pizza oven. This was a cook's kitchen, and he liked to cook.

Elvis waddled in, gave Justus a 'sup nod, headed to his water bowl, lapped up enough water to fill Lake Michigan, backed away from the bowl, and waddled back down the hallway.

"He's not a normal dog, is he?" Justus watched as Elvis disappeared into his bedroom.

"In his mind, he's the king of the world, and we lesser humans live to serve him." Elvis had started out as his brother Cinco's dog, and then he'd met Rowdy and found a kindred spirit.

Her eyes locked on the steaks sitting out on the center island. "Those are some pretty good-looking black bean T-bones." She examined the meat. "Nice cut.

He laughed. "We have an endless supply of beef, chicken, pork, and some buffalo."

"It's a carnivore's dream." She looked around, taking in every detail. "So tidy."

"I like a neat house." Some people called him anal, he preferred ordered. Not that he was defensive or anything. Okay, maybe a bit. Order equaled control, and he really liked control.

Were they just going to small-talk each other to death or were they ever going to get to the meat of the issue?

"Is your house always this clean?" She ran a fingertip along the counter, checking for dust. "Or did you hide all of the dirty dishes and Doritos bags in here?" She pulled open the top oven closest to her.

"Sorry to disappoint you, but all of my dirty dishes are the in the dishwasher, and I'm fresh out of Doritos." It was both unsettling and completely normal to have her in his house. She both fit in and stuck out. Around her, he felt himself falling into the old color-outside-the-lines Houston. Sweat broke out on his upper lip. He couldn't be that man here. Having her here in his fortress of solitude made him feel vulnerable. The man who lived on the Texas Rose Ranch was a stranger to her. Would she like him after she got to know this version?

She walked to one of the white leather sofas positioned on either side of the coffee table of his great room. "White furniture . . . interesting choice. With a dog, how to do you keep it clean?"

"Elvis hates clutter and mess more than I do. He picks up after himself." He grabbed the pepper to finish seasoning the steaks.

She turned back to him. "I appreciate the clean lines, but all of that white is just begging for some cherry Kool-Aid."

"Go ahead, it's treated. Those sofas are practically bulletproof." At least he was fairly sure they were bulletproof. The thought of a big red stain on his pristine white carpet added sweaty armpits to go with his sweaty upper lip.

"That sounds like a challenge." She walked around, examining the art on the walls. "There's never any cherry Kool-Aid around when you need it." She tilted her head to the left and then to the right. "What is this?"

"It's called *Midnight Stampede*." It was a watercolor he'd bought in one of his favorite galleries in Dallas. The colors were muted earth tones against the star-filled night sky. He'd have used richer colors, but the painting was still nice.

She leaned down, examining the signature in the lower right-hand corner. "I thought this didn't look like your work. You told me that you made wine, I just thought that was your hobby and you were a painter." She looked back at him. "I guess it's the other way around." She scanned the other artwork in the room. "None of these look like your work."

"Yes, I make wine for money and paint for fun. I don't like to display my work. My art is for my eyes only. I really just paint for myself."

She didn't look like she entirely bought his answer, but she nodded. "I still have the painting you did of me watching the sunset on the Playa." She smiled. "It's in storage now, but it used to hang above my fireplace."

"Storage?" Why were her things in storage? Had she been living with someone and then recently moved out and that's why she hadn't made it to Burning Man this year? His voice turned high and pitchy. "Were you living with someone?"

Being around her was like being in a sweat lodge.

He wanted to know and then didn't want to know.

"I've been living with someone for the last seven years." She inspected the painting over his bookcase.

There it was. She'd been involved with someone. He knew it.

She turned around and grinned at him. "He's about yea big"—she leaned down so that her hand was at her midthigh—"and is the cutest kid in the world. I put my things in storage because I'll be here for at least six months. Your mom has a few more projects for me." She watched him carefully. "Is that okay with you?"

That took his blood pressure back down to normal levels.

Part of him wanted her to stay forever. "Stay as long as you like."

That sounded lame.

Awkward silence sucked all of the oxygen out of the room.

"Wine?" She pointed to the bottle sitting on the island. "Can I have some?"

"Of course." They both could use some wine.

He grabbed a couple of glasses from the cabinet next to the wine rack and filled them halfway.

She took her glass and sipped. "Yum. You always did have the best taste in wine."

"This is our Rancho Red. It's won several gold medals." He was very proud of his wine. In a relatively short time, he'd built a brand that was well respected in the wine community.

"So is your plan to get me liquored . . . well wined up and then have your way with me?" Her laugh was forced as she took a big gulp. "In case you forgot, I can hold my wine."

"I haven't forgotten, but I have access to more wine than the average bear." He nodded to the wall of wine.

"That is impressive." She held her glass out for a toast. "To our better Burner halves, may we be able to mix real life with Playa life."

He didn't know if he was ready or willing to mix the two. Clearly when he'd made the decision to propose, he hadn't thought out the logistics, which was strange because he always worked out the details before making a decision. Would she have said yes? At one time, he'd thought he'd known the answer, but now he didn't.

He clinked her glass. "I couldn't have said it better myself."

They both took a sip.

"Okay, since we're in the getting-to-know-you phase again, hand over your phone. I need to check your playlists." She set her wine down on the island and held out her hand. "If my Houston is still in there, I better see some Def Leppard and lots of Rob Thomas."

He liked her use of "my Houston." His heart went pitter-pat, and he could stand to hear her say it a few million more times. He pulled his phone out of his front left pocket, entered the security code, and opened the Music app. She was about to get a shock, but it was better that she know the truth.

She browsed his playlists. "Very interesting." She ran her finger down the screen. "That's way more opera than should be legal." She held a hand up. "Don't get me wrong. I love me some *La Bohème*, but a little heavy on the Peter Maxwell Davies compositions. I have to say that I prefer the old masters to the modern."

"You know opera?" She never ceased to amaze him. He didn't remember them talking opera, but clearly she knew hers. Their common ground got wider and wider. Hopefully, it would be enough to bridge the gap between them.

Justus nodded and put the phone down. "So, do you need help with dinner?"

"Sure, you can toss the salad." He pointed to the colander in the sink. "There's a salad bowl in the cabinet next to the sink and some tongs in that crock on the counter." He pointed to the cabinet. "I have dressing in the small carafe, and if you're feeling extra helpful, you can rummage through the fridge for other veggies to add. The grill should be ready."

He picked up the plate with the steaks and grabbed a pair of tongs.

"Not many men know what a carafe is or how to use it correctly in a sentence, not to mention filling it with salad dressing." She turned keen green eyes on him. "I get the feeling that you're high maintenance. There's a rumor floating around that you and your dog get weekly mani-pedis."

He grinned. "We prefer to call it male grooming." He held his hands up. "My cuticles are so soft."

He couldn't help but notice that her hands showed that she was all about the hard work and had a feeling that she wouldn't sit still long enough for a manicure. Maybe he could talk her into trying it.

"I rest my case. High maintenance." She grabbed the salad bowl and dumped the baby spinach in it. She looked around. "Your dog and house are high maintenance too."

"I know Elvis is, but come on. How can a house be high maintenance?"

"So much white and not a speck of dust. It must take an army to clean. I knew you were neat, but this is taking it a bit far." She opened the fridge and prowled around. She came out with a tomato, carrot, some mushrooms, a red onion, and some strawberries. "Oh my God, I bet you're one of those people who doesn't allow food in rooms outside of the kitchen."

She made a big show of scanning the kitchen floor.

"What are you looking for?" He loved her strange sense of humor. If it weren't for the whole lied-to-him-for-seven-years-about-his-son thing, this would be a wonderful evening.

"The kitchen boundary lines. As well put-together as this place is, I'm sure that there's some sort of markings defining the border of where food is allowed. I need to know where the lines are so that I can cross them." She shrugged. "That's just how I roll."

Her non-Burner persona was a whole lot like her Burner one. He was the only one who was different. What would it feel like to be that comfortable with himself? Then again, she had omitted that fact that they had a son, so she wasn't above a little deception herself. Speaking of Hugh . . . were they ever going to speak of Hugh? It seemed best to let her bring him up.

"I know. You hate rules." He covered the steaks with plastic wrap and let them finish coming to room temp. "Maybe I just tidied up because I knew you were coming over."

She crossed her arms and looked everything over. "Since your place is clean enough to do surgery on the floor and would take a team of ten cleaning professionals at least two days to complete, I'm going with your house was already clean. You're a neat freak."

"Let's not go labeling people." True, he believed everything had a place, which made life so much easier. But around her, he could feel the control he'd so carefully constructed around himself slipping away. He looked around. His house may appear too neat to others, but he wasn't ready to disrupt the order.

"I bet you own more than one vacuum." She hunted around in the cabinets until she came up with a wooden chopping board. She grabbed a knife out of the block by the stove and delicately chopped the tomato.

"So what if I do? That doesn't mean anything." He had a Dyson upright and a handheld Dyson Animal cordless. Some messes were big and some small—a person needed vacuums equal to the mess size.

"I don't even own one vacuum. I borrow my next-door neighbor's." She scattered tomato bits over the top of the spinach.

"That sounds like a personal problem. I'm all about cleaning up the world around me, but I draw the line at lending you my vacuum. Some things a man needs to keep to himself." He leaned against the cabinet and watched her work in his kitchen.

"Do you and your vacuums need a moment? I can wait in the other room." She sliced mushrooms and tossed them into the salad.

"No, Rochelle and Tiffany know their place. They only come out after I've made a big mess." He nodded in the direction of the laundry room. "My girls are always waiting for me."

"TMI—what happened to keeping things private?" She opened a few drawers until she found the vegetable peeler and then went to work on the carrot. She peeled slices directly into the bowl. "I hope you don't get their names mixed up. There's nothing worse than a vengeful vacuum."

They'd always been good at banter. She kept him on his toes, and he loved to see how her mind worked.

Now if only they could address the big elephant in the room, they could get on with life.

# CHAPTER 11

Getting to know someone Justus thought she already knew was like going backstage after a play. Once, after a local performance of *The Sound of Music*, she'd gone to a cast party and had seen Mother Abbess knocking back shots and dirty dancing with Captain von Trapp. She had lost her innocence to a nun's habit and lederhosen.

This felt the same way, only she didn't know if today's version of Rowdy was the real thing or the character he was playing. When Lefty had asked her to dinner on Rowdy's behalf, she'd been more than a little surprised and relieved. She'd wanted to believe that it had all been Rowdy's idea, but she wasn't so sure.

"So, tell me about the wine business." She slipped off her Stuart Weitzmans as she sat on his white sofa, tucking her feet under her. They needed to talk about Hugh. It was selfish, but she didn't want this tentative intimacy to end. She'd wait for him to bring it up.

His aqua eyes followed her every movement. "You did that whenever we'd sit down to dinner."

She looked down. "What?"

"Fold your feet under you." He slipped off his shoes and tried to shuffle his lanky, muscular body into the same position as hers. Long legs and an over-six-foot frame didn't bend easily. He looked like a stiff pretzel.

"You haven't been doing your yoga." She waggled her right index finger at him.

"No." He swung his legs out in front of him.

"Why?" He loved yoga, or at least he had. Was that another lie?

"It's sort of a Burning Man only thing for me." The you-dropped-off-the-face-of-the-earth this year hung in the air unsaid.

"I'm here now." She stood and held out her hand. "Let's get you loosened up."

He took it and stood. "Go easy on me, I'm more than a little rusty."

She stepped behind him and gently moved his arms until they were straight over his head. At touching him, the same old familiar zing raced through her system. She'd forgotten how good he smelled—lemony with something under it that was all male. "Let's start with mountain pose." She dropped her arms. "Hold it, and now on to hands to heart." She guided his arms. The was something both personal and primal about human touch. Being near him again soothed something deep inside her. Was it the same for him? "Forward bend."

She ran her hands up his back and urged his shoulders down. He couldn't make it all the way over. His golden-blond hair was a bit too long and was starting to curl at the ends. "You are rusty. You used to be able to touch your nose to your knee."

"You just want me to bend over so you can stare at my butt." He grinned up at her.

"I'm not going to lie; I've checked it out several times tonight." And every other part of him. She stepped back and gave it a good, long look. It had always been this easy between them, well, as long as they didn't bring up the elephant in the room. "Nice."

He tried to shake his booty but his mobility was limited. "Stop admiring my Armani-clad ass. It's embarrassing." He tried to wiggle it some more, lost his balance, but caught himself before he face-planted into the fluffy white rug covering the white travertine tile.

Everything in here was a variation of white. More evidence that he didn't want children, because white anything wouldn't be white any longer. His world was clean and white, and he appeared to like it that way. She'd been waiting for him to bring up Hugh, but the longer this went on, the less likely that was to happen.

"Whoa there, Cowboy. Let's stick to yoga and leave booty-shaking to *Dancing with the Stars*." She'd meant to bring up Hugh, but when she'd opened her mouth, her baby boy hadn't come out. "Armani? Out here I would expect Wranglers and cowboy boots."

Light subjects . . . nothing too personal. That's what they'd cover tonight. She glanced at his shoes. "Are those Gucci?"

He was so different . . . they were so different. He was Gucci and she was Goodwill. There was a reason they'd been Burning Man Only. The loafers weren't bad, but she liked him better in Birks. Which ones did he like? Did he even know?

"Somebody knows her designers." He grinned at her. "I don't remember you liking the finer things in life."

"Or you." She really wasn't into the finer things, but she had become more materialistic in recent years. Being a mother made her crave stability for herself and her son. Like the house she wanted to buy and all of the furniture and trappings that went with it. Gone were her nomadic days when she could throw all of her possessions into two cardboard boxes and hit the road. Freedom wasn't all she'd once thought it to be. Staying put and building a life was her plan now. "I may not wear Gucci, but I can spot it a mile away."

"This from a woman who uses an old T-shirt as a coffee filter." He pressed down farther, stretching his back.

"Hey, it works. Why buy coffee filters when you have an old shirt laying around?" She may be moderately materialistic, but she wasn't about to squander her hard-earned money on one-use items.

Multitasking was important, and she insisted on using items that worked as hard as she did. There was materialism and then there was madness. "Unfortunately my recognition of the finer things is in my DNA. Believe me, if I could turn it off, I would."

"I don't understand." He watched her.

"Move into half lift." She stood beside him and bent over into half lift. "My mother is all about the Chanel and Dior."

Surely, they'd talked about this. She was almost certain that she had. Then again, she kept that hurt pretty close to her breast. Having the world know that her bio mom hadn't wanted her didn't make her feel all happy, happy, joy, joy.

"Maeve?" His eyes squinted up like he was trying to figure out the mysteries of the universe. "I thought she was a potter."

"Maeve is my stepmother. My real mother, or the egg donor as I like to call her, is Katarina Smythe-Herringdale—"

"Wait a minute." He stood up. "The *Rich Housewives of Beverly Hills'* Katarina Smythe-Herringdale? I love her British accent."

"The fact that you know who she is further proves that I don't know you at all. And she's not British. She's from Longview, Texas." She'd never watched the TV show where her mother reigned as queen bitch, lording over all of the lesser queen bitches.

"I'm a complex man." He moved back into half lift. "Besides, *Rich Housewives* comes on after *Million Dollar Real Estate*. Those dudes would eat their own young to sell a house."

"Reality TV? I think I liked you better in cutoffs and T-shirts as a starving artist." Or at least she'd assumed he'd been a starving artist. She glanced around. She'd been wrong.

"Everyone has their own version of starving artist. Mine's more of an internal starvation than an outward one." He grinned at her. "You know that some people believe that doing yoga opens the mind for communing with Satan."

"People used to believe that the world was flat and that the common cold was caused by evil spirits—what's your point?"

His eyes locked on to the hem of her dress like he was using a mental tractor beam to move it up. "I don't know about Satan, but your skirt is riding up, and I admit that some of my thoughts might be running to an impure nature. I can't wait for down dog."

"What is it with men and down dog?" She rolled her eyes.

"It's nothing sexual . . . not at all. We're just amazed by your flexibility." He was all seriousness.

"Yeah, right." She moved into down dog, and he followed. "So instead of doing yoga you watch endless, mindless hours of the Gossip TV channel. Sounds lonely."

"Are you kidding? With Gossip TV, I'm never alone." His eyes stayed on her short skirt and ever-growing amount of skin showing.

"That's what most people say about God." She shook her head. Reality TV actually fit his personality . . . even at Burning Man, he was all about the pop culture current events.

"Stan Goldberg is the Gossip TV god. He holds the ladies accountable for their misdeeds, doles out tough love, and baptizes them in the cocktail of the night. Think about it, if more people worshipped him instead of God, wars would consist of bitch-slapping and table flipping, and then after we could all hug it out over cucumber margaritas." He nodded slowly like he was completely serious.

"Clearly, you've thought this out. Move into plank." This version of Rowdy was so different from the version that she thought she knew, but she still loved his crazy sense of humor. "Seriously, you need to get out more. The thought of you rambling around in this huge house watching *Rich Housewives* marathons with Elvis makes me sad." She looked around. "Where is Elvis?"

"He's in his bedroom, watching Animal Planet." He moved into high leg right and she followed. Looked like yoga was coming back to him. "He only hangs around me if I'm watching Animal Planet."

She put down her right leg and raised her left. "I bet there's a lot of fighting over the remote."

"Not since I moved him into his own bedroom." Rowdy shrugged. "It made sense, he was no longer a puppy. It was time for him to sleep in his own big-boy bed."

Good God, she hoped he wasn't serious. That was both pathetic and sweet.

"Some people take pet ownership way too seriously." She moved into lunge and he followed. "You really should exercise him more. I noticed that his backside is approaching billboard size. That can't be good for him."

"Elvis doesn't really do exercise or nature or sniffing other dog's butts. He's more of a homebody who likes chilled Evian water and chardonnay-poached chicken breast." She hoped he was joking, but Rowdy didn't look like he was kidding.

"Yep, high maintenance." She moved into crescent moon. She could imagine them rattling around in this house, choosing a long list of TV shows to DVR, and eating caviar and wine-poached whatever. "That's just sad."

He needed an intervention, and if she was being honest, she could use one too. "It sounds like we need a little Towanda."

"Oh, no." One eyebrow arched. Did he get his eyebrows waxed? Because they looked like Anne Hathaway's. "I finally watched *Fried Green Tomatoes*, and there will be no Towanda-ing tonight." He checked his watch. "My mom has a surprise for you . . . they will be—"

"Catch me if you can." She took off running for the door that led to the backyard, flung it open, slipped out of her dress, shucked out of her bra and panties, and jumped into the swimming pool yelling, "Towanda!"

Warm water sluiced over her body. She dived under the water and swam around. She did a few laps and then dived down to the bottom. Her head broke the surface to find four faces staring down at her. Bear and Lucy accounted for two of the faces, but she didn't know the other two. Thank God the lights were off outside.

Rowdy stood next to the shallow end of the pool, holding her clothes and trying not to laugh. "Justus, you already know my parents, but I'd like for you to meet Pastor Green and his wife, Janis. They dropped by to meet you and to ask if you'd have time to take a look at the church grounds and see if you could do something with them."

Holy shit. This might have been a little too much Towanda.

She swam to the side of the pool to minimize the frontal nudity and plastered on a smile. "Nice to meet you. Would tomorrow morning be convenient? Say nine o'clock?"

"That would be fine." Pastor Green looked anywhere but at her.

"Why don't we go to the main house for dessert?" Lucy stepped between Justus and the others, blocking her from their view.

Justus made a mental note to bake Lucy some extra good oatmeal, raisinless cookies as a thank-you gift.

Lucy ushered the visitors out the backyard gate, and then a car engine fired up.

"Towanda strikes again." Rowdy sat on a teak chaise with a thick blue cushion. "I have to hand it to you. You pulled it together in the end. Impressive."

"Thank you." She pulled away from the side of the pool. The water was nice, and she wasn't in a hurry to get out. "Expecting any more visitors?"

He made a big show of checking his watch. "The Mormon Tabernacle Choir should be here any minute, followed by the pope. I'm sure they'll appreciate the female anatomy lesson."

"Ha-ha, very funny." She swam to where it was shallow enough for her to stand on her tippy-toes. "Water's nice. Why don't you join me?"

His Adam's apple bobbed up and down. "No, I'm good here."

"Do I detect a hint of chicken in your voice?" She bent her arms into chicken wings and flapped them around. "Chicken bawk . . . bawk chicken."

"Not even you can goad me into getting in my pool naked." Carefully, he folded her dress and laid it at the foot of a teak chaise.

"This from a man who spent more time naked on the Playa than he did clothed." She wanted her Houston back . . . at least some part of him.

"Somebody's inhibited." She singsonged.

"That's not it." Just as carefully, he folded her bra and panties. "I don't feel like swimming tonight."

So Rowdy was a careful folder. Come to think of it, so was Houston.

She walked to the side of the pool and propped her head onto her fist. "Are you sure you're not a patent lawyer or a CPA? I'm willing to bet that all of your socks are neatly folded in little bundles and arranged by color."

"I happen to like order . . . so?" He sat on the chaise and leaned back comfortably. "Order is good."

"So is chaos." She smiled up at him. "Guess what? I don't fold my socks. When I take them out of the dryer, I just throw them in the laundry basket I have full of socks. When I need a pair, I rummage around until I find two that kinda look the same."

"I can't believe you're willing to admit something so shameful." He shook his head. "No wonder you wore only flip-flops at Burning Man."

She moved back enough so that he could see her breasts. That was one way to get him to do whatever she wanted. "I dare you to take off your clothes and get in this pool with me."

The man couldn't pass up a dare. Once, she'd dared him to strip down and cartwheel down the Playa. His cartwheeling skills left a lot to be desired and he'd gotten some sand in some very unfortunate places, but he'd done it.

She could see his inner turmoil written on his face.

"I'll close my eyes if it helps." She walked up the shallow end until the water came only to her waist and stood so that her upper body was out of the water. "Or I could turn my back."

She turned around. "Wait, before you strip down, can you go inside and grab some condoms? I didn't bring any."

When she'd booked this job, the last thing on her mind had been sex.

"Already grabbed them." Behind her, she heard the rustling of clothes and then the rustling of plastic. The water rippled as he made his way down the steps into the pool.

"The water does feel good." His warm arms slid around her waist, pulling her against him so that her back and butt rubbed up against his front. With one hand, he brushed her hair off her left shoulder and traced her collarbone with his tongue. "You taste so good." His right hand slipped up from under the water and found her right breast. He played with her nipple. "I'd forgotten how good you feel against me."

She could feel how good in the middle of her lower back. He was hard and ready.

"Houston, I've missed you." Her heart wanted what they'd had before, but her mind knew that wasn't likely. As always, she listened to her heart. "I've missed this."

"Daisy, you drive me crazy." He kissed his way up the side of her neck to the little spot right behind her ear. She melted inside. The hand at her breast slipped lower, dipping under the water to find her center. She spread her legs ever so slightly, giving him access. His finger found its mark and drew tiny circles.

"I have a long-standing fantasy that involves you and a pool." His fingers dipped inside of her, bringing warm water with them. "Indulge me?"

"As long as it doesn't involve you stopping, I'm good." She was pretty sure that made sense, but her mind had shut down the second he'd touched her. Her eyes fluttered closed and she was steeped in sensation.

His left hand snaked around her waist while his right continued exploring her. She felt herself being lifted, and then sun-warmed concrete was under her butt.

"Open your eyes. I want you to watch me." He parted her legs wide.

She opened her eyes to find that she was sitting on the side of the pool. Rowdy smiled up from between her thighs.

"I want you to watch me as I make you come." His eyes were hooded and sexy and locked on hers.

He liked to make her lose control. She sucked on her bottom lip. "Deal."

She put her hands back and angled her body toward him, offering herself up.

His mouth was gentle as he lapped at her, but his eyes stayed on hers. He dipped two fingers inside and massaged in time with his tongue. The strokes were long and slow. Her hips fell into the rhythm and her hand cupped her breast. She rolled her nipple between her thumb and index finger.

Rowdy's eyes turned eager. He loved watching her touch her own body. She licked her lips and blew him a kiss. His tongue turned urgent, and she cupped her breast harder, enjoying the feel of the building orgasm. Her hand left her breast and tangled in his hair, urging him to go faster. The orgasm broke and she rode the crest until her body was spent.

When she felt confident that she could form words again, she said, "Nice fantasy. Any other ideas you have floating around in that pretty little head of yours?"

"The fantasy isn't over yet, and you have a very important part to play in the next act." His voice was strained, like he was holding himself back.

She spread her legs even wider. "What did you have in mind?"

He stood, circled his waist with her legs, and lifted both of them out of the water. "I want to hear you moan again."

"I didn't moan." Had she?

"Yes, you did. You always do right before you lose yourself." He sat them down on the closest chair. His long legs bumped the armrest of the chair while she straddled him. She unwrapped her legs and tried to slide down and return the favor, but his hands clamped on to her ankles and wound them back around him. "My fantasy . . . not yours."

His hands went to her hips, lifted her, and settled her onto him. She moved her hips up and down, riding him hard. His mouth fastened on to her nipple and sucked lightly. She could feel the orgasm building . . . urgent and deep.

"That feels good." Her eyes locked on to his. The delicious need there made her hungry for more. She drove harder and harder.

His hands pistoned her hips as his mouth worked her breast. Her hands fisted in his hair as she drove them harder and higher. Every muscle in her body went taut, yelling for release. The orgasm swallowed her whole, and then she felt his body follow.

She rested her head against his shoulder and felt his heart beating at breakneck speed, just like hers.

"I just want you to know . . ." His voice was a low rumble, punctuated by heaving breathing. "That we will always be together."

She didn't know that she could love him even more than she had two seconds ago, but she did.

"I've got a plan." He stroked her back. "Unlike my Burner self, I'm really a planner. I plan everything down to the smallest detail." He took a deep breath and let it out slowly. "I care about you and I know that you care about me. I want to be with you." He laced his fingers through hers. "I never want to be parted from you again." He brought her hand to his lips and kissed each knuckle. While it was sweet, he seemed to be nervous and taking his time getting the words to come out.

Oh my God, was he about to propose? Nerves kickboxed inside her stomach. He was going to ask her to marry him. It was unexpected and more than she could ever have hoped for.

She swallowed the lake of saliva flooding her mouth and waited for him to get his will-you-marry-me on.

"I'd like . . ." He did some heavy-duty swallowing too. Looked like he was as nervous as she.

Minutes drifted by in super slo-mo.

"I would like to build you a house near me so we can be together . . . you know, even if Hugh and I don't bond. I was thinking that, you know . . ." He swallowed again. "We could still be together."

And just like that, her heart died a death by a thousand cuts.

She sat back on her heels and then stood. With the molecule of hope that her soul clung to, she picked up her dress and stepped into it. So he wanted her body but not the rest of her? This was his offer . . . to make her his whore? What happened when parts of her body headed south? Would he build someone else a house next to hers or would he just simply remove her and move on? "Just so we're clear, you want to build me a house"—she waved and arm in the general direction of the backyard—"over there so that I can be your fuck buddy?"

His eyes rolled up and to the left like he was retracing his words. "No, I want to keep you close because I can't live without you."

"What about Hugh?" Her future revolved around her son, but being alone with Rowdy had sent her back into their old rhythm of laughter and sex. How had she ever thought he wanted a happily ever after as a family?

"What about him? If we get along, then great, we can hang out. But if we don't, I'll be happy to pay child support. The two of you will want for nothing." He actually believed that this was a well-thought-out and agreeable plan.

Justus had never felt the need to hit another human being. Violence seemed like a great hobby to take up right about now. She wanted to pound on him until she got her Houston back. Anger wasn't a strong enough word. She wanted to rip him limb from limb. How could she ever have loved him?

"You know, I never realized how much of an asshole you really are." She looked around for her shoes, couldn't find them, so she stomped barefooted to the back gate that she hoped led to the driveway and her truck. Screw her bra and panties, he could keep them. One more second in this man's company was two seconds too long.

"What is that supposed to mean?" He followed after her.

"If you really thought that I would agree to be your kept woman while you throw little scraps of attention at my son, you really don't know me at all." She rounded on him but kept her hands fisted at her sides. Burning Man seemed a lifetime away and some many lifetimes wasted. "I will be here for six more months. This is a huge ranch, so stay out of my way. I don't ever want to see you again, and if you come within one hundred feet of my son, I will kill you with my bare hands. Are we clear?"

"Crystal." Rowdy stepped back and slammed the gate in her face.

He was a far cry from the man she'd known at Burning Man, and she'd been kidding herself to ever think they could be together.

There would be no mooning over Houston. There would be no mourning the loss of what they'd had. There would be no happy ever after with a mommy, a baby, and a daddy.

Their life together was over.

From now on, it was her and Hugh. That was all the happy ever after she needed.

# CHAPTER 12

The next morning, Rowdy's long legs chewed up the pasture behind his house. Long walks had always cleared his mind, and since he couldn't sleep last night and Justus was back to hating him, his mind needed some serious clearing.

He just didn't get it. Everything had gone so well last night and then Justus had stormed off. Okay, he was willing to admit that he'd done a less-than-graceful job of explaining the plan to her.

It was a good plan. Didn't Justus want to be with him?

He kept running over last evening in his mind. What was he missing? Conversation was good, dinner was good, the sex was good . . . and then bam, she was gone. He'd been so angry and, okay, depressed that he'd eaten the whole coconut pie in one sitting, which now that he thought about it was probably why he hadn't slept well. Too much of a good thing was a bad thing.

"You look like a man with the weight of the world on his shoulders." His father's voice came from behind him.

Rowdy really didn't feel like company right now, but his dad wasn't one to walk away until he was good and ready. There was no point in even asking for some time alone, because he wasn't going to get it.

His father caught up with him.

"Based on the way that your legs are chewing up the pasture, you're mulling over something very serious."

"You could say that." Rowdy set his jaw. How did he start? Where did he start? He guessed that it was best to get it out there as quickly as possible. "Last night, Justus turned me down flat. I have this whole plan and everything."

Rowdy waited for some reply, but all he got was quiet contemplation. A man of few words, his father had always been a good listener.

"I offered to build her a house next to mine."

After a good ten seconds, his father slowed his pace, which forced Rowdy to slow his. His father clasped his hands behind his back. "Sounds like a good plan. What about Hugh?"

"He lives with his mother. If we get along, then good, if not, we stay out of each other's way." Men had been dealing with each other like this since brontosaurus was on the menu.

"You realize that Justus and Hugh are a package deal." His father's voice was calm as he kept his head down.

"Of course, that's why he's going to live with her." Hello, was he the only person in the world who was making sense?

"So what you're saying is that you'd like to sleep with his mother whenever you want and be a dad only if you like it?" His father just kept on walking. No judgment, just a steady stream of footfalls.

"No . . . well, partly. I mean, what if Hugh and I don't get along? I'm in love with Justus and I can't see spending the rest of my life without her." The fact that there was a possibility that he'd have to was a kick to the gut.

"Son, it pains me to say this, but your mother is right. Men are stupid."

Rowdy's head whipped around. "What?"

If his dad had just said, "Look, son, there's a kangaroo," he couldn't have been more surprised.

"Your plan sounds logical . . . sort of, but maybe we should look at it from Justus's end. Did you tell her that you loved her?" His father always had been the voice of reason . . . damn it.

"Well, no, not in so many words—"

"Let me get this straight, you told her that you wanted to build a house for her so she could be near you, but you didn't tell her that you loved her." His father peeled off his straw cowboy hat, smoothed down his hair, and carefully placed it back in the exact position he'd worn it in for as long as Rowdy could remember. This was his thinking pose. He and his brothers called it the "hat trick" because their father always did it when he was ordering his thoughts before dispensing some profound piece of advice or when reasoning with the unreasonable. "You need to man up when it comes to Hugh. Fatherhood isn't like shoes that you try on to see if they fit. You fathered a child, so do the right thing."

"So you want me to marry her?" He'd fathered a son out of wedlock . . . yet another thing that didn't fit his family. It wasn't that he didn't want to marry Justus, it was more that he didn't know what to do about fatherhood. "I think marrying someone should come from love and not an obligation." Rowdy leaned down and picked a tall blade of sweetgrass. Although obligation wasn't why he'd wanted to marry her a few days ago. "I want a marriage like you and Mom have."

His father threw back his head and laughed. "Good God, I hope so and not. Your mother and I have a solid marriage, but it takes work. According to her, mostly on her part."

"Yes, but you got married because you wanted to . . . because you love each other." Rowdy had fantastic role models in the marriage department, and that's what he wanted in his own life.

"Son, do the math. Your mother was six months pregnant with Cinco when we got married." His father grinned like it hadn't been a hardship at all.

"Pregnant when you got married?" The foundation Rowdy had built his entire life around rumbled with a 7.0 on the Richter scale. A shotgun wedding? His parents had a shotgun wedding? Shocked, flabbergasted, overwhelmed—he couldn't think of a word strong enough to express his feelings about that. His mom had been pregnant and they'd had to get married. But they'd made it work and were still making it work. Wait a minute. This was one of those life-lesson things. "This isn't like the time you convinced me that you had magical powers over the windshield wipers but in reality you just had them on delay? I'm not six years old anymore. You don't need to make up things just so I'll feel better."

"I don't know why y'all haven't figured it out by now. Yes, I love your mother and have since the very first time I saw her, but convincing her to marry me was almost impossible." His father grinned. "She used to say that I knocked her up on purpose so she'd have to marry me." He shook his head. "Think about it, have you ever known your mother to do something she didn't want to do?"

"No." His mother was the poster child for headstrong. Seeing his parents as real people was disturbing. "How did you get her to say yes?"

He'd never heard this story. He knew that his father had met his mother when she was working in the emergency room and he'd brought in an injured ranch hand.

"A bet. One hand of blackjack. I won." He shrugged. "I cheated, of course—couldn't leave my future to fate."

"Mom agreed to marry you because of a bet?" Rowdy really didn't know his parents at all. "Wait, doesn't Mom always say don't bet unless it's something you don't mind losing?"

"Yes. I'm pretty sure she didn't mind losing." He patted Rowdy on the back. "Life isn't as black-and-white as you'd like to make it."

"Justus should have told me." He felt like he'd been forced into his current situation and he hadn't had a choice. But what if Justus had told him that she was pregnant? What would he have done? He had no idea.

"When your mom first told me that she was pregnant, I freaked out. I knew that I wanted to spend the rest of my life with her, but I hadn't planned on the whole family thing. I insisted that we had to get married right away . . . mainly because I wanted to marry her, but also because I wanted my child to have two parents." One side of his mouth turned up like he was lost in memory. "She told me that she didn't have to do anything and that she would marry for love or not at all. She made me jump through some serious hoops. Headstrong women do things in their own time, and if we're lucky, they allow us to stand beside them."

God, he hated rational people. For once, why couldn't his father skip the levelheadedness and get on board with some serious female bashing? Rowdy needed a brother-in-arms to rail with him at the unfairness of life, not the voice of reason.

Could he and Justus make things work . . . correction, could he, Justus, and Hugh make things work? His parents didn't seem to resent having to get married. They really enjoyed each other's company.

"Son, it took me a long time to realize that being in a relationship isn't about me, it's about us. Somehow women get that right off, but as your mom is fond of saying, it takes men twice as long to understand half as much. Your mother wouldn't marry me—not because she didn't love me, but because I hadn't figured out that I only wanted her on my terms. I wanted to get married, so therefore, she was supposed to fall in line. Everything was I instead of we. I want this, I need that . . . she not only had to look out for herself, but the child she was carrying." His father draped an arm around him. "You have a right to be hurt, but before you wrap yourself in years of anger, think about what Justus went through largely on her own. Children are a blessing, but they're also a lot of work. I can't imagine being a single parent."

Just playing devil's advocate, he might have only been thinking about what he wanted and not what Justus and Hugh wanted . . . maybe. Family members with an overabundance of common sense were starting to get on his nerves.

"I don't know everything and I don't need to know it, but there is a reason that she didn't tell you about Hugh. You need to think about that. You don't need to make any decisions about the future right now, take all the time you need . . . only don't burn any bridges that you'd like to cross again. Think hard and tread carefully. A woman protecting her cub is a ferocious thing, and God knows that women hear and remember everything. They tend to take words said in anger to heart."

"When did life get so complicated?" Rowdy felt closer to his dad than he'd remembered feeling. His father had always been wise and kind, but today, seeing his father as a regular person instead of a role model was comforting. He knew that his father loved him, but it seemed that he liked him as a person too.

"I'd say things start heading south about the time a man hits puberty. Before women entered the equation, life was so simple." Laughter rumbled out of his father's mouth. "Once you notice the difference between girls and boys, life gets to be so much more fun."

"Sometimes it's a little bit more fun than I can handle." What was his next step? How did he make things right?

"I like that. Sometimes it's a little bit more fun that I can handle." His father nodded to himself. "That describes your mother to a T. Did you know that I was engaged to someone else when I met your mother?"

It was hard to imagine his parents as real people who had real lives before he'd come along. His father wanted to marry someone who wasn't his mother? In the puzzle of his life, this was the piece that didn't fit anywhere. "No. Who?"

"Annabelle-Marjorie Atherton. She was a debutante from Dallas. My mom was a deb so I thought that's the life my parents wanted for me. Your mom changed all of that. I called Annabelle-Marjorie on the way home from the hospital on the night I met your mother and called the engagement off. I've never looked back. Your mom challenges me, infuriates me, and makes me insanely happy. Every single day, I fall a little bit more in love with her. She is the one for me, and I knew it the second I laid eyes on her."

The second he'd seen Justus walking down the Playa, handing out fresh daisies to everyone she met, had been a lightning bolt to the heart. He remembered thinking that he'd finally found the part of himself that he'd felt had always been missing.

"I hear you and Hugh are working on a mosaic for the hospital." He tried to get the words "I'm a painter" out but they stuck in his throat.

"It's coming along. I'd love for you to take a look at it. You mother says that you're a very talented painter. My father painted. He loved the ranch in spring with all of the bluebonnets. Used to say that Mother Nature did her best work in the spring."

"Papa Tres painted?" He couldn't believe it. He didn't remember much about his grandfather except that the old man wore denim overalls and always had lemon hard candies in his front pocket. It seemed that art was in his DNA. Maybe he wasn't so different from his family after all.

"Yes, he loved to paint landscapes in spring. Bluebonnets were his favorite." His father always smiled when he talked about his father.

"Have I ever seen any of Papa Tres's work?"

"Nope. My father was a wonderful man with many talents, unfortunately painting wasn't one of them. He did it because he loved it. My mother didn't appreciate his rather modern and creative version of bluebonnets. She told my father that she gave them away to family, but I'm pretty sure she threw them all away." Rowdy's father frowned. "My mother liked things her way."

That was the closest thing to an unkind word he'd ever heard his father say about his mother.

Nerves roller-coastered around in his stomach. What if his family felt the same way about his art? Was it good enough to show them? Could he risk their rejection if it wasn't?

His father checked his watch. "Now, if you'll excuse me, I have a date with my seven-year-old grandson to play checkers. I like to think of it as making memories together." His father was about to head back to the main house when he turned back around. "Oh, just so you know, I could use a few more grandchildren. A sassy little girl would be nice."

More grandkids? Hell, he'd only found out he was a father two days ago. "I'll see what I can do."

His parents had really taken to Hugh. For their sake and his . . . he hoped that everything worked out.

"That's all a parent can ask for." His father grinned at him. "In this life, happily ever after isn't guaranteed. If Justus is your one, don't screw it up."

It was time to track her down and beg for forgiveness . . . again.

# CHAPTER 13

The next morning, Lucy had taken one look at her, hugged her, and then promptly invited Hugh to go fishing with Bear. Thank God Pastor Green had rescheduled their meeting until next week.

Right now, she vibrated with the need to destroy . . . destroy . . . destroy.

It was over. Justus needed to come to grips with that. She kicked a limestone rock out of her way. What was between her and Rowdy was over. She wouldn't settle for anything but a life with Hugh and Rowdy, and he wasn't willing to give her that. Her teeth gnashed together so hard they should have been nothing but dust. She wanted to yell and scream and pound on things. She wanted to throw out some cheesy martial-arts moves and kill something with nothing but the power of her hatred. She wanted to march right over to Rowdy's house and paint the inside of it with red dye #7 and fill his expensive Gucci loafers with dog shit.

She threw open the barn door and made her way to the Bobcat. She needed to tear some things down so she could recreate the land in the image that she chose.

Rowdy . . . the bastard. Like hell was she ever talking to the man again. Had he really thought she'd come willingly to the be-the-good-little-mistress-and-I'll-leave-money-on-the-nightstand-for-you plan?

Right now she wanted to scratch Rowdy's eyes out and feed them to him with some fava beans and a nice Chianti.

She would do everything in her power to make sure that Hugh never felt unwanted. And when she'd finished her work here, she and Hugh would go back to Austin, buy a damn house, and live happily ever after if it freaking killed her.

Knowing that she wasn't wanted by her biological mother had taken years for her to work through, even though it kicked her in the heart from time to time. One of the few memories she had of her egg-donor mother was overhearing her tell her father that Justus's name should have been Abortion Jacobi.

Rowdy didn't want Hugh—he didn't even know him. And wasn't particularly eager to get to know him. If a lover of hers showed up with a kid that was hers . . . she'd what? Well, first she'd remember giving birth, so it was hard to sneak a secret baby on a woman. Maybe if she were a lesbian, but still it seemed really complicated for a lesbian to have a secret baby considering that whole lack-of-sperm thing. She gritted her teeth to keep from rolling her eyes so hard she strained something. What it boiled down to was that she would love Rowdy's secret baby . . . no matter what. What if he'd had a child with another woman?

She'd like to believe that she'd love that child as Maeve loved her, but she wasn't 100 percent sure. Certainly she would take the time to get to know his child.

She shook her head. She was done with far-fetched secret babies.

Hugh would never know that his father didn't want him, because she wanted her son and loved him enough for two parents. And now that he had Bear and Lucy, and the rest of the Rose family, he would know only love.

It had never occurred to her that in not telling Rowdy he was Hugh's father that she'd been depriving both her son and his father's family of a relationship that they both needed.

Justus balled her fists and kicked a large rock with her boot. She would keep her head down, get the job done, and take the money that she made and buy a small house. She could provide for her son. He didn't need a father. Screw Rowdy Rose. She didn't need or want him in her life.

So now she was lying to herself?

God, she hated when her mind wouldn't let her get away with being unreasonable. Levelheadedness was usually one of the things she liked most about herself, but today she really wanted to lobotomize the levelheadedness right out of her brain.

Oh, God. Guilt pulled up a chair and stayed awhile. Last night with Rowdy, she hadn't even thought of her son. She stopped dead in her tracks.

A warm tidal wave of guilt pulled her down into the depths of a bottomless ocean of despair. From now on, she would avoid Rowdy like the plague. Never again would she put her son second to anyone. He was her life.

Now she had some real guilt to work off.

She opened the metal cage covering the front of the Bobcat, climbed in, and pulled the cage down. The other day, Lefty had explained how to start the machine. Since it was keyless and a diesel, she needed to hit the run button, type in the five-digit password, hit Enter, watch the display for the glow plugs to warm up, and then finally hit the start button. She grabbed one joystick with her left hand and the other with her right and positioned her feet one on each pedal. Gently, she eased both joysticks forward and the Bobcat Loader moved straight ahead. She drove it out of the barn and headed to the main house.

Normally she worked with a crew and didn't get to play with the machinery, but she couldn't get her crew out until next week. If she weren't in middle of an epic episode of self-flagellation, she might admit that this was kind of fun.

She pressed the pedals and played with moving the bucket up and down and tilting it forward until she got the hang of it. This was just like playing a video game.

Following the orange spray paint she'd used to outline the beds the other day, she graded the land and then used the excess dirt to build up the lower points. She cut a path for the French drain and then dug out as much of the flowerbeds as she could. Once she'd scooped out two inches of topsoil and hit solid rock, she used the bucket to break up the larger white limestone rocks and pry them loose. Painstakingly, she worked the bucket back and forth until she finally worked the rocks out of the ground and piled them off to the side. The larger ones she'd use as focal pieces in the beds, the medium ones she'd use to line raised beds, and the smaller ones would be carted off.

Next week she had eight dump trucks of good, organic garden soil coming, so she needed to be ready to spread all of it. Because the Texas Hill Country had lots of limestone and granite, it made for some of the most beautiful and scenic vistas, but it also made growing things difficult. Most people in the world didn't have to buy their dirt, but here dirt came at a premium.

She wiped the sweat off of her brow and glanced up. The sun was directly overhead, so it was close to noon. She hit the "Stop" button and the Bobcat's growl ceased. She lifted up the cage and climbed out.

Reaching to the sky, she stretched her back, and her stomach rumbled. It had been hours since breakfast. She rolled her shoulders as she made her way to the small, red Igloo cooler that held her lunch. After grabbing the white handle, she made her way over to a huge pecan tree and sat with her back against the trunk.

As she pulled out her sandwich, it occurred to her that she really didn't need to pack her lunch because the cottage was close by, but she'd been packing her lunch in a cooler for so long that it was force of habit.

She pulled out her insulated metal water bottle and drank long and deep. The only thing better than solitude and shade for lunch would be having Hugh there to enlighten her with interesting facts.

The giant mess she'd made of the yard bolstered her mood. She loved demo almost as much as she loved putting things back together and making them new again. There was nothing better than having total destruction to show for a morning's work. No one could ever accuse her of being lazy.

After eating the sandwich, some strawberries and grapes, and a bag of carrots, she closed the cooler, stood, and stretched. She was tired, but definitely not finished for the day. Giving her customers their money's worth had always been the motto she worked by.

With the exception of some trench digging that needed to be done with a shovel, there wasn't much more she could do on this site today. All of the sprinkler pipe was due to be delivered tomorrow, along with the field stone. The trench digging would take her maybe twenty minutes, if that. She could start on the backyard, but she wasn't scheduled to work on that for two more weeks. If she demoed it today and tomorrow morning, she'd have to leave it all torn up until she could get back to it. It didn't seem right to have Lucy's front, back, and side yards look like a bomb had hit them, forcing everyone to have to traverse potholes, mounds of dirt, and piles of rocks to get to their cars.

She glanced up and found her next target. The graceful old pecan tree had probably been planted around the time Texas was its own country. She walked around the tree. The circumference had to be at least fifteen feet around. Judging by the height of the house, which was four stories, this old pecan had to be eight or nine stories tall.

If this lovely old tree could talk, she'd bet that it had some crazy stories.

The canopy was at least as big around as the tree was tall. The only other pecan tree that she'd ever seen that came close to the size of this one was in San Antonio, planted on the grounds of the Alamo.

Shading her eyes from the shafts of sunlight breaking through the canopy, she walked around and around, taking stock of the tree. For the most part, it was in good shape, but some of the lower-hanging branches appeared to be dead. While technically it was okay to prune a pecan tree at any time of the year, it was definitely better to prune in late winter, when the tree was dormant.

She walked around the tree again and squinted, trying to get a better look at what was going on with it. It was hard to tell this far away, but she thought she saw round holes in some of the limbs. Some sort of borer? Or maybe just a woodpecker? A woodpecker wouldn't damage the tree, but a case of the borers would do permanent damage.

She wasn't a tree expert, but she couldn't just stand here and watch this lovely old tree slowly die. Maybe if she took a closer look, she could figure out if they needed to bring in an arborist or if it was something benign like a woodpecker.

The lowest-hanging branches had to be at least twenty feet in the air. There was a twenty-eight-foot fiberglass extension ladder in the barn. It couldn't hurt to climb up there and take a look.

Ten minutes later, she had the ladder leaned up against the tree trunk. She made sure that it was anchored properly and stable before starting her climb to the top.

Heights had never been a problem for her, but she did wish that she had a climbing harness. She glanced down. She'd probably break her neck if she fell from this height. Then she wouldn't fall. It was as simple as that.

When she finally reached the lowest limb, she wanted to weep. It was borers all right, and this poor tree had a bad case of them. She climbed to the top of the ladder and surveyed the damage. As far up as she could see, the branches were infested. She didn't see much trunk damage, though, so there was that.

They needed an arborist here, like yesterday. Maybe she could talk Larry the Tree Guy into coming all the way out here from Austin. He was the best. Once she explained how old and majestic the tree was, she wouldn't be able to keep him away.

While standing on the second-to-top rung, she reached up as far as she could and grabbed for one of the limbs. It was the smallest in circumference and would be easy to break off and bring down with her. Larry needed to know what he would be dealing with. She worked it back and forth, but she couldn't get it to break. Up on her tippy-toes, she grabbed it with both hands.

"What in the holy hell do think you're doing?" It was a male voice . . . Rowdy's voice.

She glanced down and lost her footing. She bear-hugged the tree branch for dear life, but it cracked under her weight. As she tumbled backward, the canopy got farther away.

Am I going to die?

Hugh. She thought of her precious baby boy. She was going to miss of all of his firsts: first love, first heartbreak, first car, first graduation. He was so young now that after he grew up, he would barely remember her.

As tears filled her eyes, she hit the ground with the thump. Pain tore a hole in her left leg, and the back of her head felt like she'd been poleaxed. The world moved in slow-motion as her mind registered that she'd fallen. The pecan tree loomed over her as a light breeze fluttered the leaves and shafts of sunlight danced around her.

White-hot pain burned down her left leg and radiated out from the back of her head. A mockingbird chirped in the distance and someone called her name. The varying shades of green leaves faded to gray and then to black and then to nothing at all.

# CHAPTER 14

Rowdy died a thousand deaths in the millisecond of forever that it took for Justus to fall from the top of the ladder to the ground. He was at her side and taking her pulse. "Justus?"

She wasn't moving and her eyes were closed, but her pulse was steady. She had to be okay, please let her be okay.

"Don't move her." His mother came running from the front porch. "Is she conscious?"

"No, I don't think so." He wanted to shake her awake, but his mother just told him otherwise. "Justus. Justus. Daisy."

His hands shook. He willed her to be okay. He'd make a deal with God or Jesus or Buddha or whomever to make sure she was all right. This was his fault. He'd startled her.

"Call nine-one-one and get my medical bag off of my desk." His mother was on her knees, analyzing Justus's head.

"Her pulse is strong. She hit the ground hard." Rowdy gulped in air like it was in short supply. He should be doing something . . . he needed to do something to make this right. He's startled her and she'd fallen.

His mother slapped him hard across the face.

He shot to attention.

His mother was calm. "Call nine-one-one. NOW. Get my medical bag."

He sprang into action, pulled out his smartphone, dialed 911, and ran toward the house.

"Nine-one-one. What is your emergency?" The female voice was crisp and efficient.

"A woman fell from the top of a ladder. She isn't conscious." He hit the house at a dead run. It seemed to take forever to get to his mother's study. He scooped up the bag and ran out.

"Is she breathing?" The operator was typing furiously. "What's your address?"

"Yes she's breathing and my mother is a doctor. She's examining Justus . . . um, the lady." He gave her the address and directions as he ran through the open front door.

"Don't move her. The ambulance is en route, but it will take them a little while to get there because you are on the edge of our service territory." The operator typed some more. "You said that there is a doctor on scene."

"Yes." Rowdy sprinted down the front steps. He deposited the bag next to his mother, dropped to his knees, and touched Justus's face. She was so still. Why was she so still?

"Put the phone on speaker and lay it next to me," his mother barked. "You can hold her hand, but be gentle and don't jostle her."

"This is Dr. Lucy Rose. Patch me through to the paramedics." His mother was in ER mode. She gently felt around the back of Justus's head.

"Yes, ma'am." The operator put them on hold and then came back. "I have the paramedics on the line."

"This is Dr. Lucy Rose. The patient fell from a height of thirty or so feet. She's unconscious but breathing and her pulse is strong. She appears to have double compound fractures of the left tibia and femur. Both bones are visible, but the bleeding is minimal. I've examined the head as closely as I can without moving her and I can't see any trauma. My best guess is concussion."

He glanced down at her mangled leg and thought he might vomit. Justus didn't need a pussy looking after her, she needed a man, so he kept his eyes on her face.

"Yes, Dr. Rose." The male voice was calm and monotone, like he was taking notes for his next history exam. "This is Mike and Bev. We'll be there in ten or so minutes. We were actually out in your neck of the woods on another call." After a brief pause, his voice was back. "Besides the leg, is there any other bleeding?"

"No, but she's lying on her back." His mother pulled out her stethoscope and popped the ends into her ears. She moved the round end to Justus's chest. "Her lungs are clear." She moved the little metal end around. "I am worried about some broken ribs."

Broken ribs?

She hooked the stethoscope around her neck and gently palpated the chest area. "I can't tell for sure if any are broken."

"Spinal involvement?" Mike called out like he was checking things off a list.

His heart stuttered in his chest. Spinal involvement? Did that mean paralysis? This was all his fault. Justus might not ever be able to walk again.

"I can't tell. Nothing's at an odd angle, but I won't be able to palpate until you get a C-collar on her." His mother's hands moved down to Justus's waist and then hips. "I think the pelvis is intact, but with the angle of the left leg, I can't be sure. On the left leg, I don't see any arterial blood flow."

"We just turned onto the private road. Be there in five minutes or less. Want us to call ahead and have the OR prepped for you?" It was a female voice now . . . Bev?

He heard sirens getting closer.

"Yes, and I need an ortho . . . Dr. Murray. He's a leg man. If he's not on call, make sure he knows it's a favor for me." His mother's eyes scanned up and down Justus's body like she was trying to use X-ray vision to see inside.

"Will do, Dr. Rose. I'm going to hang up now and call the hospital." Bev hung up.

"Go to the road and wave them over here." His mother sounded grave, and she never sounded grave. He sucked in gulps of air as he stumbled but caught himself.

Gently he laid Justus's hand down and ran to the copse of trees that opened out onto the dirt road the family used to go in and out of the ranch. Flashing red and blue lights barreled down the two-track. He waved them over to the main house. The ambulance skidded to a stop not ten feet from Justus.

Mike was out of the passenger's side and opening the back doors, pulling out the stretcher before Rowdy made it back to Justus.

The paramedics wrapped a plastic collar around Justus's neck and carefully slid her onto a backboard. Mike got an IV started and attached a bag of clear liquid to a metal pole that he'd extended from the back of the stretcher.

An unholy scream cut through the air. It was Justus. She was awake. Rowdy turned feral. He tried to push and claw his way through the paramedics to get to her. Her terrified eyes stared straight ahead.

"Justus, it's Lucy. You've been in an accident. You're on a stretcher and we're taking you to the hospital. I know you're in a lot of pain, but I need you to stay still. I'm about to administer something for the pain, but you have to stay still." His mother grabbed the syringe and bottle offered by Mike. She drew back on the plunger and filled the syringe and then stuck it into the IV port.

Slowly Justus's screaming dialed back and her eyes turned vacant.

She was conscious—that was a good sign, right? It had to be.

His mother pulled the syringe out but didn't recap it. "I'm concerned that you've injured your back, so I can't stress this enough, you need to stay still. How is your pain level?"

"Not bad." Justus's voice was breathy and weak.

"Rowdy, follow in my car." His mother tossed him the keys to her Tahoe. "I'm riding in the ambulance."

"Like hell." He caught them. "I want to ride—"

"Tahoe, now. There's no room and we need to tend to Justus." She shot him a do-what-I-say-or-else look. "Tahoe."

Bev and Mike rolled Justus to the back of the ambulance and loaded the stretcher inside. Mike climbed up and then offered his hand to Rowdy's mother, who climbed inside.

Rowdy ran to his mother's black Chevy Tahoe, clicking the "Unlock" button on the key fob. He opened the driver's-side door and practically jumped behind the wheel. He fired up the engine and pulled up behind the ambulance.

Justus was awake now, that was good, but spinal involvement? His eyes stung with tears. What if she was paralyzed or had brain damage?

He'd been so angry with her that he hadn't thought, he'd just seen her up in the tree and yelled out. What the hell was she doing in that damn tree anyway? He couldn't think what to do now. His brain went on autopilot as he followed the ambulance to Roseville Regional Hospital. He pulled into the ER patient parking, found the first available space.

A few seconds later he was right alongside the stretcher, watching as Justus's frightened eyes tried to take it all in. They found his gaze and she whispered, "Rowdy, I need to talk to you."

He touched her arm. "I'm here."

"Take care of Hugh. I need you to take care of Hugh." She drifted off.

"Okay." It was the least he could do for her. He would take care of Hugh, hell, he'd move the kid in with him. And her too, now that he thought of it. "I'll take care of him."

"We need to finish examining her and prep her for surgery. You can wait in the waiting room. Call your father and tell him what's going on. He took Hugh fishing. Tell him not to say anything to Hugh. I don't like lying to children, but I don't think he should know about his mother until we know the extent of the trauma." His mother gave him a quick hug. "I'll take care of her. I promise."

He just stood there and watched as they rolled Justus down the hall. Extent of the trauma. Extent of the trauma. He'd just found Justus again, and now he'd ruined everything. If only he could trade places with her—take her pain. He lifted his left thumb to his mouth and bit down hard on the cuticle. He'd given up nail biting in middle school, but now seemed like a great time to pick it up again. It was either that or smoking. She was going to be okay. She was going to be okay. She was going to be okay. He moved to his index finger. Fear gnawed at him like he gnawed on his fingernail. He kept going until he tasted blood, and then it was on to the next fingernail.

He turned around, walked around the nurses' station, and out the emergency room bay doors into the waiting room.

Justus had asked him to look after Hugh, and by God that's what he was going to do. He checked his front left trouser pocket, where he normally kept his phone, but it was missing. He'd left it on the ground by his mother. He tunneled his fingers through his hair. He couldn't do anything right.

Okay, time to go old-school. He walked up to the reception desk and knocked on the glass partition that separated—he looked down at her name tag—Wendy, patient coordinator, from the rest of the world.

"May I help you?" Wendy had a deep, gravelly voice that was more suited to TV voice-overs than to emergency room check-in. Maybe Wendy was short for Wendell?

"I need to borrow the phone." He pointed to the overly large, multiline, way-too-many-flashing-lights phone next to her.

"Sorry. That's against hospital policy." Wendy crossed her arms. "You'll have to use your cell." She pointed to a white piece of copy paper taped to the glass above her, reading "Cell phone usage is prohibited inside the hospital. Please take it outside."

"I left my phone at home. This is an emergency." He was, after all, standing outside of the emergency room.

"Sorry. Hospital policy states—"

"Screw hospital policy. Look, I've had a bad morning, the woman that I love might have a spinal cord injury, I need to get ahold of our son, so hand over the phone." If he had to crawl through that little hole to get to the phone, that's what he'd do.

"Sir, I'm sorry, but it's against hospital policy." Wendy shot him a look that said she was not budging on the subject so move on.

Most people thought Rowdy was charming. It was time to put away the vinegar and move on to the honey.

He leaned in closer to the circular hole in the glass that was the only way to communicate with Wendy and smiled his most charming smile. "I'm Rowdy Rose and my mother is Dr. Lucy Rose, a physician on staff here, please let me use the phone."

His mother had taught him that honey was always better than vinegar when it came to getting things done, but his honey supply was running out. If he had to tie Wendy to her chair with the Scotch tape he saw next to the phone, he would.

Wendy heaved an exasperated sigh and handed him the receiver though the hole in the partition. "What's the number?"

He blinked. "Number?"

Crap, he didn't know anyone's phone number. That's what the contacts icon was for. "Can you look up the main number to the Texas Rose Ranch?"

Wendy looked at him like he was skating on thin ice, but she typed something on the keyboard next to her and then dialed a series of numbers on the phone.

It rang twice. "This is the Texas Rose Ranch. I'm sorry we're unable to take your call right now, but we're out tending the cows. If you're interested in a tour, please check our website for times. All others, please leave a message and we'll get back to you as soon as we're able. Have a wonderful day."

He shook his head and handed the receiver back to Wendy. "No answer."

Maybe his mother had a phone?

"I need to see my mother, Dr. Rose." He nodded toward the ER bay doors. "Can you buzz me in?"

"Nope." Wendy sucked in a breath so deep the oxygen content in the room dipped. Either she was having a stroke or she was debating doing something she didn't want to do . . . like paying her taxes or taking a class on origami or possibly helping him out. At this rate, Rowdy would be a member of AARP before she got around to making a decision. "Look, my ex is a ranch hand at the Texas Rose. It might be uncomfortable, but I'll give him a call."

His whole body wilted with relief.

"That would be wonderful, thank you." Wendy was good people. Maybe he'd shoot the pope an email about sainting her.

She bent down, opened a drawer, rummaged around in a purse the size of a small suitcase, and finally pulled out a pink iPhone. She tapped a few things on her phone and then handed it through the round hole in the glass to Rowdy. It was ringing.

"Wendy, baby, I knew that you'd finally come to your senses." Rowdy didn't recognize the voice.

"This is Rowdy Rose, to whom am I speaking?" He was all business.

"Sorry, Mr. Rose, I thought you was Wendy. It's Dean McGraw." Dean sounded a little nervous.

"Hey, Dean. I need a favor. I left my phone on the ground under the pecan tree at the main house. Can you go get it for me? I need for you to text my father's contact info to Wendy's phone." Normally the family didn't use employees to run family errands, but this was an emergency.

"Right away, Mr. Rowdy." Dean snapped to attention. "Hold on a second."

There was some mumbling or maybe Dean had put his hand over the phone.

"What's wrong?" It was his older brother Cinco's voice. "Some of the hands saw an ambulance?"

"Yes, Justus fell and broke her leg. There may be other injuries, but we don't know yet." He couldn't get his mouth around the words "spinal injury." "Is CanDee there?"

"She's right here." Cinco mumbled something.

"I'm here, Rowdy." It was his soon-to-be sister-in-law. "What happened?"

"Justus fell from a tree and she's hurt. Can you call Dad? He's with Hugh. Can you, Cinco, and Dad take care of Hugh until we get things sorted out here? Mom says that we shouldn't tell Hugh about his mother until we know what we're dealing with." Guilt plowed through Rowdy's stomach. This was all his fault.

"We're on it. We will keep Hugh entertained. In fact, Cinco and I will move him in with us so that you can stay at the hospital." CanDee's voice was high and frantic. "Is she going to be okay?"

"Her leg is broken and she was unconscious for a while . . . right now, we don't know." Rowdy paced back and forth. He'd never felt this helpless.

"Take care of her for me and we'll take care of Hugh." CanDee sounded desperate and afraid. He knew how she felt. "I'll call her parents and let them know."

"Don't worry about anything, just stay at the hospital." Cinco was back on the line. "Dean went to get your phone. He's going to bring it to you. I'll call the rest of the family and have someone bring a change of clothes for you and Justus. I'll stop by your office and speak to Margie and find out what's important and what can wait. You worry about Justus and we'll take care of everything else."

"Thanks." He might not feel like he fit into the Rose family, but when crisis hit, the Roses circled the wagons and did whatever it took to support each other.

# CHAPTER 15

Justus woke to organized chaos. There seemed to be people scurrying around in a room painted the exact shade of green that her blond hair turned in the summer when she didn't wash the chlorine out of it.

"Hello, Justus, how are you feeling? I'm Lorraine, and you're in the recovery room of Roseville Regional Hospital. I'm your recovery nurse. You just had leg surgery to repair the two compound fractures in your left leg. Any nausea?" The woman was short, had wiry gray hair that could have passed for a Brillo pad and green eyes that matched the walls.

"Hospital?" Her fuzzy mind recalled something about a pecan tree and an ambulance.

"Yes. You're in the recovery room. Any nausea, blurred vision, or headache?" Lorraine analyzed her face. "You took quite a fall and were unconscious for a while."

"Fall?" Oh, yeah, she fell from the pecan tree. "My son . . . where is my son?"

"CanDee and Cinco are bringing him here." Lucy stepped into Justus's line of sight and placed her hand over Justus's. "He knows about your leg. The surgery was fairly straightforward and you're going to be okay. No spinal injury. You do have a concussion, and we need to watch that, but that's about it. Things could have been worse. I'm so relieved that you're going to be okay."

"Thank you. I remember you in the ambulance with me." Her voice was scratchy like sandpaper against wood. "Can I have some water?"

"As long as you're not nauseated, you can sip some water." Lucy glanced at Lorraine, who scurried off to do the doctor's bidding.

"Is Hugh okay?" She was having a hard time making her brain work. "Is Rowdy okay?"

"Both of your boys are fine. Your son is taking it a whole lot better than my son. I thought I was going to have to sedate Rowdy after he tried to barge into the operating room to get a progress report." Lucy patted her hand. "His brothers are standing guard over him. When I left them about ten minutes ago, Worth had gone out to his truck for some duct tape. It wasn't clear whether they planned to use it on Rowdy's mouth or simply tape him to the chair." She shrugged. "Either way, I'm sure he'll find his way out of it. Rowdy's rather determined when it comes to you."

Angry was more like it. Just because she refused to fall into his stupid plan. She liked him better when he didn't plan things. "How long will I be in the hospital?"

Reality was seeping into her foggy brain. Health insurance–wise, she was screwed. Yes, she had coverage, but it had some giant deductible like ten thousand dollars. She looked down at her leg. How was she supposed to work now? Self-employment didn't come with workers' compensation.

"I'd like to keep you at least three days. We need to keep an eye on your concussion and that leg. I don't anticipate any problems, but there's always a chance." Lucy was very efficient when in doctor mode . . . well, she was also very efficient in her regular life too.

Three days. What was that going to cost? Tears burned her eyes. It probably didn't matter, no doubt she'd already hit her ten-thousand-dollar deductible. There went the money she'd been saving up for a down payment on a house. Well, some of the money she'd saved up. She'd planned on earning the rest while she was here. Since she wasn't able to work, she could kiss that money goodbye. It looked like it would be a while before she'd get back on her feet financially and physically. "How long—" Her voice shattered into a million pieces. "How long before I can get back to work?"

"Six to eight weeks minimum." Lucy's gaze zeroed in on Justus's face. "You're crying. How's your pain level?"

She thought the tears were from pain. Nope, these tears were from life.

"Not that bad." Physically, she didn't feel anything . . . at all.

What the hell was she supposed to do now? She was about to be broke, she couldn't work, and technically she and her son were homeless. Would the Roses let them stay in the cottage while she recovered? She certainly didn't want to assume anything. There was always her father and stepmother's house. All because of a stupid pecan tree. She'd been reckless, and that wasn't like her.

Lucy thrust a handful of tissues at her. "Don't worry. We'll take care of everything. CanDee, Bear, and the twins are all fighting over who gets to take Hugh. My money's on CanDee. She can take them all with one hand tied behind her back."

She couldn't help but notice that Rowdy's name hadn't been in the arguing-over-Hugh list. Obviously he had no intention of ever getting to know his son. The tears came faster. Her little boy would never know his father. This was ridiculous. She needed to pull it together. Maybe she could hire a crew to finish up the Rose projects. She could supervise. That was it. Hiring out would cost her a pretty penny, but at least she could keep the job.

"I'm sorry about the landscaping. It looks like it's going to take me longer than planned." She took the tissues and wiped her face. She needed to pull it together.

Lucy waved her hand dismissively. "Don't worry about that. Your health is more important."

Logically she knew that, but providing for her son was the most important thing in her life. Right now, she felt like she was drowning. She blew her nose.

"Let me get those." Lorraine took the used tissues and held out a small, white, disposable plastic cup of water with a straw sticking out of the top. "Here you go."

She sipped deeply, and the water felt thick against her dry throat. Right now, she couldn't do anything until she was out of the hospital. One thing at a time. She'd get out of here and then find a crew. How long could it take? A week, maybe?

"I'm thinking that I can hire a crew to finish the landscaping work. It might take me a week or so to—"

"Stop. You don't need to worry about that. You need to get better. The landscaping job will still be there when you recover. Rowdy has already had your things moved to his house. He's insisting that you stay with him. He's having a ramp installed as we speak because you're going to be in a wheelchair for a bit." Lucy looked down her nose at Justus.

Again, no mention of Hugh. She refused to move away from her son. All Rowdy wanted was her. "What about Hugh?"

"What about him? He's being spoiled by every person on the ranch." Lucy grinned. "When you get home, it's going to take some time to unspoil him."

"Can I move in with CanDee? That way Hugh and I can be together." The family was being so nice to her. She didn't feel right making demands, but she wasn't moving away from Hugh.

"Why? He'll be staying at Rowdy's with you." She shook her head. "I'm sorry I wasn't clear. Rowdy moved your and Hugh's things into his house. Hugh is only staying with CanDee until you and Rowdy get home. Whether you like it or not, Rowdy is staying here with you. When I suggested that you might not like that, I thought he was going to bite my head off."

"Okay." So Rowdy had moved Hugh's things over too. It was . . . something. But she wanted Rowdy to want to get to know his son instead of feeling like he had no choice in the matter.

Lucy leaned down and whispered, "You need to tell Hugh the truth about his father before someone else does. Maybe you and Rowdy could tell him together?"

"I know. I'm just not sure how that's all going to play out." They were all about to start living together. She really didn't want to have the Rowdy's-your-dad conversation until she was sure that Rowdy really wanted to be Hugh's father. Sperm donation did not a father make. When Hugh had first asked about his father, all she'd told him was that his father was a good man who loved him but that they couldn't live as a family. He knew that his father had painted the picture of her that had hung over her fireplace. Hugh must wonder about him, but he'd never asked for specifics.

Lucy slid her hand into her white lab coat pocket and pulled out a smartphone. She glanced at the screen. "Your father just sent me a text. He's trying to get a flight out at their next port of call."

"Oh." Of course CanDee would have called them. "They're probably worried sick. Tell him that I'm going to be fine."

"I'll try, but if one of my boys were in the hospital, I'd move heaven and earth to get to them." Lucy thumb typed something and then slipped her phone back in her pocket.

"You just described my stepmother to a T." Nothing stood between Maeve and her family. Justus smiled. She'd call her parents and try and talk them out of a visit.

"Let's get you into a room so everyone can see for themselves that you're okay." Lucy turned on her heel and walked to a bank of computers. "Looks like room two seventeen is ready and waiting for you."

Lorraine began unhooking things and moving wires around.

"Since you're alert, let's get you up to your room and comfortable." With her right foot, Lucy clicked some lever under the bed, and it began to move. She and Lorraine pushed Justus down to the end of the long, narrow recovery room. A pair of huge metal doors swung open, and they rolled her down a hall to a bank of elevators. Lucy hit the up arrow and the elevator doors in front of them slid open.

"I've got this, Dr. Rose. I can take her the rest of the way." Lorraine rolled the bed into the elevator.

"If I don't make sure she's comfortable myself, my son is going to have my head." Lucy smiled down at Justus. "I like my head right where it is, thank you very much."

"I don't like all of this fuss over me." Justus believed in being as low maintenance as possible. Being the center of attention made her uncomfortable. Thank God she'd gotten her father's hatred of the dramatic instead of her mother's flair for self-aggrandizement.

She stared down at her leg. She couldn't feel much of anything, but her left leg was in a cast from upper thigh to just under her toes. She tried to wiggle them, but they didn't move. "Why can't I feel my leg?"

Oh, God. Was she paralyzed? How would she support herself and Hugh? She could move her arms, so that was something. Her mind whirled through the possibilities at a mile a minute. Did they make wheelchairs meant for heavy outdoor use? She could still draw out plans and lead a crew. Maybe she could even do some of the planting, provided the beds were raised.

"You have a nerve block with a pain pump so your left side is numb from the waist down." Lucy pulled back the blankets and showed her the thin tubes implanted in her left hip. She tucked the blanket back down and picked up a small black bag that was hanging from the side railing of the hospital bed. "Don't be alarmed. The pump will stay in for about forty hours, and then the numbness will wear off. I guess you don't remember when the anesthesiologist gave it to you. You were conscious but really enjoying the pain meds I gave you."

"Huh. I don't remember much." There was a pecan tree and Rowdy shouting her name. There was something wrong with the tree. Oh, yes . . . borers. "Did you know that your pecan tree has a pretty bad case of the borers? You need an arborist out ASAP."

Lucy looked down at her like she couldn't quite believe her ears. "My yard really isn't the priority here."

"But borers will kill that beautiful old pecan tree." Justus couldn't stand the thought of it. It wasn't the tree's fault that she'd been stupid.

Lucy shrugged like it was just another crazy thing she'd heard from a patient. "Any suggestions?"

"Larry the Tree Guy is the best. I'll give him a call." Justus glanced around. "Where's my phone?"

"Did you know that's the most popular question we get from accident victims?" One corner of Lorraine's mouth turned up.

"I'm sorry, but your phone was in your back pocket when you fell. I'm afraid it didn't make it." Lucy had excellent sarcasm skills. No wonder she and Justus got along so well. "Rowdy has most of it."

Crap. Add that expense to the ever-growing list. Wait. "Most of it?"

A look passed between Lucy and Lorraine.

"When there's an accident like yours, pockets are the worst place to have a phone." Lorraine checked the IV bag.

"I don't understand." Clearly she was missing something.

"What she's trying to say is that I dug most of the screen shards out of your backside." Lucy patted her shoulder. "You're going to be fine."

"Any other injuries I need to know about?" She was grateful for the pain pump.

"No, I think we've covered them all. Concussion, broken leg, stitches in the gluteus maximus." Lucy nodded. "All in all, you were very lucky."

Lucy appeared to be all calm and collected, but there was a bone-deep weariness in her eyes. It hit Justus like a two-by-four. She could have died. She could have had a severe head injury or been paralyzed.

Who would have taken care of her little boy then?

# CHAPTER 16

Rowdy now knew what a death by a thousand cuts felt like. Every second that ticked by when he couldn't see for himself that Justus was okay was a new cut to his soul.

He looked up to find Hugh riding on Cinco's shoulders as they both ducked to make it through the emergency waiting room door.

Jealousy sneaked up on him and punched him in the gut. That was all wrong. Hugh should be riding on his shoulders. Hugh was his son. He could see his, Justus's, and Hugh's life so clearly. In the mornings, he would get up early and make breakfast for them as Hugh packed his backpack for school and Justus fussed over her landscape drawings. And later in the evening, they would talk about nothing and everything over dinner. Their lives together would be loud and happy and filled with love. His house would be messy with the things a family used every day—no, not messy—lived in. The thought should terrify him, but it felt comfortable . . . like that's what had been missing all of these years.

Justus was right, his house was high maintenance. It needed a little boy to make it a home.

Elvis might like having a little boy around all of the time . . . maybe. Although with Justus and Hugh moving in, there would be two more people to wait on Elvis hand and paw. The dog certainly couldn't argue with that.

"Is my mom going to be okay?" Hugh looked down at CanDee, who was standing on Cinco's right.

"You bet, buddy." Cinco's eyeballs rolled up, trying to get a look at Hugh.

"She's going to be fine. She'll need a little time to heal, but she'll be back to her old self in no time at all." CanDee patted Hugh on the leg.

"Now, hit me with some facts, because I know you have some stored in the huge brain of yours." Worth waggled his eyebrows at Hugh.

Rowdy was grateful that his little brother was going out of his way to take Hugh's mind off of his mother.

"Did you know that reindeer eat bananas?" Hugh sounded so small and weak.

"Where do you suppose they get bananas at the North Pole?" Cinco laced his fingers behind Hugh's back like a seat cushion.

"Don't be silly. Everyone knows Santa Claus goes to Jamaica right after Christmas and stays for like six months. That's when he fills the sleigh with bananas. Clearly these Rose men don't take Santa Claus as seriously as we do. It's very sad." CanDee shook her head. "I think we're talking a coal-in-the-stocking situation here."

"Now wait a minute. Santa Claus loves me." It was Dallas. "Last year he got me a pony." He looked around. "I can't speak for the rest of you."

"I got a brand-new truck," Worth chimed in. "I still haven't worked out how he fit it in his sleigh, but I'm going with a teleporter like on *Star Trek*."

"A new truck?" Hugh's eyes turned half-dollar size behind his tortoiseshell glasses. "Wow."

"So, Mr. Hugh, how old are you now?" Dallas held his arms up to Hugh, who slid down into them.

"I'm seven and a quarter." He giggled.

"I think it's time we taught you to drive." Dallas swung him around in wide arcs. "Heck, you're practically a grown-up."

When had Rowdy's family become so comfortable with Hugh? He and Justus had only been here like a week and a half. But they had gotten to know Hugh and seemed to really like him. There was no pretense here . . . no acting. They seemed to adore the little boy. It should have made Rowdy happy, but he felt cheated. His family had had more time with his son than he had.

"Really?" Hugh giggled some more.

"Sure. We'll use Worth's new truck. Santa won't mind. I'm sure he meant it to be driven by all the good little boys and girls." Dallas threw Hugh up in the air and the little boy laughed and laughed and laughed.

That wasn't fair. He should be the one to make the boy laugh.

"I'm not letting you drive my new truck." Worth eyed his twin. "I don't care if Jesus comes down from heaven and personally asks me to turn over the keys to you."

"How's that for family?" Dallas rolled his eyes as he held Hugh upside down. "What happened to share and share alike?"

"Yeah, that doesn't apply to vehicles, underwear, or girlfriends." Worth sat down and crossed one steel-toe-booted foot over another. "All of which I'm pretty sure you've helped yourself to at one point or another in my life."

"It was all done out of love." He set Hugh down on the chair next to Worth.

Worth shook his head. "Do you actually listen to the words that come out of your mouth or do you just open your piehole and hope for the best?"

Dallas put his hand on his chest, mortally wounded. "Now . . . that's just mean."

"Mean? You want to see mean?" Worth stood and reared back his right fist for a good, solid blow to Dallas's jaw.

Rowdy stepped between them. "Let's not get carried away. Hugh might get hurt." He nodded down to the boy.

Worth dropped his fist and glanced down. "The H-man is all good."

He held up his hand for a high five. Hugh slapped him a good one.

It wasn't fair, Rowdy thought. He should have been the one to give Hugh a pet name.

He sat down next to the boy. "So, it looks like you're going to be staying with me when your mom comes home from the hospital."

Hugh's eyes darted between Worth and CanDee like he really wanted to ask to stay with either of them. "Okay."

Awkward silence beat like a heart between them.

What was he supposed to say to a seven-year-old? Did he discuss music, art, fine wine? What were the seven-year-olds listening to these days?

"Arrr," Rowdy said in his best piratey voice. "Let's all talk like pirates and make this little boy walk the plank. Or feed him to the crocodiles?"

The whole room went still as Hugh's eyes turned round with terror.

"Please, Aunt CanDee, let me stay with you." Hugh's voice quivered.

"I'm sure Uncle Rowdy was kidding." CanDee whisked Hugh up into a hug.

She shot Rowdy a WTF look.

Rowdy felt his whole body slump. He was a failure as a parent. Hugh loved everyone but him.

Cinco patted Hugh's back. "Don't mind Uncle Rowdy, he has no sense of humor at all. Dad won him in a poker game when he was a baby. We keep trying to return him, but they won't take him back."

"If only that were true. Somewhere out there, my real family is searching for me. I just know it." He was jealous of the bond the rest of his family had with Hugh.

Rowdy decided to take a different tack and go in for the save. "What I meant to say was that we should build a pirate ship out of couch cushions in my living room so we can sail the seven seas."

"Rowdy does make the best forts." His father, ever the peacemaker, stepped in. "Interesting fact, pirates actually never made anyone walk the plank."

Hugh looked like he was weighing the information. "I don't know anything about pirates." Cautiously, he looked over at Rowdy. "I guess making a fort would be okay."

It was a start . . . a lame one, but everyone had to start somewhere.

The doors to the waiting room burst open and Rowdy's mother made an appearance. "Okay, everyone, Justus is fine and has been moved from recovery to her own room." She turned to Hugh. "Okay, big man, you and Rowdy can go in first. She can have more visitors later."

Rowdy stood and held his hand out to Hugh. The little guy looked at it for a couple of beats, and then, like he was being led to the executioner, he finally slipped his hand in Rowdy's. Great, so he was one step above an executioner, which was only slightly better than being the monster under the bed.

He shortened his gait to match the little boy's.

"How is she?" Rowdy was desperate to see Justus, but he didn't want his mother to scare Hugh.

She smiled at Rowdy and held her arms open to Hugh, who dropped Rowdy's hand and allowed her to pick him up. After settling the little boy on her hip, she said, "She's going to be fine. She's insisting on seeing you, Hugh." She tickled Hugh's tummy, and he giggled.

Did she want to see him too? What if she didn't want to see him because all of this was his fault?

"Okay, I need both of you to be very brave. She's got a cast on her leg and she can't move it for a while." She hugged Hugh tightly. "Especially you, big guy. She's going to need your help getting around. She'll be in a wheelchair for a while and then crutches, so you're going to have to help her with things."

Hugh nodded importantly. "I'll take care of her."

Rowdy raised his hand. "Me too. We'll wait on her hand and foot." He smiled at Hugh. "Won't we, H-man?"

The nickname felt awkward rolling off his lips, but no one seemed to notice.

"I'm going to get her whatever she wants." Hugh nodded and then looked up at Rowdy. "Did you know that eosophobia is the fear of dawn?"

"I didn't know that. Eosophobia is a really long word." Rowdy had the insane desire to hold Hugh. He wanted the connection with the only other person in the world who might love Justus more than he, but he didn't want the kid to feel uncomfortable.

"The longest word in the English language has one hundred eighty-nine thousand eight hundred nineteen letters." Hugh was chock-full of information just like Rowdy's father. Had Hugh gotten that from his grandfather? Was there a fact chromosome?

"Whoever invented it must have gotten paid by the letter." Rowdy kind of liked the random facts.

His mother nodded. "That makes sense. Lots of medical terms have way more letters than seems necessary."

His mother settled Hugh more firmly on her hip and held him with one arm. With the other hand, she reached into her lab coat pocket and pulled out a purple Sharpie. She handed it to Hugh. "You should be the first to sign her cast."

The little boy took the marker and grinned. "I can do that."

"Purple is her favorite color." Rowdy pointed to the elevators. "Second floor?"

It seemed obvious that she was on the second floor since the hospital only had two floors and his mother had led them to the elevator.

"Yes." She hit the "Up" button and the elevator on the left dinged open. "She's in room two seventeen."

Rowdy committed that to memory. "How long will she need to stay here?"

"At least three days." His mother placed an absent kiss on the top of Hugh's head. The little boy didn't seem to notice.

Rowdy liked that. Maybe in time she'd come to see Hugh as a grandson. Because that's what he intended . . . for them to be family, which surprisingly didn't shock him or even feel uncomfortable. It felt . . . right. Why had he been resistant to having a family before? At that moment, being a family man seemed like the most natural thing in the world. He waited for anxiety to strike, but a sense of calm came over him.

"Justus has a pain pump attached to her hip. It keeps her leg numb while it begins to heal. She needs to stay until that is removed." His mother was in clinical mode. "She also has an IV and a catheter, but she's going to be okay."

He knew his mother was preparing them for the machinery that surrounded Justus. He needed to be strong for Hugh and for himself. She was probably pretty banged up, and he didn't want Hugh to be scared by his reaction.

They stepped onto the elevator.

"I'm planning on staying with her at night. Can they bring in a cot or something?"

"Already in there waiting for you." His mom smiled up at him.

"Thanks." He nodded.

"Do I have to spend the night here too?" Hugh's frightened tone conjured images of monsters and dragons lurking under hospital beds, waiting to eat little boys.

Rowdy wanted to reassure him. "No, sir. Only grown-ups can spend the night with patients. Sorry, I don't make the rules."

"Okay." Relief poured off of Hugh in waves. "I guess I can stay with Aunt CanDee."

"I have it on good authority that she makes the best pancakes around." Rowdy patted the boy's back just like his mother had done and planted a kiss on the top of Hugh's head. The little boy smelled like baby shampoo and sunshine. Hugh didn't seem to mind.

"I know, she always makes them for me when I stay with her. Sometimes my mom has to go out of town for work." Hugh reached over and pressed the "Two" button.

Did she really go out of town or was she on a date? It's not that he was jealous or anything, it was just that he was jealous. Justus had a whole life that didn't include him, and he wondered how or if she'd let him fit in.

The elevator lifted them to the second floor, and they walked down the hall to room 217. Rowdy opened the door for his mother and then stepped in behind her.

Justus was sitting up, and her eyes were bright but ringed in dark circles like she hadn't slept in days. "Hey, little man."

Rowdy would give anything to change places with her. He was humbled by her strength. He had to be strong now for Hugh and for her. Brave face in place—he could do this.

"How's your leg?" Hugh's gaze flickered between Justus and Rowdy's mother like he wasn't sure what he was supposed to do.

"Not too bad. Look at all of this fun stuff." She pointed to the gadgets around her. "And the bed goes up and down."

"And she gets all of the Jell-O and chocolate pudding she can eat." Rowdy's mother placed Hugh in the chair beside the bed. "We need to be careful not to hit her leg. Even by accident."

Hugh nodded. "Okay."

The little boy's movements were stiff and overly thought-out. It was like he was making sure that none of his molecules touched his mother.

Rowdy leaned down and whispered close to his ear, "Want some Jell-O? I bet we can sneak a couple."

"Can I have chocolate pudding?" He looked up at Rowdy with huge, soulful eyes. "I like chocolate pudding."

Rowdy ruffled his hair. "H-man, I'll bring you an armload."

He kissed Justus on the cheek and went in search of chocolate pudding. She was okay, and he finally felt like he could breathe again. She was okay. He pulled in air like it was going out of style.

He would take care of her forever if she'd let him, but he was willing to start with right now.

# CHAPTER 17

Seeing Rowdy and Hugh together did more for Justus's recovery than the meds pumping into her veins.

"I'll leave you in Hugh's capable hands." Lucy smoothed Hugh's hair down.

"Thank you so much. I don't know if I said it before." Justus would never be able to repay Lucy and the whole Rose family for rallying around her and taking care of her son.

"No need. You're family." The door swung closed behind Lucy.

Family . . . she was family. It meant so much.

Justus turned to her son. "How is my little man?"

His huge, aqua eyes took in her cast and then the surrounding machines. He held up a purple Sharpie. "Mrs. Lucy says that I can be the first one to sign your cast." His eyes narrowed. "Only I'm not 'posed to move your leg or anything, so I don't know how to sign it."

"I'm sure I'll be fine. I can't feel my leg right now." It was a struggle to keep her head clear enough for coherent conversation. "Why don't you climb on up here with me?"

There was plenty of room for him in the bed beside her, but he looked hesitant.

"I can't. Mrs. Lucy said I can't touch you." He scooted his chair to the bed and then climbed up onto it. He leaned over as far as he could, making sure no part of him grazed her and uncapped the marker. Contorting his body like he was playing Twister, he drew the letters of his name onto her cast.

"It looks lovely. Thank you." She watched him cap the pen and carefully place it on the rolling tray next to her bed. Slowly, he sat down cross-legged in the seat of the chair.

"How come your cast goes all the way up your leg?" He nodded to her thigh. "When Mrs. Taylor broke her leg, hers only went to the knee."

Mrs. Taylor had been their downstairs neighbor.

"I was lucky enough to break both the top and the bottom of my leg. It's like two casts in one." Her gleeful voice sounded like she'd just won a car on *The Price is Right*. Must be the pain meds.

The door swung open and Rowdy burst into the room with an armload of chocolate pudding.

Hugh's eyes were the size of Oreos. "That's a lot of pudding."

"I took everything they had in the fridge and then made a run for it." He dumped ten pudding cups onto the rolling tray table. He looked over his shoulder dramatically. "If anyone asks, we have no idea how all of this pudding showed up here."

Hugh laughed and then looked around. "Did you get any spoons?"

Rowdy froze. "Um . . . no. I was too busy procuring all of these pudding cups."

Hugh's eyebrows hunched together. "What does 'procuring' mean?"

"It's a fancy word for getting." Justus yawned.

"I'll go back for the spoons." Rowdy glanced at Justus. "Need anything?"

"Nope, I'm good." She had a mind to ask for vanilla pudding just to see if he'd go take some more, but no doubt there were others on the floor who needed some pudding, and she didn't want to be the cause of a hospital pudding shortage.

Rowdy headed out the door for spoons.

"What do you think of Rowdy?" she whispered to her son. It felt like her entire world was riding on whether they got along.

"He's okay, but I like Dallas and Worth a lot more. They let me have SweeTARTS." He looked like he was weighing the merit of all three men. "But Rowdy and I are gonna build a pirate ship out of couch cushions when we get to his house."

She couldn't help the smile. Rowdy was making plans with Hugh.

"Sounds like you're a popular man around the Texas Rose Ranch." She grinned.

"What does 'pop-u-lar' mean?" He pushed his glasses back up his nose.

"Lots of people like you." He was so much like his father in more than just looks. He had all of Rowdy's charm and magnetism. People flocked to Hugh just like they flocked to Rowdy. Hugh could talk anyone into doing anything for him.

Why hadn't she noticed that before?

The door flapped open and Rowdy breezed in. "Whew. I just made it past the nurses' station without them seeing me." He produced three spoons from his back pocket. It was all very cloak-and-dagger.

Hugh glanced over his shoulder at the door and then took one of the spoons super fast, like he was afraid someone was going to come in and take it.

Rowdy made a big show of moving the trash can in front of the door. "So we'll know they're coming."

Hugh giggled.

With their left hands, both he and Rowdy picked up a pudding, shook it exactly five times, slammed it down on the tray table, peeled the cover all the way off, licked it, and then placed it to the left of their pudding. It couldn't have been more choreographed if they'd . . .

well . . . choreographed it. Score one for nature over nurture. Clearly Rowdy's chocolate pudding DNA had won out over hers.

So much like his father. She sucked on her top lip to keep from laughing. It was a wonder that the two of them didn't see it.

Rowdy looked up and caught her staring. "What?"

"Nothing." It was like looking in a mirror, albeit a somewhat smaller mirror.

Father and son . . . she never thought she'd see them in the same room. The possibility had always been so remote that it had never crossed her mind. The juxtaposition of the two was so surreal that it made her head spin. The reality and drugs were starting to hit her. When she went home, they were all going to live together. A month ago if someone had told her this was about to happen, she'd have called them crazy.

Sleep pulled at her, and she closed her eyes.

"I think we should leave your mother alone so she can sleep," Rowdy whispered.

Her eyes shot open. "Nope, I'm good."

She wanted to see them together, needed to see them together, but her eyes drifted closed.

When she opened them again, a nurse with scraggly black hair scraped back in a ponytail was checking her blood pressure. Justus looked around for her boys but neither was in her room.

"Where is my son?" Her voice cracked because her throat was scratchy. She swallowed a couple of times and gave it another try. "Have you seen my son?"

The nurse smiled. "He left hours ago. You've been out for quite a while. Rowdy went down to the cafeteria for coffee."

"What time is it?" She squinted at the sunlight streaming through the window.

The nurse glanced at her watch. "Six thirty-seven in the morning."

Wow, Justus had been out for a while . . . like the whole night.

"Will I be going home soon?" Justus really didn't feel that bad or feel anything at all.

"Only your doctor can discharge you, but you aren't going home until that pain pump is out." The nurse slipped off the blood pressure cuff.

"Pain pump?" Justus's eyes went to the little black bag hanging on the side of the bed. "Oh, yeah, I remember now."

The door swung open and a rumpled Rowdy walked in, carrying a cup of coffee in each hand. "You're awake . . . good."

He handed one of the cups of coffee to the nurse, whose name badge read "Carla."

"Thanks." She grinned up at him. "Our patient is doing well. I'll just get out of your hair." She turned back to Justus. "Push the call button if you need anything."

"Thanks." Justus smiled as the woman pushed the door open and left.

Rowdy took a sip of the coffee and winced. "I don't get it. In this day and age, there is still bad coffee. For the love of God, it's the twenty-first century, we've cured wrinkles and the chicken pox, so a decent cup of coffee shouldn't be a problem."

He eyed the coffee like it was toxic waste as he set it down on the tray table.

She picked it up and took a sip. The gag that overtook her body was completely involuntary, and she had to fight to make her throat swallow. "That is awful."

He pulled up a chair. "Never fear, I'll have someone bring the cappuccino maker from my house."

"You have a cappuccino maker?" She hadn't noticed the other night.

He looked as if he'd slept in his trousers and white button-down. His five o'clock shadow was nothing short of downright sexy. "Did you sleep here last night?"

She had a vague memory of waking up and seeing him sleeping next to her bed.

"Yes." He pulled the chair closer to the bed and sat. "It's my fault that you're here, so I need to make sure that you're okay."

She was horrified. He was here out of responsibility. That was actually worse than breaking her leg.

He watched her face and his eyes turned huge. "That didn't come out right. Yes, I'm responsible, but I'm here because I care about you."

Care about . . . not love. And then there was that indecent proposal he'd made to her last night . . . no, the night before. That hurt quite a bit more than the felt responsible part. He had loved her once, and she didn't have a right to expect it again.

"It feels like I'm digging an even bigger hole." He covered her hand with his. "I'm here because I want to be here. You're important and what we had is important. I'd like to start again."

That made her heart go all pitter-pat. "You've always been good with words, but I need to know that you really mean it. I have Hugh to consider. We're a family, and no, I'm not living next to you so you can have a booty call whenever you want one. Either you take me AND Hugh or leave this minute."

She'd never been into taking shit from anyone, and today didn't seem like the best day to start.

It felt like her life and her happiness hung in the balance.

"Hugh and I are still feeling each other out, but I like him. He's a great kid. My family loves him. We just need to get to know each other. That's all." He sounded so confident, but confidence wasn't what she wanted to hear. She wanted to hear that he loved Hugh. It would take time. Intellectually, she knew that. They'd only met a couple of days ago, but she wanted them all to be a family. It was funny. She'd never really thought that would ever happen, and that had been okay . . . then. But now, she wanted it . . . wanted all of it. She'd glimpsed how they would be as a family and she didn't want to settle for anything less. She wouldn't be that selfish mother who thought her happiness was more important than her son's. It would break her heart, but if Rowdy didn't come to love Hugh, she would leave Rowdy forever.

"I think we need to change the subject. Like say for instance . . ." He pointed down at her cast. "Why my name is on your cast."

"That's Hugh's real name."

"You named him after me?" His eyes filled and somehow tears on a man with a five o'clock shadow and rumpled clothes were even more sexy.

"Yes." She covered his hand with hers. "I never thought you'd meet, so I wanted him to have something that was yours."

"I am truly honored." He bowed his head. "Thank you."

"How's my patient this morning?" Lucy stepped into the room.

"She looks good, right?" Rowdy beamed. "I've been taking really good care of her."

"Yep." Lucy leaned up and kissed her son on the cheek. "It was all you. Those nurses out there didn't do a thing."

Rowdy grinned. "I'm so glad that you're finally recognizing my talents." He turned to Justus. "My mom, she's proud of me."

"Hit the road, my sweet boy. I need to examine Justus." Lucy thumbed in the general direction of the door.

"I'm staying." He relaxed back in the chair, crossed his feet at the ankles, and knitted his fingers behind his head. Like a gentleman at leisure.

"Nope, you're out of here. I need to examine her, and while I understand that you've seen each other naked at least one and hopefully more times than that, I don't examine patients in front of other people." She shot him a mom glare. "Leave. Now."

"I'm beginning to feel unloved . . . maybe I should leave . . . now." He didn't move. "But I think I'll stay."

"Don't make me have you forcibly removed from this room, because I can and will." Lucy might be small in stature, but she was mighty.

He turned to Justus. "Do you see this? This is family for you. This is why I've had years of therapy."

"What therapy? I wish. You've never set foot in a therapist's office." Lucy shook her head.

"Well, I've thought about therapy, but my self-worth is so low that I truly believe that I don't deserve it." He picked at a string on the side of his trousers.

Lucy leaned down and hugged him. "My poor, sweet, unloved little boy." Her voice was syrupy sweet. "You're the smartest and best boy that I have." She patted his back. "Now, if you don't leave, I'm going to drag you out."

"She starts off all kindness and love, and then the claws come out." Rowdy sighed heavily.

"Okay, you've forced me to this." She stood and crossed her arms. "Your dad and I had the most incredible sex this morning. Just as I was waking up, he stuck his—"

"I'm out of here." Rowdy jumped up and was out of the door in the blink of an eye.

"Works every time." Lucy raised the hem of Justus's hospital gown and checked the thin wires at her hip. "Your pump looks pretty good. How are you feeling?"

"Not bad . . . I don't feel anything at all, really." Justus looked down at her leg. "How long will I have the cast?"

"Minimum of six weeks, but you'll probably be in plaster for close to three months." She moved to Justus's toes and pinched her big toe. "Can you feel that?"

"Nope, my leg is nothing more than deadweight." Three months in a cast. Her heart sank to her knees. She could go ahead and kiss her future home goodbye. In fact, she should have already done it, but dreams never died, they just kept coming back to taunt her with her own inadequacy.

"The loss of sensation is good in this case. The pain pump is working. I don't think you have any nerve damage, but only time will tell." Lucy covered Justus's feet with a warm white blanket.

She sat in the chair Rowdy had pulled beside the bed. "So, about you and my son."

"Yes?" She wasn't sure where this conversation was headed.

"Do you love him?" Lucy watched her with sharp aqua eyes.

"Yes." No hesitation. Justus knew that Rowdy was the man for her, but she would leave him if he couldn't love Hugh.

"Good. He loves you too." Lucy checked her watch and stood. "Just so you know, Bear and I could use some more grandchildren."

"Okay." Justus drew out the word. She wasn't so sure that Rowdy would be in favor of that plan.

"Hugh's at the age where everything is wonderful and exciting. I love that age." Lucy smiled to herself. "But I could do with some babies. Bear loves babies. I used to have to talk him into giving me a turn at holding my own children." Her eyes turned distant, like she was recalling several treasured memories. "I had this Maya Wrap thing that winds around you and holds the baby to your body but keeps your hands free. He'd wear that thing with the baby strapped to his chest and take them everywhere. In the saddle, feeding the livestock, to the grocery store. My man loves him some babies."

Maybe there was hope for Rowdy yet. He came from people who loved children. "That sounds nice." She pictured Bear, the big and burly man, with a tiny baby strapped to his front. "And funny."

Lucy grinned and nodded her head. "Such a sweet man." The older woman stood. "I've got to go, dear, but I'll be back later today." She leaned down and kissed Justus on the cheek and walked to the door. "Oh, we were thinking that maybe sometime in the next month or so, we could take Hugh to Disney World. You know, if that's okay."

"If course it's okay. He would love it." And there was zero chance that she'd ever be able to afford to take him. It would be wonderful if she could be there with him, but it looked like she was going to be out of commission for a while.

She wasn't doing anyone any good lying around. This was going to be the longest couple of months of her life. Well, no . . . the weeks after Burning Man when she'd first found out that she was pregnant had been pretty awful. Not that she'd ever thought of not having Hugh, but adjusting to the idea of being a single parent and puzzling over how and whether to tell Rowdy the next time she saw him at Burning Man . . . made for some tense and uncertain times.

But life was funny and had other plans for her, and fate didn't ever follow Justus's plans. She should just give up and stop trying to control her life, but she really wasn't a wait-around-for-fate kind of girl.

# CHAPTER 18

Rowdy might have left the room, but he was right outside listening to every single word. Well, not every one since his mother tended to use her quiet hospital voice when talking to patients, but he'd heard most of the conversation.

He couldn't help the joy radiated out of him. His parents thought of Hugh as a grandchild. That was the best news he'd had in a while.

Except, well . . . his shoulders slumped.

Could he treat Hugh as his son? Not that he really knew what that meant, but he already liked the little guy. He really didn't know Hugh that well, but he was willing to try.

The door started to open and he sprinted toward the nurses' station so that it wouldn't look like he'd been eavesdropping. His mother stepped into the hallway and eyed him suspiciously.

"Don't even bother to pretend that you weren't listening at the door." His mother was as no-nonsense as they come.

"How did you know?" He'd never understood how she could read him like a book.

"All of my children have tells. That's why I beat you all at poker." She smiled sweetly.

"Extorting money from your own children . . ." Rowdy put his hand over his heart. "I'm appalled."

"Extorting . . . ha. I won all of that money fair and square." His mother pulled out her smartphone, pulled up a program, and thumb typed something. "I have to see the rest of my patients." She leaned up on her tippy-toes and kissed him on the chin. "See you later."

He grabbed her arm. "Wait . . . how is Justus? Is she healing okay?"

She patted his hand as she unhooked it from her arm. "Ask her. I can't discuss my patients. That's a HIPPA violation. She hasn't given me permission to talk to you."

"Come on." He rolled his eyes. "I'm her family."

And he was, or wanted to be. Now all he had to do was apologize for insulting her and nearly killing her, and they could get on with their lives.

"That's funny. I didn't see a ring on her finger." His mother arched one perfectly groomed eyebrow. "Show me the marriage license and then we'll talk."

His mother lived to torment him. Was the ring comment her blessing? Did he care about getting her blessing? Of course he did.

She slipped her phone back into her lab-coat pocket and waved as she walked down the hall.

He pushed the door open and walked into Justus's room. Her color was better today. As long as he lived, he didn't think that he'd ever be as frightened as he had been yesterday.

She smiled at him. "Your mom and dad want to take Hugh to Disney World. Your parents are so great. You never spoke much of your family, I didn't know what to expect." She played with the ID bracelet the hospital had slapped on her wrist yesterday.

His parents were pretty great, and now he was beginning to see that the only one putting pressure on him to fit into ranch life was him. "Sounds like fun. We should go too."

Now that he thought about it, it would be fun. Never in his life had he thought to go to Disney World, much less take a child.

Her smiled drooped around the edges. "I'd love to go, but I don't think I'll be able."

She pointed to her leg.

Another thing she would miss because of him.

"I'm sure we can figure something out." Like hell was she going to miss the Magic Kingdom. He sat down in the chair next to her bed. "So, what do you want to do today?"

"Hiking Enchanted Rock would be fun, and then after you can take me tap dancing." She grinned. "Or we can just sit around doing nothing." She cupped her hands and wiggled them up and down like she was weighing something. "I don't know. Tap dancing or sitting around."

She was trying to be funny, but it hurt. She wasn't intentionally throwing her broken leg in his face, but there it was . . . all white-casty and broken.

"Did I mention that I'm sorry about that?" He was like 90 percent sure he had, but just in case he hadn't or she'd been too drugged up to remember, "I'm so sorry."

She waved his apology away. "If I hadn't been doing something completely stupid, I wouldn't have been up there in the first place." She pointed to a plastic cup with a straw on the rolling tray just out of her reach. "Can you hand me that, please?"

He would hand her the world, if she let him. He held the straw to her lips and she drank deeply.

She pulled back. "Thanks."

"Also, I need to apologize about the offer I made you. It was very self-centered and self-serving and completely not what I want." He wanted them to live happily ever after. Only now, he wasn't sure what that looked like anymore.

He moved the tray closer to her and set the water within her reach.

"So, we need to talk borers." She leaned back against the pillows.

"Borers?" He really needed to have the pillows off his bed brought here. They were much better than the thin ones provided by the hospital. "I don't understand."

"In the pecan tree. There is a borer problem. I think I mentioned it to your mother, but I want to make sure that someone calls an arborist."

"Let me get this straight: you're worried about the tree that almost killed you." If it were up to him, he'd have the damn thing chopped into kindling. He was all about survival of the fittest, and this tree was fit to die. All its limbs for her limb, that was fair.

"Yes, and the tree didn't almost kill me, I did that all on my own." She shot him a yeah-right look.

She'd forgotten that he'd done his part. "Okay, so borers?"

"Yes, that tree is several hundred years old and was here before Texas became a state. It breaks my heart that it's dying." She turned her leaf-green eyes on him. "Can you get my laptop from the cottage? I need Larry the Tree Guy's phone number. Apparently, my phone is toast."

He was one step ahead of her. He opened the cabinet under the TV, pulled out her laptop and the white box holding the new iPhone he'd had Dallas pick up in Fredericksburg for her. "Here you go."

"I'd give you a big kiss, but I'm not going to lie, my teeth feel a little furry. Don't suppose you brought my toothbrush?" Her gaze went to the small rolling suitcase he'd stowed in the cabinet.

"I just happen to have picked it up for you." Making her happy made him insanely happy. He'd forgotten that. Hell, just being with her made him insanely happy.

She puckered up to blow him a kiss, smelled her own breath, crossed her eyes, and groaned.

"That bad?" He hadn't noticed, which was odd because he had a super sensitive nose.

She mashed her lips together, no doubt because she thought she would pollute the air with her words.

He cleared off her plastic cup of water and laid the suitcase on the rolling table. He unzipped it, fished around for the Ziploc she used as a toiletries bag, and finally pulled it out. "I'm buying you a toiletries bag as soon as I have a minute."

"Why?" She pointed to the bag. "This works just fine."

"If you're freezing leftovers." He looked honestly scandalized.

"Don't be ridiculous. That's a regular Ziploc. The freezer bags are way too expensive to waste on toiletries." She was dead serious. He'd forgotten how frugal she was. That was something that he planned on breaking her of. Perhaps she hadn't realized that he was a wealthy man?

"I can afford to buy you a toiletries bag. In fact, I can afford to buy you the factory where the toiletries bags are made." He didn't like to toot his own horn, but there it was.

"Good for you. I can afford to buy my own Ziploc bags, so we're even." She looked down at the toothbrush and toothpaste he held out to her. She glanced at the sink and then back to the toothbrush. "How is this supposed to work?"

He'd never realized how having two working legs made it possible for him to brush his teeth. "I've got this."

He laid the toothbrush on the tray, smeared a dollop of toothpaste on the bristles, and wet it at the sink. "You brush and then you can rinse and spit into the cup. I'll pour it down the sink and wash out the cup."

She nodded and took the toothbrush. After she was finished and the cup was rinsed, he came to sit down by her again.

"There's another thing." She shifted uncomfortably from side to side.

"Are you in pain?" He had a powerful need to make it go away. "I'm sure we can get you some more pain meds."

"No, that's not it." She bit her bottom lip and then held her right hand up with the IV in it. "With all of these fluids, I need to pee."

"That makes sense. They took your catheter out while you were sleeping." He reached over her and pushed the nurse call button.

There was some static, and then a tinny voice said, "Yes."

"Our patient needs to pee." Rowdy glanced back at the open bathroom door. "We aren't sure how to accomplish that."

"I'll be right there." The nurse's voice faded and then there was a knock on the door. "Here you go."

The nurse handed him a pink plastic bottle-type thing with a wide white capped mouth on one end.

Justus took one look at it and shook her head. "You know what? I can hold it."

The nurse shook her head. "How long do you plan on holding it?"

"Until I get to pee in a toilet." Justus eyed the pink urinal like it was plutonium.

"Once, I saw her hold it for twenty-two hours straight because she didn't want to use a port-o-toilet. It was impressive." Rowdy didn't like public toilets either. Back then, they'd been at a daylong concert on the Playa.

"Yeah, we really don't like for you to do that." The nurse held up the urinal. "It's either this or the catheter. What's your poison?"

"If you unhook me, I'm fairly certain I can crawl to the toilet. Really, I'm an excellent crawler." Justus threw back the blankets. "If someone can just help me to the floor, I can do the rest."

She was completely serious. She'd rather crawl on the hospital floor than pee into what amounted to a giant plastic cup.

There was only one thing to do. Carefully, he slipped one arm around her waist and the other under her knees and gently scooped her up. Two things were immediately obvious—one, she still weighed close to nothing, and two, her hospital gown was open from top to bottom and her bare ass bumped against the front of his trousers.

The nurse ran over and untangled all of the various wires and followed along with the IV pole and the pain pump bag. "Be careful."

Like he was going to be reckless?

Slowly, they made it into the bathroom and he set her down gently on the toilet and then carefully lowered her cast leg to the floor. The nurse rolled the IV pole over so that everything was in Justus's reach.

Both he and the nurse stepped back, waiting. Rowdy wasn't sure what to do now.

Justus rolled her eyes up to glare at both of them. "I realize that hospitals aren't a place of human modesty, but I'd sure like some right now."

"Oh." He stepped outside and waited for the nurse.

"I'll stay in here in case she needs something." She closed the door.

After what felt like an hour, the toilet flushed and the nurse opened the door. "She's ready."

He went to Justus and scooped her up. The nurse followed with the IV pole.

"Sorry about all of this." Justus sounded embarrassed.

"No big deal." It was his fault. The least he could do was take care of her. "I don't mind."

And he didn't, which was strange. He hated hospitals, but he didn't seem to mind this one, because she was here and she needed him. It felt good to be needed.

# CHAPTER 19

Two days later Justus was released from the hospital. She was on the mend. Rowdy had never been so relieved in his life.

He walked into his kitchen and said to Hugh, "I just got your mom settled in comfortably. She's sleeping."

"Okay." Hugh pulled out one of the clear polycarbonate Louis XV kitchen chairs. "How come your chairs are see-through?"

Rowdy hunched his shoulders. "Seemed like a good idea at the time."

Hugh nodded as he placed his Spider-Man backpack on the table and sat in the chair. He unzipped the backpack and pulled out several sheets of manila construction paper.

Man that brought back some memories. Rowdy hadn't seen manila paper since he was in elementary school.

"Did you know that kite flying is a professional sport in Thailand?" Hugh set the manila paper down in front of him.

"I did not." Was he planning on making a kite out of manila paper? It might be a touch heavy. Rowdy pulled out the chair across the table from Hugh. Making a kite sounded kinda fun. He hadn't made one since, well . . . he couldn't remember the last time, if ever. "What are you doing?"

"Making Mom a get-well card." The little boy reached into the backpack and came out with a battered package of Crayola markers.

So okay, kites were out the window.

"Can I help?" He didn't know why he hadn't thought of making her a card.

"I guess." Hugh didn't sound at all enthusiastic.

Rowdy didn't know whether to stay or go.

Slowly, Hugh slid a piece of construction paper across the table and placed the markers in the middle right between them. It was more of an olive branch than an invitation, but it was better than Hugh telling him to hit the road. They had to get used to having each other around at some point, might as well be now.

"What's your plan for the card?" Rowdy watched as Hugh debated over the markers. Did little kids plan things? He had for as long as he could remember.

"Don't know. Maybe a pirate ship." Hugh pulled out the pink marker. He drew a large, fat semicircle with a pole coming out the top. He picked up the yellow marker and added a boxy sail.

"Aren't pirate ships usually brown because they're made of wood?" Rowdy understood artistic license, but this was a little too much. "It should be brown."

Rowdy picked up a piece of construction paper, and *Color inside the lines, Rowdy*, reverberated around in his head. He could hear the voice booming inside his brain like it was happening right now.

*You have to color inside the lines.*

Mrs. Laramey, his kindergarten teacher, was glaring down at him. Instead of coloring a picture he'd been given of a horse brown or black or white like the rest of the students, he'd chosen every color in the rainbow and had even mixed a couple of the crayon colors together to give it a little something extra special. To him, his horse was bright and cheerful and lovely.

*Horses aren't multicolored and you colored outside the lines.*

But it had been so pretty and colorful.

Mrs. Laramey snatched up the paper, wadded it up, and tossed it in the trash can. She slapped another picture of a horse down in front of him. *Try again, but this time, do it right. Color inside the lines and make it look like a horse.*

*Color inside the lines.*

So he'd made the horse brown, but when she wasn't looking, he'd taken his colorful horse out of the garbage, smoothed out the crinkles, and stuffed it secretly in his backpack. Later, when he'd gotten home, he'd tried to show it to his mother, who hadn't even looked at it on her way to work. The next day, it had been wadded up again in the trash.

Tears stung his eyes for the little boy. Coloring outside the lines had gotten him nothing but heartache. That soul-crushing rejection he'd felt at having his beautiful horse once again wadded up was just as fresh today as the day that it had happened. He wanted to go back in time and tell his little-boy self that the horse was beautiful, but it seemed that his wounded inner child was beyond repair.

He'd been coloring inside the lines ever since. Until now, he'd never noticed how forcing himself to conform to the world around him had cost him bits and pieces of his soul. Every time he put on his Armani suit of armor, a fraction of himself was lost.

But surely his mother hadn't thrown the picture away on purpose. She wasn't like that. She may be tough, but there wasn't a malicious bone in her body.

As an adult, he could look back and see that she'd probably been stressed out and tired from work and pregnancy, but his little-boy self had only seen the picture as trash. Hindsight had given him clarity, but healing was another matter.

"Are you okay?" Hugh stared up at him, his tiny tortoiseshell glasses slightly magnifying his aqua-blue eyes.

Rowdy swiped at the warm tears running down his face. "I'm fine. I just realized something about myself."

"Did it hurt? 'Cause you're crying." Hugh watched him like he was judging whether he needed to go get help.

"I'm fine." Rowdy pointed to the pink-and-yellow pirate ship. He wouldn't inflict the same conformity on Hugh. The boy deserved to create pink pirate ships and rainbow horses. "Forget the brown. I like the pink. More pirate ships should have been pink." He would never, ever tell Hugh to color inside the lines.

"Mind if I use the green?" Rowdy waited for permission.

"Okay." Hugh colored inside and outside of the pirate-ship lines with a purple marker.

Rowdy picked up the green marker, uncapped it, and sketched Hugh as the little boy concentrated on his drawing. He was so lost in his pirate ship that his tongue peeked out between his lips. This little boy—his son—was absolutely charming.

Ten minutes later, Hugh looked up and saw Rowdy sketching him. "Is that me?"

"You bet it is, H-man." The nickname was starting to roll off his tongue with little effort.

"You're a good draw-er." Hugh added some blue clouds and a red ocean.

"Thanks." He put the finishing touches on his portrait. "You're a really good drawer too."

Hugh grinned. "Thank you very much."

Elvis waddled in, checked his food dish in case some fettuccini Alfredo showed up while he was napping, found nothing, and waddled over to Hugh.

The little boy got down on the floor with Elvis and rubbed his belly.

Elvis was acting so doglike that Rowdy did a double take. Usually Elvis went out of his way to avoid any doglike behavior. The dog's head lolled back and he gave in to the bliss of a belly rub.

Hugh picked up Elvis's top lip and peeked inside.

Rowdy couldn't believe that Elvis was okay with this. Then again, it had never occurred to him to peek into Elvis's mouth.

"Good boy." Hugh continued to rub the dog's belly. "You're such a good puppy."

Rowdy didn't equate "good boy" with Elvis. Not that the dog was bad, it's just that he thought Elvis viewed himself as his intellectual equal, and there was nothing puppyish about him.

Elvis caught Rowdy looking at him. The dog rolled from side to side, trying to get enough momentum to roll from his back onto his feet. Finally he got up on his feet, refused to make eye contact with Rowdy, and lumbered down the hall to his room.

"Can I stay with Elvis?" Hugh pushed his glasses back up to the bridge of his nose.

"You bet." Rowdy wasn't so sure that Elvis would be okay with that plan, but maybe the dog would surprise him.

"Good. I'm gonna go move my stuff over to his room." Hugh shoved the unused pieces of manila paper into his backpack and rushed down the hall after Elvis.

Thank God he had a couple of extra bedrooms in case Hugh and Elvis didn't make it as roommates.

Rowdy picked up the drawing he'd done of Hugh. It was pretty good, if he did say so himself. He grabbed the pirate ship and took both to the refrigerator. He needed to buy some magnets. In fact, he wanted lots of drawings on his fridge, and a calendar, and maybe even a grocery list. Refrigerators with mismatched magnets showcasing accomplishments and highlighting moments of a family's life were exactly what his house needed.

And exactly what he needed.

A little bit of chaos in his ordered life wasn't so much coloring outside the lines as it was finding a happy medium.

# CHAPTER 20

Three hours later, Justus was propped up in Rowdy's bed with the TV remote, her phone, her Hydro Flask full of water, and a plate of home-made chocolate chip cookies.

Right now she was willing to bet that Rowdy was on the other side of the closed door, hovering and waiting for her to call for him. Not that he wasn't thoughtful, but his attention was a little stifling and somewhat overwhelming.

Just like his house . . . sort of. It needed color and a little mess. It felt like a model home. His house was a place to look at and not to live in.

She looked around at the art displayed on the white walls and then down at the white comforter and then finally to the white area rug over the blond oak floors. She felt like she was sitting in the middle of a giant cotton ball. What in the holy hell was she supposed to do now?

She'd never been one much for TV or reading. Maybe she could take up knitting or sewing or arts and crafts? Those things still required her to work with her hands. But it wasn't the same. She needed to be outside and getting her hands dirty. She needed sunshine on her face and ground under her feet. She glanced down at her cast. That wasn't going to happen anytime soon. She checked out her fingernails. Sure enough, they were dirt-free. She'd always been able to measure her worth as a person based on the dirt under her fingernails. If they were too clean, she wasn't working hard enough.

It felt like the walls were closing in on her.

Six weeks in a cast wasn't a lifetime. Maybe if she repeated it over and over, she wouldn't notice that she wasn't outside . . . or working . . . or able to do anything but sit on her ass.

That wasn't strictly true. She could manage short distances on her crutches, but for anything beyond hobbling to the bathroom, she needed a wheelchair. Thanks to years of heavy lifting, she could haul herself in and out of it without assistance.

Never in her life had she felt this helpless.

She grabbed the remote and clicked on the TV.

"Tonight on *Medical Mysteries*, a woman falls out of a tree, breaks her leg, and dies two weeks later. It's a medical phenom—"

She clicked it off. That certainly wasn't helping.

She picked up a hank of her long blond hair and held it up to the light, checking for split ends. Ten minutes later, she gave up. Glancing up, she counted the light bulbs in the white ceiling fan. There were four. And then her gaze landed on the cookies. There were seven of those. Three watercolors hung on the back wall, all lined up like windows to a vibrant watercolor world. Speaking of windows, there were four floor-to-ceiling ones that looked out onto the swimming pool on the left wall. A white loveseat, two nightstands, and one ginormous king-size bed with no less than six pillows rounded out the room.

Her eyes rolled up to the ceiling fan again. Yep, still had four light bulbs.

She flopped back on the three pillows that Rowdy had fluffed for her. This was going to be a long six weeks. The clock on the nightstand next to the cookies taunted her with its big red numbers. It was all of one fifteen in the afternoon.

She had nothing to do and nowhere to go. Hell, she didn't even need to go to the bathroom. This was going to be the longest day of her life. She checked out the floor. With nothing else to do, she counted the blond oak floorboards.

Out of desperation, she clicked on the TV again and immediately changed the channel. Her mother's face filled the screen. Tears ran down Katarina Smythe-Herringdale's perfectly powdered and blushed cheeks. Her makeup was flawless. Where in the world had her egg donor found waterproof base and blusher? For all she knew, Katarina used spray paint and epoxy to hold her face together, or maybe sheer evil and narcissism gave her that dewy, twenty-one-year-old skin. After all, evil doesn't die, it just gets a face-lift.

Justus's thumb was poised over the "Channel Up" arrow, but she couldn't get her thumb to change the channel.

"If only I'd been able to give Lars children, then maybe he wouldn't have turned to another woman," her egg donor said in her faker-than-fake English accent as she wept prettily. This must have been some sort of reunion show, because while the scene played out in some restaurant, there was a small inset picture of her mother in the lower left-hand corner of the screen. Her mother was watching the scene as they replayed it. "But my body just isn't made for childbearing."

Except you have a child that you'd rather forget than acknowledge.

A brunette with huge cantaloupe-size breasts and lips that looked like cocktail wienies patted Katarina on the back. "It's not your fault. He's the one to blame, not you. You didn't cheat on him."

"Please." Justus rolled her eyes. There wasn't a chance in hell that Katarina had been faithful to her husband. Fidelity wasn't in her genetic makeup. Clearly her egg donor had gotten the bigger, better bank-account gene, because her vagina honed in on the man with the most money.

"I know. But I wish that I'd been able to give him children." Katarina dabbed daintily at the corners of her eyes. "I feel like such a failure."

If the failure shoe fits, she should feel free to strut around in it.

"Stop punishing yourself," Cocktail Wienie Lips cooed.

Katarina wasn't capable of punishing herself, so Justus knew this was an act for the cameras. Katarina was all about Katarina. Whatever she could do to manipulate people, she did. The world revolved around her, and everyone else was just along for the ride.

"I'm so sorry that you've never been able to have children." Wienie Lips put her arm around Katarina. "Bliss and Caress are such a joy."

Her kids' names were Bliss and Caress? Weren't Bliss and Caress two brands of shower gel? Those poor kids. Justus shrugged. She guessed they were lucky not to be named Dial or Irish Spring.

"I do have a child . . . a daughter, but she hates me." Katarina's voice was small and vulnerable.

Justus's heart nearly stopped. Was she talking about her? A craving for her biological mother's love, one that she thought she had buried deep, welled up. She should be over this—but she couldn't bring herself to change the channel.

The larger scene faded away as the small insert of Katarina blew up to full size. Her mother was overly made up and sitting on a purple velvet couch next to Wienie Lips, who was also overly made up.

The camera panned out, and a man's face came into view. "That was this season's bombshell moment, and we'll be right back to discuss it. I'm Stan Goldberg, and we're live with *The Rich Housewives of Beverly Hills* season ten reunion."

They cut to a commercial, and she clicked the "Mute" button. Was Katarina talking about her? Did she have another daughter? Did Justus have a half-sister?

After what seemed like an eternity of product ads, the purple velvet couches full of dressed-to-the-nines women filled the TV screen.

She clicked the "Mute" button again and Stan Goldberg's voice said, "We're back live with *The Rich Housewives of Beverly Hills*, and we're talking about Katarina Smythe-Herringdale's admission that she has a daughter." He turned to Katarina. "Tell us. We're all dying to hear about her."

Even though tears ran in rivers down her mother's face, her makeup wasn't even smudged. Maybe if Justus bought her makeup somewhere other than the grocery store, it would be waterproof too. "It was my first marriage. I was only nineteen when I had her. She lives with her father."

Wienie Lips put her arm around Katarina and pulled her in for a hug.

"Does Lars know?" Stan passed her egg donor a tissue. "Why haven't you mentioned your daughter before?"

Katarina nodded. "Lars does know and he's been supportive. I don't talk about my daughter out of respect for her. We have no contact and she didn't agree to be on the show."

"What's changed? If she didn't agree to be on the show, why did you mention her now?" Stan sounded like he didn't quite believe Katarina.

Score one for Stan. At least he didn't appear to let her egg donor get away with her usual drama.

"Since I'm not able to have any more children, I'd love to have her in my life, but I don't know how to go about it." Katarina was all teary and contrite.

Stan appeared to be trying not roll his eyes. He was fast becoming one of Justus's most favorite people. Like he knew her egg donor was full of shit, he stared her down with penetrating brown eyes and then pointed directly at the camera. "Now's your chance. Why don't you tell her how you feel?"

Katarina stopped dabbing her eyes and looked around like a caged animal.

Yep, Stan Goldberg was good people.

"Well . . . I . . ." She was back to dabbing her eyes as she looked in the direction of the camera. "I'd like to tell her that I love her and I'd like to see her."

Justus called bullshit on that.

"If I do the math correctly, you're thirty-five and you had her at nineteen. That makes your daughter sixteen." Stan didn't look like he bought her age for a second.

Yeah, thirty-five in dog years. Try forty-nine and closing in on the big five-O.

"You get her, Stan." Justus pumped a fist in the air. "Don't let her get away with anything."

"Yes . . . um . . . well . . ." Katarina's green eyes turned the size of ice cream scoops.

"She's in those difficult teenage years." Stan crossed his legs. "Don't you feel that you should help her navigate them? Not being a teenage girl, I have no idea, but I'm thinking she could use a mother." His hand disappeared into his pocket and he pulled out a smartphone. "I don't know about the viewing audience, but I think you should give her a call right now."

Justus glanced at her phone on the nightstand and then touched the info button on the remote. The show had been recorded a week ago.

"I . . . um . . ." Her mother gathered herself. "I'd like to call her in private. That is only fair, since she didn't ask to be on television."

That was a cop-out and Stan knew it. "If you didn't want her involved with the show, why mention her?"

God he was good. She had half a mind to send him a thank-you email.

"Um . . . well . . ." Katarina shot Wiener Lips a help-me-out look, but the woman wouldn't make eye contact. Her egg donor bit her bottom lip so hard that she must have been close to biting clean through, and the tears started up again, only this time they were racking sobs, which were part honking goose and part Mommy Dearest. Soon her face turned red, and it looked like she was about to pass out. All of the cast stared at their incredibly high-heeled, outrageously expensive shoes. Apparently one of their own dissolving into gasping sobs made them all uncomfortable.

Stan handed her tissues like he was on a bucket brigade putting out a fire.

This show was hilarious. What did it say about Justus that she was enjoying her egg donor's discomfort? She shrugged. Katarina deserved more than a little discomfort. If Justus were a better person, she would hope that her egg donor had changed, but people didn't change that much. The only place where people one-eightied their personalities was in fiction.

The camera zoomed in on Stan. "Unfortunately we're out of time, but join us next week for part two of the reunion show. Hopefully we can track down Katarina's long-lost daughter."

He made the last part sound about as possible as Bernie Sanders jumping ship and becoming a right-wing Republican.

"Yep, Stan, you got that right." She looked around and noticed that she'd been talking to herself. So now she was bored, lonely, and pathetic.

"Who are you talking to?" Rowdy poked his head in the bedroom doorway.

"No one." It was beyond embarrassing admitting that she'd been talking to the TV. His gaze went to the TV and one eyebrow shot up. "I thought you didn't watch *The Rich Housewives of Beverly Hills*."

"My first time. This was their reunion show and apparently they want to contact me." There wasn't a chance in hell she was going to let that happen.

Now both eyebrows smacked his hairline and then settled back into place. "That's not a bad idea."

She stared at him for a second and then blinked. "It's a terrible idea. It's an insane idea. My egg donor, as I like to call her, doesn't want to have anything more to do with me than I do with her. My mother's name is Maeve, and she's wonderful and kind and loves me as the biological daughter she never had. That's enough for me."

Why did she sound defensive?

"But is it enough for Hugh?" Rowdy stepped into the bedroom and leaned against the door jam. "Ever thought about that?"

"More times than you can possibly imagine. I don't ever want for him to feel unloved or unwanted like I did." Which was precisely why she hadn't told Rowdy he had a son for seven years.

"I didn't know it was as bad as that." He sat down next to her on the bed and took her hand, his thumb drawing little circles on the back. "Sorry. I may not be exactly what my parents wanted, but they love me anyway."

"What do you mean not exactly what they wanted?" His parents were so wonderful and seemed very proud of him.

"I don't know." His eyes dropped to the floor. "I've never really fit in. I like wine, they like beer. I like opera and they like country music. I feel like I was switched at birth. Sometimes it's stifling trying to be the person they want me to be."

She didn't get that vibe from Lucy or Bear—granted, she hadn't spent that much time with Bear, but he seemed really laid-back. Justus knew what it felt like to not be wanted. "I'm sorry you feel that way. I don't know them as well as you, but I don't see them as anything but proud of you."

Maybe his parents were different in private, but they seemed like good people who valued family above all else. However, she wasn't part of the family, so she couldn't know for sure.

She brought his hand to her lips and kissed his palm. "I'm sorry that you feel like you don't fit in. That must have been hard growing up."

He shrugged, but she could see the hurt in his eyes. "I'm sorry you have a crazy mother . . . ur . . . um . . . egg donor."

"What can you do?" She matched his shrug and threw in a head nod. "Family can be complicated."

He chewed on his bottom lip. "Can I ask you something . . . it's kind of personal?"

"Sure." He'd seen her naked, carried her to the bathroom so she could pee, and rejoiced with her after she'd had a bowel movement and could leave the hospital. Honestly, how much more personal could it get?

"Is the reason you didn't tell me about Hugh because of what your mother did to you? You didn't want him to feel the same kind of rejection?" He watched her carefully.

"Yes. No child should ever feel unwanted." She shook her head. "I know I have issues, but now I've given Hugh my issues." Since she'd gotten home from the hospital, her son hadn't wanted to spend time with her. She'd given her son mommy issues—a mother's worst fear.

"He's fine." Rowdy kissed her cheek. "Don't worry. He's a great kid." Rowdy rubbed the back of his neck. "What did you tell him . . . you know, about me . . . well, about his father?"

She smiled to herself. "I told him that his father is a wonderful man who loves him, but that we couldn't be together."

She hoped the love part wasn't just wishful thinking.

Rowdy nodded. "Thanks for that. I'm getting to know him. I want him to like me. I'd like for him to, you know . . . look up to me. I don't know if I'm ready for a family, but I know that it's no longer off the list."

Not off the list was something . . . sort of.

Maybe one day he'd figure out that having a family wasn't a chore, it was a gift. With any luck it would be sooner rather than later.

# CHAPTER 21

Two hours later, Lucy knocked on Justus's open bedroom door. "Okay if I come in?"

"Okay." Justus wasn't fit for company right now, she just wanted to marinate herself in self-pity and possibly eat her way out of a vat of ice cream. Crap, she didn't have any ice cream.

"Bear and Hugh are just starting the checker world showdown and I need some girl time." Lucy gently sat on the edge of the bed. "Penny for your thoughts."

"Not sure they're worth that much." Maybe isolation wasn't the best plan. She could use some girl time too. "I think I broke my son."

Now she'd given her son some serious mommy issues.

Lucy's shoulders bobbed up and down with laughter. "Isn't motherhood the best?"

"I never knew I could feel so much guilt." Justus would give anything to be able to go back in time and change a few things.

"Please, you have nothing to feel guilty—wait, you kind of do. Want me to kick you while you're down?" If nothing else, Lucy was honest.

"Sure, why not?" Maybe she could get all of her guilt at once and then be over it.

"You're a good person and you've had to make some tough decisions." Lucy lay down on her side and propped her head on her fist. "I wasn't going to tell you this, but I was angry and hurt to find out now that I had a grandson."

Justus leaned forward, "I'm so sor—"

Lucy threw a hand up. "No, let me finish. Bear and I talked about this the other day. Once the shock wore off and we were able to see things objectively, we both realized that the anger and hurt stemmed from losing time with Hugh. We missed his birth, birthdays, first time he walked, his first words. Having had children, we know what we've missed. Rowdy has no idea. He may have told you that he didn't want children, but I'm not so sure that I agree with that. He loves people and family, and I can see him with lots of kids. I just wish he did too."

"You're preaching to the choir here." She appreciated Lucy's honesty. Now that the issue was out in the open, they could resolve it.

Lucy reached over and stroked Justus's hair. "Rowdy doesn't like surprises and you dropped a big one on him."

"The person I knew at Burning Man loved surprises. He was Mr. Spontaneity."

"I wish. Of all of my children, Rowdy is the least spontaneous. He's a planner." Lucy patted her hand. "Bless him, but he's so buttoned-up." The older woman smiled to herself. "When he was little, he was so tenderhearted and artistic and then he grew out of it."

It was Justus's turn to laugh. "The Rowdy I know is tenderhearted and artistic." She moved around, getting more comfortable. "I wonder which version is the real him?" She pointed to the paintings on the wall. "I've wondered why his paintings aren't everywhere. It's one thing to hide his art from his family, but another to hide it from himself."

Lucy shook her head. "I feel like I don't know my son at all."

"Me too—well, not my son, but Rowdy." It was time for her to tell Lucy the truth of why she didn't tell Rowdy he had a son. "I didn't tell Rowdy about Hugh because I didn't want my son hurt. Rowdy was pretty up-front about not wanting children . . . so was my biological mother. Katarina Smythe-Herringdale is a textbook narcissist. I should be over it by now, but clearly I still have some unresolved issues."

How could one self-involved person that she'd only remembered meeting once still be able to hurt her?

"Katarina from *The Rich Housewives of Beverly Hills*?" Lucy didn't sound like she believed it.

"Yes. That's my bio mom." Justus shot her a big, fake smile.

"Damn, she's evil." Lucy grinned. "I'm so sorry she's your biological mother."

"I know . . . right?" Justus threw her hands up. "I should be over it. I shouldn't want or need her approval."

But she did.

"Oh, my dear, every child will always want parental approval no matter how old they get or tall they grow. I know that she didn't have much to do with your upbringing, but she's still your biological mother. Children are programmed to seek approval from their parents because they are supposed to make them feel safe. It doesn't matter that your biological mother wasn't there, it's nature over nurture. Part of you still wants validation from her." Lucy continued to stroke Justus's hair. It was soothing.

"Maeve is a wonderful mother and grandmother. When I was little, every single year on my birthday, I'd blow out the candles on my birthday cake and wish that Maeve was my real mother." It's all she'd ever wanted.

"She is your real mother in every way that counts." Lucy settled Justus's head on her shoulder. "I think you need to mourn the loss of the relationship you would have had with your biological mother. You need to mourn it and let it go. It's okay for you not to love her. Not loving her doesn't make you anything like her. Not loving her won't turn you into a bad mother. I mourned the loss of a motherly relationship long ago. It's not that my mother isn't capable of love, she has too many other things she'd like to do instead. Familial sentiment isn't high on her list of priorities."

Lucy didn't sound particularly sad about this.

"What is your mother like?" Justus used the present tense, hoping that Lucy's mother was still alive.

"My mother is both an MD and a PhD. She's a clinical psychologist who most likely became a mother so that she could observe the human condition up close and personal. My brother, sister, and I were merely larger rats for her to put in a maze." Again, Lucy didn't sound particularly upset, only stating the facts.

Would Justus ever be able to step back from the situation with her mother and look at it with an objective eye? "How long did it take you to make peace with the relationship?"

"It's a work in progress. Some days I view her through the detached lens of a physician, and other days I want to poison her with tetrodotoxin. It comes from the blowfish. It's tasteless, odorless, and colorless, but very painful." Lucy grinned. "I've spent more than a healthy amount of time researching just the right poison."

"Good to know that I'm not the only person with mommy issues."

"Mommy issues are as old as time." Lucy crossed her arms. "I wonder what my children's mommy issues are?"

"I don't think they have any." With the exception of Maeve, Justus had never seen a more caring mother.

"I'd like to think that, but everyone is entitled to their own mommy issues." Lucy shrugged. "They're all male, so maybe they have daddy issues instead."

"I'm choosing to believe that too." Justus let out a long breath slowly. "Then again, I might be the reason Hugh could have daddy issues. I did kind of give them to him."

Lucy patted her knee. "Don't be so hard on yourself. You have some serious reasons for not telling Rowdy about Hugh and vice versa.

Chances are, Hugh won't remember a thing. My mother was one of the researchers who found that memory crystallization in children happens at around the age of ten. While younger children can recall past events, they generally lose that information by adulthood. The average adult has memories of nothing before the age of ten."

"Looks like I have a few more years before the damage is permanent." Justus was only half kidding. "I'm still getting the hang of motherhood."

"Me too." Lucy crossed one ankle over the other. "You're a fantastic mother. Know how I know that?"

"No." She wanted to be a fantastic mother, but she always felt like she was doing the wrong thing.

"You second-guess yourself. The mere reason that you don't think you're a fantastic mother is what makes you a fantastic mother. My mother thought she was an incredible mother." Lucy rolled her eyes. "Once I asked if her delusions included an auditory element or if they were just visual. She thought I was kidding."

"I can't wait to meet her." Justus was only half kidding.

"Don't get your hopes up. She doesn't make it out to the ranch . . . ever. She lives in Dallas with my father. He's a retired neurosurgeon who lectures all over the world." Lucy seemed as clinical about her father as she was about her mother. "Their marriage works because they are both workaholics."

"I bet Christmases were so much fun at your house." Justus laughed.

"You have no idea. When I was sixteen, I got a paperweight for Christmas. Don't even ask about Santa, because we were told that he was nothing more than a fantasy dreamed up by retail outlets to sell more things." Lucy shook her head. "That's why I still give my sons Santa presents. Santa Claus is alive and well and lives in the North Pole. I reject all other realities."

"Just curious. At the age of sixteen, did you have enough papers that needed weighing down?" At the age of sixteen, Maeve and her father had given her the truck that she still drove.

"Not that I remember. I do remember my sister, Fiona, and I riding the elevator all the way up to the roof of Parkland Memorial Hospital and dropping that damn crystal paperweight over the edge." She smiled to herself. "It shattered into a million pieces. It was a very good day."

"When it comes to child-rearing, I try to do the exact opposite of what I think my biological mother would have done. Is that what you do too?"

"Yes, pretty much. I've picked up a thing or two here and there. Bear's mother was no prize either. Suzette Louise McCloud Rose was a debutante who thought the world revolved around her, but Bear turned out okay. His father, on the other hand, was amazing. Truly one of the finest people I've ever had the privilege to know. When he died, I felt like I'd lost my real father. I've always wondered why he married Suzette in the first place." Lucy grinned absently, like she was recalling memories. "You would have liked Tres, and he would have been over the moon for Hugh. Tres always wore overalls and had lemon hard candy in his pocket. He was forever slipping them to Cinco and Rowdy. It's a wonder that my two oldest boys didn't develop type two diabetes."

"I would have loved to have met him. He sounds like a lot of fun." Justus made a mental note to ask CanDee—the family historian—for a picture of Tres. Hugh should know all about his family.

"Lefty is a lot like him, only crotchety. He and Tres were best friends."

A light knocking sounded at the door. Lefty held a battered straw hat to his chest. "Is now a good time for a visit?"

"Of course." Justus waved him inside the room.

"Speak of the devil." Lucy smiled at him. "Your ears must have been burning. We were just talking about you. I was telling her about Tres."

"Best man that ever lived." Lefty's head bobbed up and down. He turned his eye on Justus. "I brung you something. I hope you like it." A boyish smile cut across his craggily old face. "It's a 'hope you get well soon and thanks for letting me drive Imogene while you're recoverin'' present."

He walked into the room and went straight to the bank of windows. "I made it myself." He fumbled around and yanked on the cord to the blinds.

Outside was a vehicle of sorts—part ATV, part wheelchair, part riding lawn mower.

Lefty waved his arm like a game show hostess. "I took the tires off of a four-wheeler and mounted them onto an old John Deere riding mower I used to cut grass around the houses. I added them leg braces off of an old wheelchair I had in the barn. I added the frame and banana seat from Rowdy's old bicycle as a sidecar for Hugh and welded the old bike to a foot-long pole so the bike doesn't bump up against the mower."

Justus squinted to get a better look, and sure enough there was a bicycle frame and banana seat suspended in midair and mounted on the side opposite of the wheelchair leg brace. There was even a set of bicycle handlebars for Hugh to hold on to.

The whole contraption reminded her of something from Burning Man. It was fantastic and just a little bit south of normal.

He continued, "That tractor engine was kinda slow, so I took an old Honda motorcycle motor and used it instead. She can do twenty-five miles an hour on open land, fifteen uphill." Lefty pointed to the steering wheel. "I added a horn. It's also got lap belts for safety."

"That's awesome." Justus eased herself off the side of the bed and grabbed her crutches. Slowly, she hobbled over to the window. "I can't wait to drive her. She's beautiful."

Lefty blushed and shuffled his feet. "It was nothing."

Justus propped herself up and put one arm around him. "I love it. I can't wait to get behind the wheel."

She glanced at Lucy. "What do you say? Want to ride on the back? Or on the banana seat?"

"Like hell; I don't ride bitch. We'll take turns driving." Lucy looked as excited as Justus felt.

Every day at the ranch was a new adventure.

# CHAPTER 22

Back from the grocery store for supplies, Rowdy pulled into the drive-way, clicked the button to open the garage, and drove in. Having three people living in his house meant he needed more food . . . and kid food like Little Debbie snack cakes. God, he loved those. And chocolate pud-ding. He'd bought lots of chocolate pudding.

His inner child nodded. Having a little boy around seemed like a great idea.

All of those years he'd missed with his son and with Justus. He'd never been one much for regrets, but he was willing to admit that maybe he'd missed out a little on Hugh's life.

Had he been a good baby or a fussy one? What had been his first word? When had he taken his first steps? Did he go to preschool, and if so, what had his first day been like?

He froze midstride.

He really wanted to know. He wanted to know everything. When had that happened?

Arms loaded down with brimming recyclable bags, he opened his back door and stepped into his kitchen. He dropped everything on his kitchen table. Looking at his kitchen through new eyes, the clear plastic chairs were kinda stupid. He needed new ones, and Justus and Hugh should have a say in picking them out.

Damn, he really was on board with this whole domestic life thing.

His house was too quiet. The TV was no longer on and the house was silent as a tomb. Now that he thought about it, he'd had enough quiet to last him a lifetime. He was more than ready for some noise.

He walked through the living room and poked his head into the master bedroom, expecting to find Justus asleep, but the room was empty.

"Justus?" He called as he walked into the attached bathroom, but there was no sign of her. "Where are you?"

Hell, she couldn't have gotten far. He glanced back at the wheel-chair next to the bed. He walked back into the bedroom and out the door. "Justus? Are you here?"

Where the hell else could she be? He searched the house. She was nowhere to be found. His heart dropped to his knees.

Fear stabbed him in the gut.

She was gone.

She'd left.

She'd walked out of his life again.

Rationally, he knew she hadn't, but he didn't want to take a chance that history was repeating itself.

He threw open his front door and slammed it behind him. Where the hell could she be? It's not like she could navigate dirt roads on her crutches.

Off to the west, a humming noise caught his attention. He shaded his eyes from the sun as he turned in that direction.

It couldn't be . . . he squinted, trying to get a clearer view. Was Justus behind the wheel of a lawn mower?

He took off in a dead run.

For the love of God, she'd just gotten out of the hospital, and now she was mowing the grass. What in the holy hell was wrong with the woman? Was she trying to do more damage to her leg? Christ, he'd only been gone for like two and half hours and she was already back to work.

What did he have to do, tie her to the damn bed?

He cut across his front yard and down the road to his parents' house. As he got closer, he noticed that both his mother and Lefty were standing under an oak tree watching Justus. Had they all lost their ever-loving minds?

"What in the hell's going on here?" he called to his mother as he made his way to Justus. It didn't look like his mother had heard him over the hum of the mower.

Justus giggled loudly as she turned the lawn mower in a circle and appeared to be doing donuts. This was insane. Nothing made sense.

Rowdy tapped his mother on the shoulder, and she jumped as if startled.

"What in the hell is going on?" he yelled over the mower.

His mother smiled as she pointed to the mower. "Justus is doing donuts."

"I can see that, but why?" He folded his arms. "As her doctor, I'd think you'd want her to stay in bed."

"She's fine. Her leg is elevated." Lucy pointed to Justus's out-stretched leg. "Lefty made her a mobile wheelchair of sorts."

"Why is there a bicycle frame mounted to the side?" He turned to Lefty.

"Sidecar for Hugh." Lefty's tone suggested that was completely self-explanatory.

"And you're okay with this?" He glared at his mother.

"She's fine." His mother cupped her hands around her mouth and yelled, "My turn."

Justus slowed the mower and pulled right up to them. Her cheeks were flushed and she looked absolutely beautiful. Right now, he wanted nothing more than to scoop her up and kiss the grin right off of her face.

Justus turned a key and the mower's growl halted. She untied the scarf she had dangling around her neck and slipped one end under her cast. She retied it and used her neck to hoist her leg up.

Lucy rushed over with the crutches.

He was at Justus's side and attempting to lift her up when she batted his hands away.

"I got it." When she used that I'm-an-independent-woman-hear-me-roar tone, he knew to admit defeat.

He backed away.

Using her neck to hold her leg up, she carefully scooted off of the mower and onto her crutches. It took everything in him not to help her.

He turned on Lefty. "So you're responsible for this?"

"What? All I did was make Miss Justus something she and her son can use to get around the ranch. I can't help it if the woman's fiery and didn't feel like laying in bed today. I'm just the mechanic." Lefty passed a condescending gaze over Rowdy. "How people use the stuff I make ain't my concern."

"And you." He rounded on his mother. "You should know better."

"Son, don't point your finger at your momma. It's disrespectful." Lefty's tone was so sharp that Rowdy should have been missing an eye or at least an ear. Technically, Lefty wasn't family, but he'd been around for as long as Rowdy could remember.

"Medically speaking, if Justus feels she can do something, I want her to do it. Provided that her leg is elevated most of the time." His mother avoided looking at Justus's unelevated leg.

"I'm fine. It feels good to get out of bed and to get some sunshine. I've been cooped up too long." Justus yawned.

"Looks like you need to get back into bed." Rowdy tried not to sound condescending, but it was hard. "Why don't you get back on this thing and ride back to our house?"

His mother's jaw dropped to the ground. Justus looked like a deer in the headlights. Lefty's unicorn eye patch sparkled in the sunlight.

"Yep, I said our house. Don't everyone fall over with shock." His family would just have to get used to him and Justus and Hugh living together.

Justus yawned again and nodded. "If you don't mind, Lucy, I'd like to go back to bed. I'm so sorry, but would it be okay if you have a turn later?"

His mother waved it off. "I'll have a turn another day. Need some help getting back to bed?"

Rowdy stepped in between the two women. "She has all the help she needs."

His mom was acting like Justus hadn't just had major surgery.

Lefty snickered. "Never seen him this possessive. And to think that not two weeks ago, I could have sworn he was into dudes."

Justus laughed so hard that her eyes watered. "Your family thought you were gay?"

This wasn't the first time he'd heard something like this. His family really didn't know him.

"I wasn't sure, but I made every effort to tell him that he should feel free to be himself and that we were okay with him loving whoever he chose." Lucy patted Rowdy's arm.

"I can tell you that he's definitely not gay." Justus grinned up at him. At least she was looking at him again.

"We had a pool going. My money was on cat burglar." Lefty turned his good eye on Rowdy. "I was so disappointed to hear that all you do on the one week a year you sneak away is go to some weird festival. The pot was almost ten thousand dollars until your momma broke it up. It don't make no sense, you covering up going to a festival." His eyes swept down Rowdy, taking in everything from his head all the way down to his toes. "It still don't explain the hidden room you have in your house."

Rowdy felt his mouth fall open. No one knew about his art studio.

"You have a secret room?" His mother looked at him like he was a lab rat she was about to dissect. That's exactly the look he'd spent the better part of his life trying to avoid. He didn't want anyone to look too closely and confirm that he didn't fit in. "Cool. I wish I had a secret room."

Rowdy released the breath he'd been holding.

"On second thought, a secret room would be bad. I'd be tempted to lock your father in it when he did something that pissed me off. Since he does that a lot, some folks might start wondering where he is." His mother laughed and kissed him on the cheek. "One day, I hope you'll trust me enough to show me your secret room."

He did trust her. It wasn't about trust, it was about acceptance. His art studio was private . . . his art was private.

"Secret room?" Justus's eyes glowed with excitement. "Can't wait to find it."

At least she wouldn't be shocked by it. And he didn't want any more secrets between him and Justus.

"Maybe I'll show it to you sometime." Maybe he could talk her into sitting for him again. She'd always been his favorite subject.

"Nope, I'd rather find it on my own." She nodded toward the mower. "I could use a hand getting on. And if you're nice to me, I'll give you a ride on the sidecar."

"Oh, I plan on being really nice to you." He scooped her up and gently placed her in the seat and then positioned her leg in the holder. He kissed her on the cheek.

She kissed him lightly on the mouth.

Then it hit him.

She knew everything about him and loved him anyway—totally and without reserve.

Justus got him.

# CHAPTER 23

The pain meds were muddling her brain.

Rowdy had put her to bed, brought her a bowl of homemade tomato soup and a grilled cheese sandwich, and was now sitting next to her in bed, eating his sandwich.

"Okay, I'm willing to admit that I might have made a mistake in not telling you about Hugh." Justus reviewed the words in her mind. Her thoughts were fuzzy, and it seemed to take a long time to wade through them. She needed to make amends and make him understand that she hadn't meant to hurt him. "Wait, that sounds like I really don't think I made a mistake."

She wanted to show him all of the pictures she'd taken of Hugh from the day he was born until now . . . but she didn't know if Rowdy wanted to see them. She wished she had the photo album she'd made for him all of those years ago.

"Yes, I think I am sorry I didn't tell either of you." Did that make sense? She wasn't entirely sure.

"How much pain medication have you had?" He dipped a corner of his sandwich into the tomato soup and then took a bite.

"Enough that I'm pain-free and floating on a cloud of hydrocodone." She dipped her sandwich into the soup and then overshot her mouth, hitting her cheek. Using the sleeve of the red T-shirt she'd borrowed from Rowdy, she wiped the tomato soup off of her face. In getting her sleeve to her face, the bowl of soup sloshed precariously to the left and a small tidal wave of red spilled onto the white comforter.

"I'm so sorry." She plunked the bowl onto the nightstand and, using the hem of the shirt, rubbed furiously at the soup. All that did was rub the stain deeper into the fabric.

Rowdy took his bowl and poured a healthy dollop of soup on the white comforter next to him. "Now we have matching stains."

"Why did you do that?" That was something her Houston would have done. So there was a little Houston still in there.

"I thought it would make you feel better. Maybe if we splattered the whole thing, it will look intentional." Calmly, he dipped his sandwich into the soup and took a bite like he didn't have a care in the world.

Justus looked around, trying to make sure that she was indeed in Rowdy's house and not in some Twilight Zone version. "Given all of this white and your love affair with your vacuums, shouldn't you be freaking out about the tomato soup stain and frantically pretreating it with some secret recipe of cleaners you happen to have on hand for just such a stain emergency?"

"See, here's the thing. Usually I am very particular about my clothes and my home, but in the last week, I've learned that I have a son, not to mention that the woman I love almost died. My priorities have realigned. Stains are so far down on the list that I'll probably never give them much thought again." He sounded so casual.

"So you still love me?" Had he said something about loving her or had she made that part up?

"It's not like I can turn it off. I love you. Since the first moment I set eyes on you, I knew that I loved you. Does that mean that we get to have a happily ever after?" He sounded so hopeful that it was heartbreaking. "You know, now is an excellent time for you to tell me how you feel." He took a deep breath and let it out slowly. He was nervous. She didn't remember ever seeing him nervous.

"I love you. I have always loved you and will always love you." Why did it hurt her to say? Because he just told her that he didn't know if they were going to end up together.

He closed his eyes and relaxed against the pillows. Relief poured off of him in waves. "It's good to know. I wasn't sure after your accident, and then I've acted like an ass when it comes to Hugh."

She took a deep breath. Maybe it was the pain meds giving her courage, but it was time he faced the Hugh issue. "I need to know right now how you feel about being in Hugh's life. That's a deal breaker for me."

"Here's the thing. I didn't want children." He shook his head.

There it was, the truth. She didn't think he could actually break her heart more, but he was doing it. After she was healed and the job was finished, she and Hugh would hit the road.

"But now I do. I can't wait to hang out with Hugh and get to know him. We're going to build a pirate ship out of pillows. Tomorrow, I was hoping we could spend all day together and play board games. We need some family time."

Her heart smiled at his excitement.

"Family time." She hadn't realized that two words could mean so much . . . mean the world. Even in her best dreams, she'd never imagined that she could have a life with her Houston and Hugh. Tears welled in her eyes.

"You're crying. Oh, God, what did I do?" His eyes went to her leg. "Are you in pain?"

"No, I'm happy. I thought I'd never see you again. I felt like I had to give you up for Hugh, but it looks like I get to have my cake and eat it too." She mopped her face with the sleeve of her borrowed T-shirt. The pain meds were making her tired. She yawned and stretched.

Rowdy's eyes went to the *V* of the T-shirt. It showed more than a little cleavage.

"Are you checking me out?" She arched her back and stuck her chest out in case he was.

"I'm a guy, we like boobs. Can't help it." He stuck a finger in her neckline and pulled at it, looking down. "You're not wearing a bra. Nice."

"Cool it, Lover Boy, I'm injured and tired." She pushed playfully at his chest.

"We've lived together for like six hours and you're already tired of me—"

Her lips came down hard on his and she showed just how untired she was. Her tongue explored the inside of his mouth. Gently, he pressed her back against the pillows as his hand slowly pulled up the hem of her shirt.

Lightly, he bit her bottom lip, and then he trailed light kisses down her jawline. "Think we can navigate around your broken leg?"

"Thanks to yoga, I'm very flexible." Her hands fisted in his hair, pushing him into her. "Sex would be nice, yes please."

Laughter rumbled in his chest as he kissed his way down her neck. "Sex? Who said anything about sex? I was talking about playing Twister. There's nothing like a good game of Twister to cement a relationship. It's a great bonding experience."

He kissed his way down to her left nipple. He tongued it through the T-shirt.

She moaned. God, he loved that sound. He could stand to hear it a thousand times a day for the next hundred years.

"You like this." He sucked a little harder. "So do I."

"Nope, I was just thinking that instead of Twister, we could play Pictionary. The thought of Pictionary always makes me moan."

"Good to know." His hand took over for his mouth as he kissed his way to her other breast. "I hate to throw a damper on the whole

Pictionary idea, but the only thing I plan on drawing are little circles." He moved his free hand down her stomach and placed his thumb at her opening. "I'm good at little circles."

She moaned again and moved her right leg, opening wider for him. He dipped a finger inside her.

It was his turn to moan. "You're so wet." His fingers stopped their slow, easy circles as he brought his hand to his mouth and licked his thumb. "And sweet."

He ripped the comforter back and cool air tickled her exposed thighs.

"I know it hasn't been that long, but it feels like I've waited a long time for this, and I can't wait any longer." His mouth found her core as his dipped two fingers inside. His tongue lapped at her as his fingers massaged some pretty terrific places. She arched her hips up, urging him to pick up the pace, but he took his sweet, damn time.

He'd always been a generous lover, but this was bordering on cruel. That was fine, two could play at that game.

She slid her hands down to the front of his trousers. She unhooked them and would have slipped her hand inside, but he took her hand, brought it to his lips, and kissed her palm. "Later. Right now, I'm concentrating on you."

He placed her hand back in his hair. "I like the way it feels when you run your fingers through my hair."

His tongue found its mark again, and he resumed the lazy, maddening circles.

Slowly the orgasm began to build. Again she urged him to go faster, but he was having none of that. He kept his pace and his touch light. The tension in her body grew and grew until holding back the release took everything she had. He increased the pressure and his mouth found a faster rhythm. Her nails scraped against his scalp as a tidal wave of pleasure consumed her. His mouth worked its magic until she was limp and satiated.

"Your turn." She did her best to pull him down on top of her.

"What did you have in mind?" He slid up so that his head was level with hers.

"Right now, returning the exact favor could be challenging, but I'm sure we can manage something else." Her hand slid down his chest and found the button of his trousers.

His mouth came down hard on hers as her hand slipped inside and found him hard and ready. She worked him with both hands. His eyes closed and his head fell back. He bit down on his lower lip.

His hips found the rhythm of her hands and he thrust against her. His breathing turned rapid and shallow. His face was a tortured mask and then the damn broke and his whole body shuddered against her.

He rolled off and lay down next to her. "I love you and I've missed you so damn much." He kissed her cheek.

"I love you too." She relaxed back against the pillows. "I can't wait until we have actual sex again."

He draped an arm around her stomach.

"So there was no one else?" With her index finger, she traced the seam of the comforter. She'd been dying to ask, but part of her really didn't want to know. "I mean, it's okay if there was someone else. It's been a long time."

Like hell was it okay, but she'd try to understand.

"Honestly, I went out on a couple of dates, but, well . . ."

"Well what?" What kind of dates? Like one-night stands or blind dates? She had no right to be jealous, but here she was all jealous.

"They didn't work out." Was he purposefully being vague?

"Why?" It was out before she thought about it.

"They weren't you. You've ruined me for all other women." He grinned. "Once you've had prime rib, it's really hard to go back to ground round."

Slowly she turned her head to look at him. "Did you really just call me prime rib?"

It was offensive but kinda cute.

"Just saying, once you've had the best, nothing else will ever do." He zipped up his trousers and tucked in his blue button-down. "Notice how I'm not asking about your love life."

"So are you asking or not?" She pulled her shirt down. Somehow it had ended up around her neck.

He pulled the comforter up and covered her. "I don't know if I want to know. I mean, on the one hand, it's more than fair if you dated, and on the other hand, I really don't want to know if you did."

"My sentiments exactly." It wasn't like she had lots to tell, so not saying anything wasn't that much of a sin of omission.

He shot her a look. "I told you mine, now tell me yours."

"Okay, you asked for it. I went on exactly one date, and in all honesty, I didn't know we were on a date until he kissed me good night. In fact, I'm still not sure if it was a date. One of the kids at Hugh's pre-school has a single dad. The dad told me that he had two extra tickets to an Austin Stars hockey game, so we all went together. After he walked us to our car, he kissed me." The poor man had been a terrible kisser.

"Cheap bastard. I bet he didn't buy you dinner. In the very least he should have picked you up and driven you to the game." He sounded so happy that her date hadn't gone well.

"Yeah. I agree. We never went out again." She thought about it for a second. "I heard that he'd gotten back with his ex." It was amazing that there was a woman in this world who was willing to put up with a bad kisser.

She yawned. "I need a nap."

He kissed her lightly on the mouth. "Sleep well and call if you need anything."

Rowdy rolled off the bed and headed out of the room.

As she watched him walk into the hallway, she couldn't help but hope this was their new beginning.

# CHAPTER 24

There weren't many kids who could pull off a pirate costume with cowboy boots, but the look suited Hugh.

"Did you know that the world's oldest piece of chewing gum is five thousand years old?" Hugh's earnest aqua-blue eyes were all seriousness as he pushed his tortoiseshell glasses higher on his nose. He was adorable.

"I didn't know that. Let's see, five thousand years ago would have been the Stone Age." Rowdy handed Hugh the pillows from the room he shared with Elvis to add to the ones on the sofa. Elvis had been none too happy about the pillows disappearing from his bed and now lay on his fluffy dog pillow in the corner watching his prized pillows like a hawk. The making of a pirate ship took lots of pillows. "Think Stone Age people stuck their used chewing gum under tables?"

Hugh thought about it for a second. "Don't know. I guess whoever found the world's oldest gum might have found it under a stone table."

"That certainly makes sense." Rowdy had no idea that hanging out with a kid would be so much fun. Granted this was his kid, and he was cute as hell, but that's not why he was falling in love with him. He loved Hugh for himself. The kid was smart, funny, and serious, but with a fantastic imagination just like Rowdy.

"Son," he stopped. He hadn't meant for that to come out, but it felt right. He put an arm around the child. "I think we need to have a talk, man-to-man. I've got to ask you something very important."

Hugh nodded and sat down next to Rowdy on the sofa. "What's on your mind?"

Rowdy mashed his lips together to keep from laughing. Hugh was seven going on forty.

"Well, I was wondering if it would be okay if I asked your mother to marry me." He didn't need the little boy's blessing, but he wanted it.

Hugh's face screwed up like he was weighing the question very carefully. "So would we live here with you and Elvis . . . all of the time?"

"Yes, I would like for the two of you to move in with me permanently. I was also thinking . . . well, there's something I need to tell you. You're . . . um . . ." Rowdy's voice cracked to his cleared his throat. "It, um . . . looks like I'm your father."

Hugh's eyes narrowed. "Huh?"

Rowdy took a deep breath and let it out slowly. "I've known your mother for a long time. We met at a festival called Burning Man. She got pregnant with you there, and I'm your father."

Hugh still wasn't convinced. "Then why didn't you live with us?"

"Well . . . that's a good question. I just found out a little while ago that I'm your father. I didn't know before. If I had, I would have lived with you the whole time." Not until he'd said it out loud did he realize that he meant it. He actually felt sad at having missed so much of his son's life.

"So what do you want to do now?" Hugh sounded like he was weighing the facts.

"I already mentioned marrying your mother, but I was kinda hoping that maybe you'd let me be your father . . . you know . . . like all of the time. We would all live together and be a family." He was having a hard time getting the words out. It dawned on him that this might just be the most important conversation of his life. "I would really like that. Maybe one day, you might call me Dad or something."

"Dad" was just an ordinary word, but now it held so much promise and love that he couldn't wait to hear it roll off Hugh's lips. He wouldn't insist on it. Hugh needed to make up his own mind whether he could think of Rowdy as his father.

Hugh pondered this for what felt like to Rowdy like a few terrifyingly long beats. "So my last name would be Rose?"

He hadn't thought that far ahead, but yes, he wanted Hugh to have his last name. "Yes, if you'd like."

Hugh thought about it for a few more beats and then shrugged his shoulders. "Okay." He glanced at the refrigerator. "Can I have some more chocolate pudding?"

"You bet, big guy." He ruffled Hugh's hair.

Important life decisions made, it was now on to the pudding.

Rowdy grabbed two pudding cups out of the fridge, a couple of spoons out of the drawer next to the dishwasher, and stopped by the dog treat closet. He shuffled everything around and palmed a Lean Treat. He dropped the treat in front of Elvis.

The dog shot him a "seriously?" look, heaved a sigh of annoyance, and closed his eyes. Rowdy could practically hear him mumble, "Over my dead body am I touching that nasty piece of crap."

"Elvis doesn't do much, does he?" Hugh knelt down next to the dog and petted him.

Elvis glanced at the treat again and then rolled his eyes up and gave Rowdy a "WTF?" look.

"He's really more about watching the world go by instead of participating in it." Rowdy watched his dog carefully. Oddly enough, Elvis seemed to like all of the attention Hugh was giving him. Maybe there was just something special between dogs and little boys.

Elvis glanced over at Rowdy and did the one eyebrow up thing, clearly saying, "Don't judge me. This kid is good people."

"Did you know that there's a vet in Brazil who does plastic surgery for dogs?" Hugh continued to pet Elvis. "In Belgium there's a company who makes ice cream just for dogs."

Elvis's ears twitched, which by Elvis standards was practically a command to order him some doggy ice cream.

"Plastic surgery and ice cream for dogs. What is the world coming to?" Rowdy handed Hugh a spoon and his pudding cup.

The little boy took the pudding, shook it exactly five times, slammed it down on the tray table, peeled off the cover, licked it, and then placed it on the coffee table. Rowdy looked down and realized that he'd done exactly the same thing in exactly the same order.

That was interesting. So Hugh had gotten more than his aqua eyes from him. It shouldn't make him swell with pride that his son was a little bit like him, but it did.

After they'd killed the pudding and Hugh had taken both his and Rowdy's trash and spoons to the kitchen, they got back to some serious pirate ship making. After the addition of some blankets, a few clothespins, some chairs to hold everything up, and all of the pillows not currently being used in the house, the ship was finished.

Rowdy couldn't remember the last time he'd had this much fun.

"You know what we need? Some paddles. You can't have a pirate ship without paddles. Come with me." He took the little boy's hand and led him to the garage.

Rowdy flicked on the lights. Fluorescent lights blinked on. Only one of the three garage bays held a vehicle, his new Chevy 3500. The middle bay was completely empty, but the last bay held some gardening tools and sporting goods. He had a couple of kayak paddles hanging on the wall from a river rafting trip in college. Come to think of it, he liked kayaking, so why hadn't he done it since college?

He took the paddles down and handed one to Hugh.

Hugh took it and inspected it. "Fun . . . real paddles. Do you take them out in a boat or something?"

Rowdy pointed to the two-man kayak hanging on the wall. "I use these paddles when I go kayaking."

Hugh pushed his glasses up to the top of his nose. "Can you teach me someday? That looks like fun."

"You bet. We can take the kayak out on the quarry lake."

"The twins showed me the lake." Hugh looked up at Rowdy. "The water's really clear."

"I know. Lots of people use it to learn how to scuba dive." There were so many things he wanted to do with Hugh: kayaking, horseback riding, kicking around a soccer ball. It might be fun to teach him how to paint. He wanted to share his art with his little boy. He wanted to share everything with Hugh.

"Can we go on the kayak tomorrow?" Hugh was excited.

"You bet, big guy. We'll do it first thing in the morning." Now Rowdy was excited.

They carried the paddles into the living room and added them, one on each side of the sofa. In his humble opinion, they'd made an exceptional pirate ship.

Hugh climbed up on the sofa to man his paddle, but instead of picking it up, he looked up at Rowdy. "So if you marry us and are my dad, does that make Mr. Bear and Mrs. Lucy my grandparents?"

"Marry us." That sounded like the best thing in the world. "Yes, they would be your grandparents, and all of my brothers would be your uncles."

"Really?" Hugh's eyes turned tennis ball size. "I think you should marry us right now."

Rowdy put his index finger to his lips in the universal be-quiet signal. "Let's just keep the marrying part between you and me for now. I need some time to plan the proposal and romance your mother into thinking that it's her idea. Funny thing about women, they like to be the ones with the good ideas. Sometimes we men have to plant the seed of an idea and then pretend to let them come up with it."

Hugh looked like he was filing that bit of info away for later. "Can I get my new grandparents and uncles right now?" He turned huge, hopeful eyes on Rowdy.

"I don't see why not. And if, say . . . you wanted to call me Dad or something, I think that would be all right."

Hugh pondered that for a few seconds and then shrugged. "Okay."

It looked to Rowdy that Hugh had moved on. Giant life changes handled—moving on to more important things.

Rowdy said in his most piratey voice, "Captain, shall we set sail to Pirate Island and check on our buried treasure?"

"Aye, matey." The little boy stood on the arm of the sofa and pointed to the wall ahead. "I can see the island now. Row faster."

Rowdy took a paddle in each hand and rowed for all he was worth.

Hugh fisted his little hands and made binoculars. "I see Pirate Island." He sacrificed one lens to point ahead. "There's a storm brewing."

Rowdy jumped up and down on the sofa and made thunderstorm noises. Hugh bounced on the cushions, giggling.

"Oh no, Captain, we're headed for a sandbar, give her a hard turn starboard," Rowdy yelled in between thunderstorm noises.

Hugh glanced over his shoulder and whispered like he didn't want the rest of the crew to hear, "What's starboard?"

"The right side," Rowdy stage-whispered back. After all, they couldn't let the crew know that the captain didn't have his nautical terms down.

Hugh turned the giant imaginary ship's wheel hard to the right.

"Whew . . . just missed it. Looks like we're skirting the edge of the storm." Rowdy toned down the thunderstorm and pointed toward the kitchen. "Land ho, Captain."

Hugh put his binoculars back up to his eyes. "I see the beach."

"Should we land there or look for a better site?" Rowdy rowed and rowed. Pirating was a pretty good workout.

"Land." Hugh nodded once with authority as he kept his binoculars on the kitchen.

Rowdy jumped hard on the sofa to simulate a rough landing, and they were on solid ground.

Rowdy's smartphone binged with a new message.

"Captain, if you please, I need a moment." He pulled his phone out of his front trouser pocket and held it up. "There is an urgent letter from home. Please allow me to respond."

Hugh laughed. "You sound funny."

Rowdy put his hand over his heart. "I am sorry to give offense." He bowed his head in contrition.

He looked down at the message. It was from Margie, his assistant.

`911 Barrel Room NOW! Cork rot.`

Alarm bells jangled through his system. Cork rot killed wine. Once the cork rotted, the wine tasted foul and smelled even worse.

What if it was the Riesling he was due to release in a couple of weeks? Cork rot could ruin every bottle he had. They'd have to destroy their entire stock, and it would be a setback for Texas Rose Winery, for everything he'd built. They'd have to cancel the launch and their reputation would suffer.

He glanced at the door to the master bedroom, where Justus was still sleeping soundly.

"How would you like to see the barrel room? It's in a cave and where we keep all of the wine I make." He hoped he made it sound like an adventure.

Hugh nodded like a bobblehead.

Rowdy held his hand out for the little boy, who slipped his hand in Rowdy's . . . no hesitation.

Today they'd made progress. This was a beginning . . . a step in the right direction. Rowdy Rose was one proud father.

# CHAPTER 25

"Are you awake?" CanDee smiled from the open master bedroom doorway. She held up an armload of magazines. "I brought several months' worth of *People*."

"I'm so glad that fame and fortune haven't changed you one bit." Justus patted the place next to her. Recently CanDee had come into a large sum of money after her ex was arrested for fraud. He'd stolen her first novel and published it under his name. She'd just gotten the rights back and the publishing house had given her a big, fat advance for her next book. "Have a seat."

She was glad for the company. Who knew that being laid up could be so boring?

The mattress bounced a little as CanDee sat down next to her and handed her the stack of magazines.

They all had Lucy's name and address on the front. So she was a gossip addict. Justus loved finding out new facets to people's personalities. Lucy had a serious job and for the most part was a serious person, but she loved celebrity gossip. Good for her and great for CanDee and Justus. She thumbed through them but didn't find anything as interesting as the possibility of Rowdy's secret room.

"So, how nosy do you feel like being today?" She turned to look at her friend.

"Is that a trick question?" CanDee fixed her wounded golden-brown eyes on Justus. "Honestly, I'm hurt that you'd even ask me that. Of course I'm in a mood to be nosy. I'm a writer. Nosy for me equals research. What did you have in mind?"

"Nothing much. Just a little recon." The best thing about a good friend was that they never said no, no matter how stupid or unusual the request.

"Is this like the time you swear you saw Brad Pitt and Angelina Jolie shopping at the Smithville Walmart so we staked it out for two days hoping to see them again?"

"They were there. I'm telling you. We just missed them." Justus leaned over and grabbed her phone from the nightstand. "There's a rumor floating around that Rowdy has a secret room. I think we should find it."

"Before you came along, there was also a rumor that Rowdy was a serial killer, care to comment on that one?" CanDee sat back, leaning against the headboard. "Are you sure you really want to know all of his secrets?"

Justus sat back too. "I'm like ninety-nine-point-nine percent sure that Rowdy's secret room is his art studio."

"Yeah, I know he's an artist. You told me all those years ago, but . . ." CanDee's eyes narrowed. "It doesn't fit with the man I know."

A slow grin tickled Justus's face. "I'm going to prove you wrong."

"What did you have in mind?" CanDee leaned in closer.

"How about a little FaceTime snooping?" Justus picked up her phone and pulled up FaceTime. She hit CanDee's number and her phone started ringing.

CanDee nodded as she answered her phone. "I see. You FaceTime me so that I can be your eyes and ears. Let me guess, I'm going to walk around looking for the room while you watch."

"And listen. You know I wouldn't settle for video only." Justus eased back on the pillows. "I'm ready when you are."

"Got it, Boss. I'm at your disposal." CanDee climbed off the bed and walked out the bedroom door. "So where should I start?"

"Look for any locked doors." Surely a secret room would be locked.

CanDee walked down the hall and opened a closed door. Elvis lay on the edge of the bed, watching *Pit Bulls and Parolees*. "Do you think he watches this for the pit bulls or the parolees?"

Elvis looked up at the interruption and then went back to his program.

"No idea." Justus waited for CanDee to pan the camera around the room. There was a closet door and a bathroom door. Both were open. "Bye, Elvis." Justus waved into the phone, but Elvis didn't even acknowledge her.

CanDee backed out of the room and went to the next bedroom and then the next. Rowdy had five bedrooms in all, including the master. Each was neat, clean, and secret-room-free. They searched the rest of the house. No secret rooms.

"We need to try the attic." Justus was certain that his studio had to be there.

"Any ideas how to get there?" CanDee walked through the kitchen and into the garage. "I don't see a pull-down ladder."

She panned the camera around. Tucked into an alcove on the other side of the closet with the water heater was a set of stairs. They blended so well with the wall that Justus almost missed them. "There's a door there. See it?"

"Got it. I'll take the stairs, and if I don't find it here, I can look outside. Maybe he has some sort of converted bomb shelter or something." CanDee climbed the plywood stairs. They weren't exactly rustic, just unfinished. At the top of the landing, there was a closed door. CanDee tried the doorknob, and it was unlocked. She opened the door and was met with bright sunlight. It looked like one side of the ceiling was nothing but windows.

"I've been in and out of this house a hundred times. I've even barbecued in the backyard, and I never noticed the windows." She walked into the sunshine and looked up. "That's why. Because of the angle of the roof, these windows aren't visible from outside. This really is a secret room."

Slowly, CanDee walked the phone around, making sure to take everything in.

"I think it's safe to say that he's in love with you." CanDee stopped at every painting so that Justus wouldn't miss anything. "They're all of you. On second thought, maybe he is a serial killer and this is that weird memento room that all crazy stalkers have."

"He's not a serial killer." The paintings were both lovely and sad. Rowdy had surrounded himself with her. She was in vivid oils and soft watercolors and even charcoal sketches. He'd done all of these from memory. There she was on the first day she'd met him, handing out daisies, and there was another in her favorite green sundress, and one of her tangled in the sheets smiling up at him after they'd made love. He'd captured her in every mood imaginable . . . even sad and mad ones. He really saw her . . . saw everything about her. Her heart melted. This was real love. He saw her for who she really was and loved her anyway.

"I'm going to start crying. This is a lovely tribute to you." CanDee turned the phone so she could see Justus. "And I've got to be honest. It's also a little creepy. It's almost like a memorial. He never paints himself into the pictures. It's just you alone. Wouldn't you think that in at least one he would have the two of you riding off into the sunset?" CanDee scanned the room again. "Nope, they're all of you and only you."

"Well, he only saw me once a year." Justus looked at the paintings of her behind CanDee's back. "Okay, I see your point. It's both creepy and romantic . . . it's cromantic."

It was heartbreakingly beautiful.

Would he ever paint her, him, and Hugh as a family?

"I still think that it's lovely in a sad sort of way." Would he ever think of them as a family? Based on the fun she'd heard him and Hugh having in the living room while she dozed, she was hopeful.

"Okay, chica, what do you want me to do now?" CanDee waited for instructions.

"Let's see. Why don't you take pictures of all of the paintings and then text them to me? I'd like to take my time looking at them, and I don't know when he and Hugh will be back." Rowdy had so much talent that it seemed like a waste to never show it to the world.

"Okeydokey, I'll be down soon. Call me back if he shows up before I get done."

Fifteen minutes later, CanDee was back in the master bedroom with Justus. CanDee scooted onto the bed and pulled up the pictures and texted every one to Justus.

"I guess I should ask him to do my portrait in my wedding dress." CanDee ran through the photos again, looking at each one in turn. "I mean, you already outed him as a painter, so how bad could it be to ask him to do my portrait?"

"He's so talented, right?" Justus wanted to help him share his art with the world but she didn't know how.

"I can see a portrait of me standing on the front steps to our house. Or wait. He could do our portrait after the wedding with both of us standing on the front steps." CanDee smiled to herself. She was going to be a June bride and she couldn't wait.

"Thank goodness the wedding is ten or so months away. Maybe by then I'll have thought of a way for Rowdy to show his art."

"You know, next week Rowdy is throwing a launch party for his new wine, Roundup Riesling. That would be the perfect time to introduce the world to his art." CanDee beamed. "His two passions in one place."

It wasn't much time, but it wasn't like she had anything else to do. She'd figure out a way to put his show together from this bed if it killed her.

There was a knocking on the door frame of the bedroom. Lucy stood there holding a magazine. "I brought y'all the latest *People* that came in the mail. I haven't had a chance to read it yet, but I'm headed off to see some patients, so I won't get to it until tomorrow."

"Come and see Rowdy's paintings. We found his secret room." Justus extended her phone to Lucy. "Fair warning, they're all of me."

CanDee stood over Lucy's shoulder and watched as she scrolled through the pictures. "We think it's sweet that he missed Justus so much that he filled his studio with paintings of her."

"I like this one." Lucy showed the phone to Justus.

"That's the one of me on the day we met. See, I was handing out daisies." Justus shook her head. "And for some reason I thought it was a good idea to make a crown of daisies to wear around my head and as a lei around my neck, and then, as if that wasn't enough, as a chain around my waist. Now that I see it, that's a whole lot of daisies."

"Speaking of daisies, once you're done convalescing, I was hoping to talk you into doing some landscaping around our house." CanDee linked her fingers, prayer-like. "Pretty please with sprinkles on top?"

"What did you have in mind?" Justus was more than happy to do anything for her friend.

"Well, Cinco and I have been talking about getting married in our front yard." CanDee watched Lucy's response.

"Really?" Lucy grinned from ear to ear. "That's wonderful. You fell in love in that house. I love that you want to get married there."

"Tomorrow, I'll go over and take some measurements." She looked down at her leg. "Okay, tomorrow I'll ride over and you can take some measurements. Off the top of my head, I see a white gazebo in keeping with the style and age of the old Victorian house and lots of rosebushes, because they'll scent the air. I wish I had my sketch pad." She looked around like one would appear.

"Is it in your backpack?" CanDee went to the white sofa at the end of the bed. "Let me see if I can find it." She grabbed the bag and rummaged around in it. "Got it."

She handed it to Justus, along with a pencil.

Justus had such a clear picture in her head of what she wanted to do. She drew furiously. When the rough sketch was done, she tore it off and handed it to CanDee.

"I wish I had Rowdy's gift for drawing, but this is better than nothing." She pointed to the gazebo. "Roses here and here and here. Nothing too fussy, just some tea roses."

"Roses are perfect. The house was built by Cinco's great-great-aunt Edith, and she loved roses. Her journals sort of brought us together. Aunt Edith most certainly would approve." CanDee was excited. She looked at Lucy. "What do you think?"

"I think that it's perfect. I couldn't have picked two better daughters-in-law if I tried." Lucy traced the lines of the gazebo.

Justus wasn't a daughter-in-law or even slated to be, but it was nice for Lucy to include her.

"If either of you need any help with wedding planning or anything at all, I'm your girl." She pulled CanDee in for a hug. "I know that losing your mother at such a young age has made you self-reliant, and that's wonderful, but I'm here for you if you need me. I always wanted a daughter or two."

"I would love the help from anyone who's willing." CanDee hugged Lucy and then pulled Justus into the hug and looked down at her. "I thought I'd start by asking if you'd be my maid of honor?"

"Really?" She knew that her wedding gift to her friend would be the landscaping. The best gifts were those created and not bought. "Absolutely."

"Have you decided on your wedding colors?" Lucy asked.

CanDee's jaw dropped open. "Um, colors? Well, I was hoping to use Aunt Edith's veil, but beyond that, I have no idea." She looked from Lucy to Justus and then back again. "I was thinking of asking Lefty to walk me down the aisle. Think he'll do it?"

"Are you kidding? He's going to cry like a baby when you ask him." Lucy teared up. "Looks like I'm not immune either." She wiped her eyes. "By the way, excellent practical joke in rewiring his office so that when he turns on the radio his blinds go up. Awesome."

CanDee and Lefty bonded over practical jokes like other families bonded over board games.

"Thank you. I had to do something after he removed all of the labels from our canned goods. Every time I need something canned, it's a total mystery." CanDee laughed. "I've got a little something I'm working on for him. He's going to curse the day he ever glitter bombed my car. If you think rewiring his office was good, wait until I nail all of his furniture onto the ceiling and then fill his office with foam peanuts."

Lucy held her hand up for a high five, and CanDee slapped it. "That's awesome. Can't wait." She checked her wristwatch. "I've got to run." She leaned down and kissed Justus on the cheek and then leaned up on her tippy-toes and kissed CanDee on the cheek. "I'll see y'all tomorrow."

Lucy waved her way out of the room.

"I'm so excited to be your maid of honor." Justus hugged her friend. "What help do you need?"

CanDee pulled out her phone and they started making lists of what needed to be done.

Her best friend was getting a happily ever after, and hopefully, so would Justus.

# CHAPTER 26

The next morning Rowdy was practically pulling out his hair. All he wanted to do was to spend the day with Justus and Hugh. But instead he had a wine launch to oversee. More people were coming than he'd planned for, so they needed additional hotel rooms, and the caterer had threatened to quit when he'd called to double the food and drink originally planned. The list went on and on.

He'd cleaned up the breakfast dishes and his dad had come to pick up Hugh. They were going fishing again and then to have lunch with his mom. Now, as he slid onto the bed next to Justus, his phone buzzed with yet another text.

He glanced down at the screen. Damn. The Riesling launch was falling apart right in front of his eyes. He had wine critics, colleagues, bloggers, reporters, and half the damn world flying in to try his new wine, and now they were out of rooms in every single hotel in Roseville and Fredericksburg. After yesterday's 911 from Margie about cork rot, which, thank God, had turned out to have only affected a couple of cases of Riesling, he'd almost lost it. The only things that kept him from totally freaking out were Justus and Hugh. They kept him grounded.

"What's the matter?" Justus covered his hand with hers. "You look like a desperate man."

"Nothing. Just some work stuff." He shot off a text to Margie, offering the cottage as an additional place to house people. Damn the Fredericksburg Flea Market and Trade Days for taking up all of the damn hotel rooms. Three months ago, he'd blocked off several rooms in Roseville and Fredericksburg. The trouble was that now that the word was out about his new Riesling, lots of people were RSVPing at the last minute.

"Why don't you tell me? I'm good with work stuff. I've owned my own business for close to a decade. I'm a whiz at project management." She smiled at him.

"You need to concentrate on getting better. I don't want to bother you with trivial things." Maybe his parents could put up a couple of people? And CanDee and Cinco? Their house only had one bathroom, though, so that wasn't ideal. What about the bunkhouse? He shook his head. Nope, too many rough-and-tumble cowboys.

"Look, I've got nothing but time and I'm bored to death. Is this about the Riesling launch? CanDee said it was next week." She patted his hand.

What could it hurt? Besides, it wasn't like Justus was going to drop the subject until she had what she wanted. "There are no more rooms at the hotels for all of the last-minute RSVPers who now want to come to the ranch for the launch party. In addition to finding them a place to stay, I have to figure out a way to shuttle them all here, and the caterer is threatening to quit because it's now double the amount of people."

He didn't know where to start.

"Okay, off the top of my head, let's move your most important VIP to the cottage. I'll talk to Lucy about having it cleaned. We can put people up at the main house, I'm sure your parents won't mind. If I can talk CanDee and Cinco into staying with us, we can use their house. If you have some good friends coming, they can stay here with us." She grabbed a pad from her nightstand and starting jotting things down. "Who is your event planner?"

"Event planner?" He and Margie had always handled everything. In the beginning, not many people had showed up for his launches, so an event planner seemed like overkill. "Don't have one. All of my other launches have been fairly low-key."

"How long ago was your last one?" She continued to write at lightning speed.

"Two years." That was before his wine started winning awards. This time around, three times the number of people were coming. This launch was going to be a disaster.

"Okay, let me call Rosie Gomez, she's an event planner in Austin and an old college roommate of CanDee's and mine. If she's free, I'll have her come down. Can she stay with us?" Justus glanced over at him.

"Event planner? Um . . . sure. She can stay in the room next to Hugh and Elvis." His heart was pounding a mile a minute. This was his baby, and the control freak that he'd thought he put away for Justus and Hugh threatened to rear its ugly head. "I'm not so sure that I want someone else to take over."

The thought made his heart rate spike and his breathing turn rapid.

"Tell you what, how about I just give her a call and see if she's available? I'll call CanDee, and we can put our heads together to figure out what we can do for additional sleeping space. We'll run everything by you. Just give me today to work on it, and I'll report in tonight with our progress. If you like it, we'll proceed, if you don't, no hard feelings." She blew him a kiss. "What can it hurt?"

In his experience, women rarely adhered to the no-hard-feelings thing, but he was desperate. "Okay, but you promise not to be mad if I don't give it my stamp of approval?"

"Don't worry. Letting me help you isn't the end of the world." She touched his face. "You need to slow your breathing or you're going to pass out."

He focused on her face and willed his breathing to slow. The lightheadedness started to pass.

She shook her head. "No hard feelings."

This still sounded like a really bad idea, but it couldn't hurt to have her working in tandem with Margie and him. More heads were better than one.

She leaned over and grabbed her phone off the nightstand. "I need my laptop and the power cord so I can charge my phone. Also, how do I contact your assistant? She'd be a big help."

He gave her Margie's phone number and made a mental note to explain the situation to her.

Eight hours later, he walked into his kitchen and was stunned.

Justus, in her wheelchair, wearing shorts and a T-shirt, was drawing on a whiteboard she'd gotten from somewhere. Lefty, CanDee, Cinco, Worth, Dallas, and Margie all had coffee cups in front of them and were paying close attention. Clearly Margie had jumped ship.

"So where are we on the cabins?" Justus fixed her eyes on Worth.

"All of them have running water and electricity, but they are a mess. There is no way we can make them habitable by next week." Worth shrugged. "Sorry, Justus."

"Never say never. Rosie is on her way, and she'll have those cabins five-star-hotel ready before we need them." Justus held everyone's attention like a quarterback calling plays in the Super Bowl.

"What cabins?" Rowdy eased his backside up onto the gray granite island because they were fresh out of chairs.

"The old ones by the river. Justus came up with the idea to use them for your guests." Dallas laced his fingers behind his head and leaned his chair back on two legs. "General Patton couldn't have been this bossy."

"Wait until you meet Rosie," CanDee and Justus said in unison, and then they both laughed.

"Rosie makes me look like a slacker. We're lucky that the bride ran off with the best man so the wedding she had planned for this weekend is canceled." Justus cringed. "Well, sorry for the groom, but good for us."

"The cabins?" Those old things were falling down and full of junk. They used them for storage now. God only knew what vermin-infested crap was there. He shot a look at Margie.

She nodded toward Justus. "She's a miracle worker. Have you seen what she did with your parents' house today?"

The only place he'd been to today was his home and the winery. No time for traipsing around the ranch. "No. Isn't it still a mess from all of the landscaping demo?"

"Nope, I had a team out today. They finished all of the prep work and repair. Tomorrow they start planting. Everything should be in the ground by tomorrow evening. Speaking of landscaping, we really need to talk about the area in front of the tasting room, but"—Justus held up a hand like a traffic cop—"we'll get to that in a minute."

Finished landscaping his parents' house? That had to be a solid acre of work. She got it done that fast? "Wow."

He really needed to stop by and give it a once-over. Surely someone at the table would have said something if it turned out badly, but they all just looked at him expectantly.

"Can't wait to see it."

His doorbell bing-bonged.

"That will be Rosie." Justus glanced at Rowdy.

That was his cue to answer the door. "I'll get it."

He slid down from the island and walked to the front door. A lot was happing in his house and he had no idea what was going on.

He opened the door. The striking lady smiling up at him wasn't what he expected.

"You must be Rowdy." She held out her hand. "I'm Rosie Gomez."

"Rowdy Rose, nice to meet you." He took her hand. Her handshake was firm as she pumped his hand once. She bore a strong resemblance to Penelope Cruz, only Rosie's almond-shaped eyes were navy blue.

"The troops are in the kitchen getting a briefing from General Justus. Right this way." He moved to the side so she could walk into the house. She stepped inside and rolled a large, black leather briefcase behind her. He closed the door and led her to the kitchen.

"Rosie." CanDee jumped up and hugged the woman, who was a good six inches shorter than her, and then Rosie went to Justus and leaned over, hugging her.

CanDee waved to the table. "Let me introduce you. This is Cinco, my fiancé." CanDee grinned at Rowdy's older brother.

"Nice to meet you." He nodded.

"Good to meet you." She returned his nod.

"Margie Allendale, Rowdy's assistant, is on his left." CanDee pointed to Rowdy's right-hand man.

"Nice to put a face with the name. Thank you for sending me the guest list." Rosie nodded at Margie.

"The least I could do for the woman who's going to save us. Anything you need, just let me know." Yep, Margie had switched sides.

"That's Lefty on his right." CanDee winked at Lefty.

She grinned at Lefty. "I've heard a lot about you."

"It ain't all true. That CanDee is a fiction writer, so telling the truth ain't what she's known for." He shot CanDee an evil look.

"I love you too." She winked at him again. "You still can't be mad over the glitter. Really, it's hardly noticeable in this light."

"She glitter bombed my shampoo. A man's grooming products is sacred. Everybody knows that." He growled at CanDee and then blew her a kiss.

"Yeah, your scalp is glowing." Rowdy inspected it. "Is that rainbow glitter?"

"Yep, and it glows in the dark." CanDee jumped up and down and clapped her hands. "You mess with the bull, you get the horns."

"Really, we're a fairly normal family." Worth stood and held out his hand. "I'm Worth."

Rosie smiled at him and shook his hand.

Her gaze landed on Dallas, whose eyes were the size of drink coasters. His mouth hung open, and all he seemed to be able to do was stare at Rosie.

Rosie smiled at him, waiting for an introduction. She looked at Worth.

"And that's my brother. Usually he's a chatterbox, but clearly he's tired or sick, or maybe it's because Mom dropped him on his head a bunch of times when he was a baby." He reached over and smacked Dallas on the back of the head. "Wake up and shake the woman's hand."

Dallas looked around like he'd just figured out that there were other people in the room. His eyes went to her hand, but he didn't move. Rowdy had never seen his younger brother like this.

Rosie's eyebrows bounced off of her hairline and she finally pulled her hand back.

"I have to go. There's something I need to do." Dallas practically ran out of the room and was out the front door before Rowdy could stop him.

"Okay, that was weird." Rowdy pointed to the now-available chair. "Please have a seat. On behalf of my brother, I'd like to apologize. He normally has manners."

"Yes, they may not be particularly good manners, but usually he gives common courtesy his best shot." Worth waved his brother away. "Don't worry, I'll knock some sense into him later."

Rosie rolled her bag over and took the seat next to Worth. She unzipped her bag's front pocket and pulled out an iPad. "Okay, Justus's last text said that we have beds for seventeen of the fifty latecomers, so that leaves thirty-three bedless people. Are any of them couples? Are any of the single people bringing a guest?"

Margie looked down at the list. "I'm not sure."

She handed the list to Rowdy. "Do you know if these people are coming alone or are there any plus ones?"

He ran down the list. He knew all of the people by name, but that was all. "No idea."

"Okay." She unbuttoned her cherry-red suit jacket and hung it on the back of the chair. The white shirt she had on underneath was no frills, just all business. Rowdy got the feeling that no-nonsense was her middle name. She leaned over and pulled a brochure out of her bag and laid it facedown in front of her. "I'd like for everyone to think outside the box for a moment. I've done a little research into this area, and there is a record of a treaty with the Comanche back in 1847—"

"Yes, the Meusebach-Comanche Treaty. Four million acres between the Llano and Colorado Rivers was deeded to settlers by the United States. If memory serves, it was Penateka Comanche hunting grounds and the treaty guaranteed that the Comanche wouldn't harm the settlers," CanDee said as she sat beside Cinco.

"That's right." Cinco snapped his fingers. "There's a historic landmark in San Saba County. I took CanDee there on a date."

"And she still agreed to marry you? Shocker." Rowdy rolled his eyes. "Why didn't you just take her to the Walmart in Fredericksburg? Y'all could have parked in the lot and watched the cars drive by." He punched his older brother in the arm. "Cheap bastard."

"It was fun. You should take Justus and Hugh there. This land has history. It's important to know what happened before we came along." CanDee snuggled into her fiancé. "That night under the stars on a blanket, we christened that landmark and two others. A good time was had by all."

Rowdy put his hands over his ears. "Stop talking about sex. I can't know this about you two."

Worth clamped a hand over his mouth. "Sorry, I just threw up a little bit in my mouth."

Rosie smirked. "Moving on, so I think you need to capitalize on the history of this place and the ranching aspect." Rosie turned to Rowdy.

"Margie made sure to tell me that you wanted chic. So I'm proposing upscale teepees." She flipped the brochure over.

And just like that, he lost all hope and was back to feeling completely screwed.

"I can tell by the look on your face that you're having trouble with the vision. So here." She opened the brochure. "I've used this company before. Every teepee is air-conditioned, has its own bathroom, and comes with either a king-sized bed or two queens. Just take a look."

She slid the brochure to Rowdy. He'd already made up his mind to hate the concept, but he picked up the color brochure anyway. Each teepee was very spacious. He studied the room. "Is that a chandelier?"

"Yes, each room has a chandelier, flat-screen TV, luxury bathroom, and a real front door." Rosie reached into her bag again and brought out a folded map, which turned out to be several 8 ½ by 11 sheets of paper taped together. "Margie was kind enough to send me a map. Sorry that it's crudely put together, but I didn't have time to have it printed off on plat paper." She spread the map out in the middle of the table. "We can do three groupings of ten teepees. We'll have a central fire pit, and then the teepees will surround it. We do need to tap into the water and electrical lines, so the teepees will have to be near existing structures. Either by the river next to the cabins or over there." She pointed to the flat area behind the cottage where they always had the Fourth of July carnival. "Either place should work, but I have the head of the company coming out tomorrow to scout the sites."

"How did you know that I'd like this plan?" Rowdy was starting to see that Rosie Gomez knew her stuff.

"I took a chance. Since the only other option was bringing in RVs—which is ordinary and generic—I figured this was better. I'm thinking we should go for an upscale cattle ranch feel for the launch." She sat back in her seat. "After all, the wine you're presenting to the world is called Roundup Riesling. Since most of the world thinks that Texans still ride horses to work and sit on hay bales and watch tumbleweeds roll by, why not capitalize on that? I've found a chuck wagon we could rent for a big barbecue. I read that Cranky Frank's in Fredericksburg is one of the best barbecue places on planet Earth, as judged by *Texas Monthly*. I've already spoken to them, and they have agreed to cater the food. We'll make a weekend of it. The launch party is on Saturday night, so we'll pick everyone up at the airport with a glass of your Hill Country Sparking Wine, and the drivers will be wearing ranch-hand clothes. It's too late to get a fleet of limousines complete with horns on the hood, but I've found several limousine coaches that will hold fifteen to twenty people."

Rosie pulled out another brochure and handed it to Rowdy. It was a company that rented luxury buses complete with full bars and leather couches.

Rowdy went around the table to Justus, bent down, and hugged her from behind. "I never should have doubted you." He kissed her on the cheek and then looked over at Rosie. "You're hired. What do you need from me?"

# CHAPTER 27

The next morning, Justus's phone dinged with a new text from CanDee that read Is he gone yet? Ok to come over?

She texted back that yes, Rowdy was gone, and he'd taken Hugh with him. Rowdy really seemed to like having Hugh around. Between him and the rest of the Rose family, she was getting a little jealous of sharing her son with so many people.

Ten minutes later, CanDee stood in the master bedroom doorway with a tape measure in hand. "Is Rosie up yet?"

Justus shook her head. "Still sleeping."

Rosie wasn't a morning person and did her best to never schedule an event or appointment before noon.

"I'll give her a call." Justus scrolled for her number and hit "Dial."

They could hear the phone ringing down the hall. On the fourth ring, she picked up. "Hello."

"Rise and shine, valentine. It's time to get to work." If there was one thing Rosie responded to, it was work. Workaholics around the world held her up as a shining example of overachievement.

"Jesus, what is it, like five in the morning?" Rosie was an angry antimorning person.

"It's nine fifteen, and since you're up, CanDee and I require your presence in the master bedroom immediately." Justus knew to stay on the line until Rosie actually got out of bed or she'd go right back to sleep. "Don't make us come over there and sing 'The Wake-Up Song.' Because we will and it won't be pretty. You know I can't carry a tune even with it strapped to my back."

"You don't need to resort to terroristic threats, I'm on my way." There was some shuffling and then a loud bang. "Damn it, I ran into the door. Who in the hell closed it?"

"Are you okay?" Justus asked. She turned to CanDee. "Think she's awake enough for me to hang up?"

"I heard that. I'm hanging up now." A door down the hall banged open. "Is that a dog watching *The Talk*?" Rosie stumbled into the master. "Why is a dog watching *The Talk*?"

"That's Elvis. Usually he watches Animal Planet, but *My Cat From Hell* is on now, and he doesn't like that." Justus couldn't believe that she was explaining why a dog was watching TV. The worst part was that she'd been sitting in this bed so long that she knew Elvis's TV habits and didn't think they were strange anymore.

"Whatever." Rosie yawned and stretched and then sat on the end of the bed. She looked from Justus to CanDee and back again. "Why are the two of you all smiles this morning?"

Justus knew that she practically glowed. "I don't know about CanDee, but I just had some crazy-good thanks-for-saving-my-ass morning sex."

CanDee shrugged. "I just had some it's-morning-and-we're-sleeping-naked-next-to-each-other sex."

Rosie rolled her eyes. "I hate both of you. So you woke me up to gloat?" She stood. "I'm going back to bed."

"Wait, the sex was just a bonus, we got you up because we need help with a secret mission." CanDee sat cross-legged on the bed.

"Secret mission?" Rosie turned to Justus. "This isn't like the time that you convinced her that you saw Brad Pitt and Angelina Jolie shopping at the Smithville Walmart, is it?"

"Hey, this is different. And just for the record, they were there."

"Yes, honey, whatever you say." CanDee patted her knee.

Justus stuck out her tongue. "Fine, I'll just hobble around on one leg and probably kill myself trying to pull off the good deed of the century."

Rosie glanced at CanDee. "I don't know about you, but that works for me."

"Well, thanks for volunteering. I need your help hanging Rowdy's paintings. I'd like for the wine launch to also be his first art showing." Justus was brimming with excitement.

"Wait a minute. Let me get this straight. Rowdy is an artist as well as a winemaker? He didn't mention his art last night." Rosie looked like she was taking it all in.

"It's a surprise. He's sort of a closet artist." Justus couldn't wait until Rowdy saw his paintings up on the walls and people fawning over them.

"Okay." Rosie let out a deep breath. "Can I see these paintings?"

CanDee pulled the pictures up on her phone and handed it to Rosie.

She scrolled through them. "They're pretty good and all of you. I haven't had my coffee, so bottom-line this for me."

"We want to have the paintings framed and hanging in the tasting room, and we don't want him to know about it." CanDee nodded enthusiastically.

Rosie mulled that over. "Why are they being displayed?"

"He's really talented." Justus's voice was full of my-man-can-do-no-wrong pride.

"I guess we could send him out to greet the guests or have him pick them up from the airport, but we'll have to get them framed. Won't he notice that his paintings are missing?" She sat up. "I can find someone local. If I have to pull someone out of San Antonio, it might double the price."

"Oh, I didn't think of that. How much are we talking?" Justus didn't have much money, and right now all she had was her savings, because nothing was coming in. She'd already used the down payment the Roses gave her on supplies to pay the crew for yesterday and today. Well, she hadn't paid them yet, but after she did, all she'd have left was about a thousand dollars. After that was gone, she'd be flat broke. The thought made her slightly nauseated. She could talk to Lucy about being reimbursed for the workers, but it didn't feel right, considering that the woman had probably saved her life. She'd gotten half of her fee up front and wasn't scheduled to get the other half until the work was finished.

Rosie scrolled through the paintings again. "I say you pick the ten best to frame. I had some thirty-six-by-twenty-four-inch photos framed last month and it was a hundred a photo. That's just the frame, no glass."

It's not like she hadn't been broke before, but spending the money still made her uneasy. She wanted to do this for Rowdy, but it felt like she was taking what stability she had away from her little boy. She bit her top lip. It wasn't the end of the world, but it sort of felt like it. She told herself that she wasn't putting Rowdy before Hugh, and this needed to be done. She had to do this for Rowdy. She took a deep breath and jumped right in. "Okay, see if you can find someone to come out."

It was just money, right? That didn't make her palms stop sweating.

"What's wrong?" CanDee watched her carefully. "Is it your leg?"

"No." Justus waved away the idea. "Just juggling a few things around in my mind."

Once she was back on her feet, she could earn plenty of money. This was merely a minor setback.

"Why don't you get dressed?" Justus turned to Rosie. "We'll make you some breakfast and then we can map out the tasting room. I know you walked through it yesterday, but I'm sure you'd like to get a better look."

"I'll grab a shower and then I'm commandeering your kitchen table. I need a command central." Rosie stood, stretched, and headed to her room. "Now he's watching *The Price is Right*. So he knows how to change the channels?"

Justus heard the channels start flipping.

"Show-off," Rosie called as she stomped down the hallway.

Thirty minutes later, CanDee slid the tasting room's large barn door open. Justus didn't know if the building had actually been an old barn or if it was built to look like an old barn. Either way, it was charming, if a little sparse. Basically it was one giant room with concrete floors. A large, L-shaped bar ran the length of the back wall. Floor-to-ceiling wine racks took up the space behind the bar. Tall bistro tables dotted the floor space.

"Where are all of the products? You know, like wine accessories, fancy cheeseboards, and expensive soaps and lotions?" Rosie looked around. "I schedule lots of bachelorette trips to wineries, and they usually have full-on retail stores."

"Maybe he's just about the wine." Justus was trying not to be defensive about her—was Rowdy her boyfriend or just her baby daddy?—about Rowdy's business.

"It doesn't matter." Rosie walked around, getting a feel for the place. "I don't know what arrangements he's made for the launch, but I think we should open both barn doors and set up some tents with air-conditioning so that the guests can flow in and out of this space. Maybe even string quartet or a small band that plays country? They should set up outside on the patio." Rosie opened her iPad and started typing notes.

She walked around, inspecting every single inch of space and making notes.

Justus rolled her wheelchair over to the bar, and CanDee followed her.

"I'm not good with decoration, so I hope Rosie or you can figure out where all of the paintings should go." CanDee walked around to the back of the bar. "Water?" She held up a bottle.

"Sure." Justus nodded.

"I'm good," Rosie called out without looking up.

"I wish I had that level of concentration." CanDee twisted open the bottle and took a drink.

"You do. When you're writing, everything else disappears." Justus twisted off her own cap. "I've lived with you on and off for most of my adult life. Thank God I don't hate your guts."

"Ditto." CanDee took another drink and then swallowed. "You're hyperfocused when you're in work mode too. I guess everyone does it."

"Does what?" Rowdy walked in from the open barn doorway, went to Justus, and kissed her lightly on the cheek.

"Get super focused when we work." Justus pointed to Rosie. "She's making tons of notes." It sucked that she couldn't just stand on her tippy-toes and kiss him back. The world revolved around people five foot tall and above. She'd never really noticed until she was only wheelchair height. "Rosie was wondering why you don't have more of a retail business."

Rowdy rolled his eyes. "Margie has been after me for years to add retail items, and one day I will, but I've had so much to deal with getting Texas Rose Winery up and going."

"I can look into it for you." Justus needed something to occupy herself. God knew that idle hands were boring as hell.

"That would be wonderful." He rested a hand on her shoulder. "What are y'all up to this morning?"

"Just checking out the venue." Rosie closed her iPad. "We need to talk about the catering, and we still have three beds we need to find."

He pointed to a door with "Private" stenciled on the front. "Welcome to my office."

He produced a key from his pocket, unlocked the door, and opened it. "After you."

Rosie stepped through the doorway and clomped up the stairs. He looked back at Justus, and by the look on his face, he'd just realized that she couldn't navigate the stairs.

She shook her head. "I'm fine down here. I need to get my laptop and check out some products you might want to sell."

He dropped a kiss on the top of her head. "I don't know what I would have done without you."

Hopefully he'd still feel the same after she outed him to the wine-making world.

# CHAPTER 28

Four hours later, as Rowdy sat at his office desk, he couldn't believe how much Rosie had accomplished in such a short time. With any luck, everything would go off without a hitch.

All of this was because of Justus. He'd always known that she was a hard worker, but she was also willing to jump right on in and get to work. The team of twenty that she'd hired to finish the landscaping at the main house had done wonders in two days. Justus was able to manage the entire project and the cleaning of the cabins all from her wheelchair.

He owed her so much.

He looked down at the phone number Margie had written on a red sticky note and left next to his phone. There was so much he wanted to do for Justus, but he didn't know for sure if this little gesture of gratitude would be welcome. For as long as he'd known Justus, she'd always felt like something was missing from her life because of her biological mother. If he could give her peace of mind on that issue, he was willing to wade through alligators. He picked up his cell and dialed the number. After being transferred to four different people, he finally got the right voice mail.

"This is Stan Goldberg, please leave a message, and I'll either call you back or I won't. Mazel."

"This is Rowdy Rose of the Texas Rose Ranch and my, um," what was Justus to him? "Fiancée is Katarina Smythe-Herringdale's biological daughter. I'd love to talk to you about a meeting. Have a wonderful day." He hit "End."

He sounded like her manager or pimp or something.

Was the queasiness in his stomach regret or excitement? When he finally talked to Stan, Rowdy would insist that if the meeting was filmed, that Justus had final approval on what was aired. If she met Katarina in front of cameras, Justus could tell her bio mom exactly what she thought of her, and Katarina would have to sit there and take it. In this case, private wasn't the best way to go. If they met one-on-one, he was sure that Katarina wouldn't keep her claws sheathed long enough to take the ass chewing she so richly deserved.

He laced his fingers behind his head and leaned back in his office chair. Yep, a very public meeting was the way to go.

He sat up.

Fiancée?

He did see them together, but there was still that little detail of the proposal. He opened his laptop and googled romantic proposals and found everything from skywriting to scavenger hunts and romantic vacations to asking over the loudspeaker at a sporting event. He didn't want to have a chef at a fancy restaurant bake the ring into a dessert. That just sounded like a choking hazard. The hot-air balloon ride wasn't awful, but now that she'd fallen from like three stories, she was probably scared of heights. There was proposing on the Eiffel Tower, but Justus didn't seem like the Eiffel Tower type. Proposing at the first place they met was a good idea, but Burning Man was eleven months away. He really didn't want to wait that long, and he'd tried to do that this year.

Why couldn't he just get down on one knee and go for it? Too bad he didn't have the necklace he'd had made for her. An engagement ring was traditional, but Justus was anything but traditional.

A lifetime with her and Hugh wouldn't be enough.

"You look miles away."

He jumped about a foot in the air.

His mother stood in the doorway, holding an overstuffed manila folder with both hands.

"I was going over some of the details of the launch in my head." Why couldn't he tell his mother the truth? She loved Justus and Hugh, so the possibility of them staying around would make her happy. He'd kept his family at arm's length for so long that it was hard to change.

He took a deep breath and dived in. "Actually, I was thinking about how I was going to ask Justus and Hugh to marry me."

That wasn't so bad.

His mother smiled. "I have a feeling that Justus likes simple and something from the heart. She doesn't strike me as high maintenance. Have you thought about a ring?"

"I had planned to propose to her at Burning Man. I had this necklace made for her. It was a daisy made out of diamonds, but when she didn't show up, I threw it away." If only he'd kept it, but he honestly never thought he'd see her again, and having it around would have only reminded him of what he'd lost.

One corner of his mother's mouth turned up in a wry smile. "That sounds perfect. Justus is too practical to be a huge diamond ring kind of girl. She likes getting her hands dirty. She's more of a plain gold band. She values family above all else. You'll come up with something." She sat down in one of the brown leather chairs in front of his desk. "So, teepees by the river? Sounds like fun. I wish I could stay in one."

"Me too." He closed his laptop. "Have you met Rosie?"

"Yes. She's very efficient. I plan on keeping her info so she can plan future events for us. She has such great ideas." His mother relaxed back in the overstuffed chair but held the folder tightly to her chest.

"I need some advice. I just did something that may or may not be a good thing." He wasn't sure how his mother would land on the whole Katarina Smythe-Herringdale thing, mainly because he wasn't so sure how he felt about it.

"Okay. Am I going to be mad about it?" Lucy looked down her nose at him, which was something, considering he towered over her by at least a foot. "This isn't like the time you tried to dye the river green to honor our nonexistent Irish heritage?"

He'd forgotten about that. "Believe it or not, that was Cinco's idea. He was the mastermind behind most of my bad ideas."

"So you keep telling me." She crossed her legs. "Is he the one who put you up to the thing you need advice on now?"

"No, that's all me." Why was he hesitating? Because he didn't want to hurt Justus and he was almost sure that he'd done just that. "I called Stan Goldberg." Did his mother even know who that was? "He's the producer of—"

"Of the Rich Housewives franchise. I don't live under a rock." She shot him a "really" look.

"Justus's mother is Katarina Smythe-Herringdale." He waited to see if she knew who that was.

"I know."

"A couple of days ago, I walked in on her watching *The Rich Housewives of Beverly Hills* reunion show and—"

"Yep, I caught that one." His mother sat up straight. "Do you think Justus was the child Katarina was whining on about?"

"Yes, I mean as far as I know, Katarina has only birthed one baby." Here was the hard part. "For as long as I've known Justus, she's felt unwanted. I think she needs closure with her bio mother, so I left a message with Stan Goldberg. I don't even know if it will go anywhere." Now, he hoped that Stan would think it was a crank call and he'd never call back.

"Did Justus ask you to call him?" His mother's tone was so hopeful.

"No." The word reverberated between them.

"I think it's a mistake. Yes, Justus should have the platform to vent her feelings, but I don't think national TV is the best choice. Also, Justus seems like a private person to me. She is open and shares herself with people she loves, but I don't see her as a fame hound." His mother leaned closer to the desk like she was trying to get closer to him. "I don't see how TV cameras will help her find closure."

"My thinking was that if she met Katarina one-on-one, her mother would railroad her, but in front of fans, Justus could finally have her say and her mother would have to sit there and take it." Now that he said it out loud, it was a terrible idea.

His mother opened her mouth and then closed it. She looked like she was weighing her words very carefully. "I know that your heart was in the right place, but Justus needs to deal with this on her own time. She has some pretty profound issues when it comes to her mother, and I don't know that she would appreciate someone making her face something that is so deep and personal." His mother shook her head. "If you do go down this road, just remember that turnabout is fair play. Put yourself into her shoes: How would you like it if someone took something you held as deeply personal and put it out there for the world to see?"

What was it with rational people? Just once, could his mother say, "What a wonderful idea"? Then again, he'd asked for her advice and not for her praise.

"You have a point." He wanted closure for Justus, but if she'd done the same thing for him, he'd be very angry. "If Stan does call back, I'll tell him that I made a mistake." Or not take his call. That sounded like a better plan.

"Of course I don't know Stan, but he doesn't strike me as a leave-it-alone kind of guy. You've opened a can of worms that won't be easy to close." She stood. "I've got to go. We're having girls' night at the cottage. You and Hugh will be bacheloring it tonight, so don't wait up. I'll have your lady home before sunup."

"You and Justus and CanDee seem to get along really well." It was nice that his family seemed to love Justus as much as he did.

"I couldn't have picked better daughters-in-law myself." She walked around the desk, placed the folder in front of him, and then hugged him. "Your father and I could use some more grandbabies. You should get started on that."

He grinned. "I'll keep that under advisement."

"I brought you something. I thought you might like to see the file I have of some of your artwork over the years. I kept it in my desk drawer." She pointed to the folder and then checked her watch. "I need to run to Roseville, need anything?"

"No, I'm good." He glanced down at the file folder.

"I hope that you know that I believe in you . . . always." His mother walked out the door and closed it behind her.

Rowdy opened the file. The paper on top was heavy white cardstock that held tiny blue painted handprints in the shape of a flower. Where these his hands? He placed his hand over one of the prints. On the bottom, in his mother's precise writing, was *Rowdy age 3*.

They were his handprints. He'd never really thought of his mother as sentimental.

He turned to the next thing. It was a snowflake cut out of a large coffee filter. He looked for a date or name, but there was nothing. The next work of art was a dog coloring page. He'd used crayons to color the dog red with purple polka-dots. Then there was a robot made out of paper plates and what appeared to be a construction-paper turkey made out of his handprints. There were bumblebees made from fingerprints, a giant cut-out Christmas ornament covered in red glitter, a castle—based on the turrets—out of markers, an owl complete with feathers, and various coloring pages from pastoral scenes to Batman. He flipped to the last drawing and his breath caught in his throat. It was the crumpled-up picture of his rainbow horse. The paper was still creased in places, but having been mashed into the folder for so many years had ironed it almost flat.

His mother must have fished it out of the trash all of those years ago.

He closed his eyes and relaxed into his chair. He put his right hand over his heart, and he could feel the little boy from so long ago smiling.

# CHAPTER 29

"Let's go over the plan one more time." That evening at the cottage, Justus studied all of the objects on the small kitchen table. She, Rosie, CanDee, and Lucy had shared a bottle or two of wine, made s'mores in the microwave, and watched *Magic Mike XXL*. It was good to have girlfriends. She loved spending time with Hugh and Rowdy, but girl time was essential.

"Okay, at three thirty Saturday afternoon, the limo delivers the last batch of guests." She used a Zippo lighter they'd found in one of the kitchen drawers to represent the limo. She put the Hershey's Kiss that represented Rowdy next to the lighter. "I'll have Rowdy stationed out front to greet the guests. While he's glad-handing everyone—"

"I take Andre the framer to Rowdy's secret studio and help him frame the paintings." CanDee took a small, broken picture frame they'd found in the bathroom and put it next to the chunk of limestone that served as Rowdy's house.

"All the while I'm at Rowdy's side, making sure he doesn't go back to the house or into the tasting room." Justus leaned over and set the running shoe they'd taken from a Monopoly game that represented her down next to the Hershey's Kiss. True, she couldn't run now, but she was optimistic.

"Margie and I will be handing out gift baskets to the guests and spreading the word about the hayride we have planned to tour the ranch." Rosie placed her blue Sorry! game piece and the brass button that was Margie next to the upside-down Dixie cups that made up the teepees.

"I'll be stationed at the tasting room with picture-hanging supplies, waiting for CanDee and Andre." Lucy put her aspirin bottle next to the Oreo that was the tasting room.

"Okay, I think we have the plan down." CanDee picked up the tasting room and popped it into her mouth.

"Do you have another one to replace that one?" Justus couldn't believe that CanDee had eaten the tasting room. "What if we need to go over the plan again?"

"What?" CanDee threw up her hands. "We know the plan backwards and forwards. Besides, did I get all testy when you ate the Peanut M&M guests?"

She had a point.

"Oh, I almost forgot to tell y'all, but I got the weirdest phone call today." Justus pulled her phone out of the backpack she'd strapped to the back of her wheelchair. She held it up. "It was from Stan Goldberg. He'd like to talk to me about Katarina. He's the guy from the Rich Housewives reunion show."

He hadn't taken any of her bio mom's bullshit, so that made him good people.

"He's the executive producer of the Rich Housewives shows." Lucy took out her own phone and checked her messages.

"How do you think he got your number?" Rosie dismantled an Oreo and licked out the Double Stuf.

"I don't know." Justus pressed her lips together and tried to stifle the hope growing inside her. She did her best to pull off casual. "Think Katarina gave him my phone number?"

Deep down, she wanted that so badly, and it cost her to admit that to herself. Would she ever grow out of wanting approval?

"Maybe." Lucy continued to fiddle with her phone.

"What if Katarina really does feel bad about the way she's treated you? Maybe she's sorry and wants to make amends." CanDee popped another Oreo in her mouth. "Stranger things have happened."

"Why wouldn't she just call herself?" Rosie was all about the practical and never had someone else do something for her. She fought her own battles, and sometimes she staged battles just for fun.

"I don't know." Justus pursed her lips, pondering that. "Maybe she doesn't know what to say, so she needs his help."

"What do you plan on doing?" Lucy looked up. "Do you want to see her or not? What if the meeting involves cameras?"

There was no denying the part of her that desperately wanted to see her mother, but there was also the part that couldn't take more rejection. "I don't know. For Hugh, and I guess also for me, I'd like some sort of relationship with her, as long as it's not negative, but part of me doesn't want the hassle."

"Did you talk to Stan?" Lucy put her hand over Justus's and patted her lightly.

"No, he left me a message." She thought about it for a couple of seconds. "I guess I don't have call him back. I really need to sit down and think about this, for my sake and for Hugh's. I don't want him to be confused or to ever feel like he isn't loved. My egg donor has a talent for making people feel unloved."

Perhaps seeing Katarina wasn't such a good idea.

"Just keep an open mind and mull it over for a few days. The answer will come to you." Lucy squeezed her hand lightly. "Do what your heart tells you to do."

Justus leaned over and hugged the older woman. "You always know the right thing to say."

"I'm glad you think so. I'm pretty sure my husband would disagree." Lucy grinned.

Justus would take some time and listen to her heart. Right now, her heart was telling her that she'd created her own sort of family with the women around this table and that she no longer needed Katarina Smythe-Herringdale's approval.

Lucy squeezed her hand. "I just want to go on record as saying while your heart is in the right place about Rowdy's art, that he might not agree. Forcing someone to face something they want to keep private can be both good and bad." She patted Justus's hand again and then let it go. "Just putting that out there."

"So you think it's a bad idea?" Nerves played eight ball in her stomach.

"I didn't say that. I just want you to be aware that the consequences may outweigh the payoff." Lucy smiled. "As long as you are willing to weather the storm, I think it's a wonderful idea."

"I guess I am." Now Justus was second-guessing herself.

"Put yourself in his shoes. What if someone . . . say . . . spoke to your bio mom on your behalf and forced you to deal with her?" Lucy was all voice of reasony.

Justus sat back. It would be terrible to have to face her bio mom if it wasn't on her terms. She would like to think that she was a strong enough person to handle it, but she didn't know for sure. "You're right. Maybe I could cancel the art show?"

It would certainly be easier on her bank account.

"I disagree. I think the art show is a fantastic idea. I just want you to be certain. He may love it or he may hate it." Lucy's voice definitely indicated that she was on team love it.

Justus took a deep breath and huffed it out. "I guess we go on as planned while I puzzle it out."

# CHAPTER 30

Launch day was finally here and Rowdy didn't know whether to jump for joy or throw up. Both options seemed appealing. As CanDee flipped the last pancake on the griddle and Cinco pulled a sheet pan of bacon out of the oven, Rowdy tried to find solace in being surrounded by his family. His brother and fiancée had gladly moved in to Rowdy's house for a few nights and given over their house to the launch party guests. Elvis and Hugh sharing a room turned out fine. He'd seen Elvis snuggling with the little boy when he thought no one was looking.

Justus, who was seated next to him at the kitchen table, kissed him lightly on the cheek and whispered, "Everything's going to be wonderful. Don't worry."

How could he not worry? The future of his business hinged on today's success. The wine business was more than just making great wine. Yes, the product needed to be stellar, but promotion was equally important.

"We got this." Rosie smiled and shot him a double thumbs-up.

"Don't listen to her. That was a fake smile. She's probably more nervous than you." CanDee popped the last pancake on the plate with the others and brought them to the table.

Hugh put his tiny hand on top of Rowdy's. "I'm gonna help people around with their bags and stuff. Rosie says that I'm the head concierge."

Rosie put her arm around Hugh. "I hope you have a piggy bank ready, because I bet you're going to get lots of tips."

The little boy's face fell. "I left it at home."

"Never fear, Aunt CanDee is here." She held up a gift bag. "I got you these in Fredericksburg yesterday."

His whole body brightened as he took the bag and ripped it open. "A piggy bank and a special hat." He pulled out a black baseball cap with "concierge" embroidered on the brim and an ugly lime-green ceramic pig with a slot on its back for money.

He slapped the hat on his head and ran over to CanDee to give her a hug.

"Don't forget about me. I need some love too." Cinco held his arms open wide. "I found the piggy bank."

The boy let go of CanDee and hugged Cinco with his entire body. Cinco scooped him up and planted the kid on his hip. "So, are you coming to help me today? I've got a couple of steer wandering around in the wrong pasture that I need to get back to the herd. Feel like spending the morning in the saddle?"

Hugh's shoulders slumped. "I can't. I already promised the twins that I'd help them blow up some stuff at the quarry."

"I'm not so sure that's a good idea." Rowdy loved his little brothers, but they weren't exactly the best role models. "That doesn't sound safe."

"Just fireworks. Dallas and Worth are planning a fireworks show this evening for your guests. Worth had some extras left over from the Fourth of July." Cinco shifted Hugh to his other hip. "Worth is setting everything up around the quarry lake and Dallas is setting the show to music."

Rowdy's family was all helping out where they could. He didn't even have to ask, they just started working. Why had he never realized that before?

"That sucks." Rosie dug in her left suit jacket pocket and pulled out a five-dollar bill. "Here's a tip for helping me get the cabins ready yesterday. I was hoping you'd help me finish them this morning."

"I'm rich." He stuffed the money into the slot at the top of his piggy bank. "Sorry, but Momma says that when I make a promise, I have to keep it."

Rosie grinned down at him. "That's a very good thing to learn."

"I smell pancakes." Dallas stepped into the kitchen. "Did CanDee make them?"

"Yep, have a seat." CanDee scooted her chair over to make room for him.

"I don't mind if I do." He brought a bar stool over from the kitchen island and set it across the table from Rosie. His eyes landed on her and turned huge. He stood back up. "I just remembered that I already ate breakfast."

Awkward silence filled the room.

"I have to go. I forgot I had a thing." He continued to stare at Rosie. "Can one of you run H-man over to the quarry after breakfast?" He didn't wait for an answer but practically ran out of the house.

All eyes turned to Rosie.

She shook her head. "Don't ask me. I have no idea why he hates me. I only met him last week, and he treats me like an ex-boyfriend who owes me money."

"I'm sure it's not you." Justus didn't sound so sure. "He's probably just tired or something."

"It hurts me to say this, but I'm really the only sane one in the family." Rowdy put his hand over his heart. "All the others my kindly parents took in after a visit to the crazy farm."

Cinco bounced a piece of bacon off the side of Rowdy's head. "I'm sitting right here."

"Thanks for the bacon." Rowdy picked it up and munched on it.

"We all know that you were switched at birth. The hospital sent you home with the wrong parents." Cinco shoveled in a huge bite of pancake.

He used to think that too, but he was coming to see that his family accepted and loved him for who he was. He didn't have to pretend with them. They would love him no matter what.

"I'll take that as a compliment." Rowdy snagged another piece of bacon from the plate his brother had set on the table.

"You would." Cinco shoveled in another large forkful of pancakes.

"Tell me about the barrel room yesterday." Justus pulled Hugh onto her lap. "You never told me what you and Rowdy were doing."

"We were testing the wine." Hugh reached over Rowdy's plate and grabbed a piece of bacon. "You have to test it sometimes to make sure that everything's okay inside the barrels. You have to taste every barrel even if the same wine is in lots of barrels. So Rowdy pours a little bit into this glass and tastes it." He relaxed back against his mother. "And then he spits it on the floor."

The kid had asked a thousand questions about wine making. He was damn proud of his son. And he really saw him as his son. He winked at Hugh. He'd gone and fallen in love with Hugh.

"He let me taste a teeny-tiny little bit." Hugh clamped a hand over his mouth. "Oops, Dad." His eyes were giant blue pools of "I'm sorry."

Rowdy ruffled his hair. "No big deal, kiddo."

He'd called Rowdy "Dad." His heart went pitter-pat. He glanced at Justus, who'd also heard the "Dad" part. Tears pooled in her eyes.

She smiled so brightly that NASA could probably see it from space. "You told him?"

She didn't seem mad, more like she was in awe.

"Yes." Was it okay? Should he have asked her first?

"Thank you." She planted a big smacking kiss on Hugh's cheek. "What do you think about having Rowdy for a dad?"

Rowdy heard the raw hope in her voice and it tore at his heart. His ears perked up, wanting to know the answer more than Justus.

"I like him." Hugh traced the grain of the table's wood. "He said I could call him Dad. Is that okay?"

"Buddy, I think it's wonderful." Justus swiped at the tears running down her cheeks.

He thought it was pretty wonderful too.

"Sorry I told her about the wine." Hugh refused to make eye contact. "I can keep a secret . . . I promise."

"It's okay. No harm done." Rowdy waited for Hugh to look up, and when he finally did, Rowdy winked at him.

Hugh relaxed. "At least I didn't tell her that you wanted to marry us."

The whole room went silent as Justus turned to look at Rowdy.

Thanks a lot, H-man.

"Um, well . . . Hugh and I have talked about it." Rowdy's palms started to sweat so he wiped them on his gray trousers. "You know, I wanted to see if he was okay with the idea because, um . . . it affects him too, and, well . . . um—"

"Cinco and I have something that I just remembered that we needed to do." CanDee shoved two forkfuls of pancake in her mouth.

"Yes, that's right. We have that stuff that needs doing." Cinco took a handful of bacon and scooted back from the table.

CanDee and Cinco made a beeline for the front door.

"And I'm going to go do something in my room." Rosie looked like she was searching for a thing she needed to do but gave up and just stood. "Hugh, why don't you help me with it." In one hand, she picked up his plate and she offered the other to him. "You can finish these in my room."

He took her hand and they walked out of the kitchen, and once again the front door closed.

"Next time I need to clear a room, I know just what to say." His attempt at humor didn't even make it to lame.

He cleared his throat, which seemed to be closing in on him. "I was working on some elaborate plan to do this, but the only one I could think of involved waiting until Burning Man, and that seems like forever. In fact, I had this all planned out for Burning Man this year, but you didn't show. Really, I had this daisy necklace made for you because you don't really seem like a flashy ring kind of girl, but then when you didn't show, I threw it into the street in front of where we always park the RV." Christ, now he was rambling.

Should he get down on one knee or what?

Justus looked stunned. She licked her lips and cleared her throat too. Her hand shot out, probably looking for her water glass, but landed on the small glass measuring cup that held the warmed-up maple syrup. She brought it to her lips and downed the whole thing. She didn't seem to notice that it wasn't juice or water.

She was as nervous as he was. That gave him strength. He slid out of his chair and was about to get down on one knee when the perfect ring came to him. He ran into the dining room, pulled open the middle drawer of the buffet, and pulled out a sterling silver napkin ring. A napkin ring was better than nothing. He ran back into the kitchen, got down on one knee beside Justus's wheelchair.

With the sleeve of his blue shirt, he shined up the napkin ring. "Daisy, I have loved you from the very first time I saw you. I want to spend my life with you and Hugh. I asked you to marry me all those years ago and you never answered me. So now, I'm asking again, will you marry me?"

He held the napkin ring out to her.

She slid her ring finger into the napkin ring. "For your information, I did answer you all of those years ago, but you were so busy trying to convince me that you weren't a crazy person that you didn't hear me. My answer is the same, yes—absolutely and always. I love you and I can't wait to spend the rest of my life showing you just how much."

She kissed him hard. She tasted of syrup and tears and happiness.

After a minute or so, he pulled back and cupped her face with his hands. "So you mean that we could have been married this whole time?"

"Sometimes I think you like to talk just to hear your own voice. I'm not complaining or anything." She held out the napkin ring. "Let's go tell our son that his parents are getting married."

"Rowdy, help!" Rosie called from down the hall.

He took off in a dead run. Had something happened to Hugh? As soon as he hit the hallway, he noticed one of Hugh's boots floating down the hallway. Floating?

Water was rushing out of Hugh's and Elvis's room. If it weren't for the step down into the hallway, his living room would be flooded.

He shucked off his shoes and socks and rolled up his pants. "What happened?"

He stepped down and sloshed his way to Hugh's room. The water was coming from the bathroom. The toilet was Niagara Falls-ing all over the floor. He turned off the water.

"Oh my God, what is going on?" Justus called from the other room.

"Toilet overflowed." Rowdy threw open the cabinet doors under the sink and tossed a heap of towels on the floor. It was like putting a Band-Aid on a gushing wound.

"I'll call a plumber and a cleaning service. If we can get the water up and the floorboards dry soon, it will minimize the water damage." Rosie sloshed into the bathroom.

"Just what in the holy hell happened?" Today of all days, he didn't need this.

Hugh shuffled into the bathroom with his head down and his entire body wilted. "I flushed some rocks down the potty."

Huge tears gathered in the little boy's eyes as he hung his head.

Rowdy did his best to rein in his temper. "Why would you flush rocks down the toilet?"

He was doing his level best to calm down.

"Yesterday, I helped Mr. Bear install a new toilet in one of the cabins. He said it could flush a whole bucket of golf balls." Hugh pointed to the toilet. "I wanted to see if ours could do that too . . . only I don't have any golf balls, so I used rocks."

Rowdy took several deep, cleansing breaths and then finally nodded. "Okay, mistakes happen."

What was he going to do? His guests would start arriving in a couple of hours and every bedroom except the master was under water.

"Rowdy, Justus and I can handle this." Rosie nodded. "Don't worry."

"I'm so sorry." Hugh was crying quietly to himself.

Rowdy picked up the little boy and hugged him tightly. "It's okay, little man, but from now on, let's only flush toilet paper, poop, and pee down the toilets."

It looked like fatherhood was a multifaceted experience that included plumbing crises and tearful hugs. He could deal with life's little messes, it was all part of the job.

He patted Hugh on the back as the little boy hugged him tight. "Just wanted to let you know, your mom and I are getting married."

"Okay." Hugh turned his head and looked sheepish. "Does that mean that you're not mad about the rocks?"

He reached down and swooped Hugh up into his arms. "Well, I'm a little mad, but if this is the worst thing that happens to me today, it will be a pretty good day." Hopefully.

# CHAPTER 31

Rowdy smiled. So far the launch was going off without a hitch. Well, apart from the plumbing issue, which a plumber had fixed, and a fire/flood restoration company had come out and wet/dry vacuumed most of the house. The Sheetrock was toast, but the floors had been saved.

As the last of the limo coaches turned onto the road that led to the front gate, Rowdy couldn't have been more pleased with the day.

"Can't wait to taste this new wine of yours." Larissa Van Burton elbowed him in the side. She'd practically thrown James Rider and Bart Mendol out of the way so she could sit next to him on the ride from the San Antonio airport. If *Larissa Knows* wasn't one of the most influential wine blogs in the country, he'd have moved to the back of the bus. She'd been hitting on him for the better part of the hour it had taken to get to the ranch from San Antonio.

"I can't wait for you to try it. It's one of my fiancée's favorites." With any luck, she'd take the hint. He was off the market. Come to think of it, he'd been off the market for a long time. He was still reeling from her saying yes.

This was turning out to be a perfect day, plumbing aside.

Because Larissa was sulking, he had five gloriously silent minutes before they pulled through the main gate of the Texas Rose Ranch.

Every new group of people arriving at the ranch for the launch had been stunned by the beauty, size, and scope of the operation. They really had something unique and historic here, and it was a shame that the family were the only ones who got to experience it.

Maybe it was time to open a bed-and-breakfast on the ranch, or maybe keep the teepees. Everyone staying in them was enchanted. He didn't have time to run it, but he could do some research and talk it over with his family.

As the bus pulled up to the tasting room, he checked his watch. "Okay everyone, your bags will be taken to your rooms, so if you'd follow me to the tasting room, we have just enough time for a glass of wine before dinner."

He stepped off of the bus and waited for his guests to follow.

Roland Hopkins, pompous wine aficionado and self-important windbag, bounded down the bus steps, his sterling silver tastevin around his neck bouncing against his rotund body. Tastevins had gone the way of gaslights with the advent of electricity, but Roland was never without his.

"I trust the Riesling is extraordinary for you to have brought us all this way." His snotty tone suggested that civilization was a couple of continents away.

"You won't be disappointed." He hoped.

"What a lovely place you have here." It was Marsha Carter from *Wine Spectator*. At least she was fairly normal, although she had brought two giant suitcases for an overnight stay and insisted on a three-quarter-size refrigerator in her room for some mysterious reason.

"Thank you, we enjoy it." He offered a hand to help her step down.

Alphonse Girard followed. He fanned himself with a baby-blue pocket square. "It is very hot." His fake French accent made the last word sound like "aught." Everyone knew he was from Cleveland, but that didn't stop his long-winded stories about his family's château in France.

Larissa finally stepped off the bus and refused his offered hand. Apparently she was still miffed about the whole fiancée thing.

Once all of his wine-loving little duckies were off the bus, he led them to the tasting room.

"We have some lovely cheese, pâté, and pork belly appetizers for you to try with the Riesling. Later, we're having an old-fashioned barbecue. I hope you enjoy the Riesling as much as I do." Rowdy gestured to the open barn door like a game show hostess revealing what was behind door number two.

Loren Hyde, who owned one of the largest wine distributorships in the United States, stepped out of the tasting room. "Oh, there you are, Rose, the Riesling is fantastic. I've already spoken with your assistant about placing an order." He shook Rowdy's hand. "Say, is any of that art for sale? My wife would love the desert landscape."

What piece was he talking about? He had a couple of ranch-inspired cow watercolors, but nothing with a desert landscape.

"I'll talk to my retail manager and see what we can do." By retail manager he meant Justus.

A couple walked out of the tasting room—the Merkins. If memory served, they owned a large chain of liquor stores. Mrs. Merkins saluted him with a glass of wine. "Riesling is out of this world, and the artwork. Wow. I'd love to buy the lady at sunset. Who's the artist? The paintings are only signed HR."

Rowdy's heart flinched. It couldn't be. Sweat dotted his upper lip.

He smiled dismissively at the couple and headed into the tasting room. It was crowded with people milling around with glasses of Riesling in one hand and hors d'oeuvres in the other. Little crowds of people were clustered around paintings hanging on every available wall space. It was so crowded that he couldn't quite see the artwork. Two men broke off from the cluster across the room from him and one of the paintings came into view. It was the watercolor of Justus on the day that he'd met her.

Holy crap. His knees felt like they were going to buckle. His paintings, his work, were hanging around the tasting room for all of the world to see. He managed to make it to one of the tall bistro tables and hung on to it for dear life. Somehow his paintings were framed and hanging all around. Being naked couldn't make him feel this vulnerable. But how?

He scanned the room for Justus.

He found her by the mosaic birdbath his father had done that was now for sale in the tasting room. Her excited smile made her eyes look greener. She'd done this.

Why?

His artwork was private . . . she knew that and still hung it up.

Anger burned through him. Why couldn't she have left it alone? Wasn't it enough that she'd told his family about his art, but now she had to show the whole world? It was personal and only for him. He didn't want to show it to anyone, but that choice had been taken away from him. How could she?

He looked away.

This was too much. Wasn't it enough that she'd waltzed into his life and changed everything? Hell, even his house wasn't really his own anymore. Who had he been kidding? Justus would never fit into his life. He liked order and she thrived on chaos. They would never make it as a couple.

Only she did fit into his life . . . perfectly. He glanced down at the slacks and button-down he wore. No tie or suit jacket, because he'd realized that he didn't like ties and suit jackets. In fact, he hadn't worn either since she'd shown up.

It dawned on him that he'd lost himself in her—well, the detail-oriented, anal part that had gotten lost since he'd bumped into her on the ranch and muddied up one of his favorite Hugo Boss suits. He looked around. For someone who'd recently let go of the minutiae, he had to admit this party was running smoothly.

But for how long? He'd given over the planning to someone else. When had he become a delegator instead of a do-it-all-er? He tunneled his fingers through his hair. He needed to pull it together. He had 150 guests that he needed to impress, and he didn't think watching him go ballistic was the best course of action.

Cinco clapped a hand on his back. "Looks like you need some Riesling." His older brother grabbed a couple of glasses off the tray a waiter was carrying and handed one to Rowdy. "Wine's really good."

"Thanks." He took a sip and the peachy notes caught him. The wine was good, and by the looks on the faces of his guests, they thought so too. But his stomach went queasy when he saw everyone milling around and inspecting his paintings.

"I didn't know you could paint." Cinco glanced at the painting across from them.

Rowdy sucked in short, shallow breaths. This was where his brother made fun of him. He'd been waiting for this most of his life. What were the chances that his older brother wouldn't embarrass him in front of all of his guests?

"You're really good. The only artistic ability I have is . . . wait, I don't have any artistic ability, but thank God I got all of the looks and the brains in the family." Cinco was serious.

Rowdy waited a few beats for the ribbing to begin, but all Cinco did was admire the painting.

"You should stop listening to the voices in your head that tell you how smart you are. They're lying," Rowdy teased as he watched his brother very carefully. He wasn't making fun of his art and really seemed to appreciate it.

"I don't suppose I could convince you to do our wedding portrait? I'd love to give that to CanDee as a wedding gift." His brother took another sip of wine. "I thought I'd ask nicely before I beat it out of you."

The deepest, darkest part of Rowdy's soul, where all of his self-doubt and fear of his family's rejection lived, felt lighter. He might have been different from the rest of his family, but that didn't make him an outsider. There was only acceptance and love in his brother's face.

And hadn't his entire family pulled together to help him? Would they have done that if they hadn't thought he was worth the trouble?

"That makes me feel all warm and fuzzy inside. I'll do your wedding portrait, but only because I like CanDee. I guess you can be in it too." Rowdy made a big show of rolling his eyes.

His brother liked his art. He'd never felt more vulnerable than he did right now . . . and not a single member of his family had said a negative word about him.

"Darling." Cynthia Rand floated by on impossibly high heels, and wearing a red pantsuit. The giant diamonds at her neck glittered in the fluorescent lighting. "The Riesling is to die for and the artwork is out of this world. I simply must have the girl at sunset." She pointed to the painting he'd done of Justus at sunset that she'd said used to hang above her fireplace. Now that he looked at it again, it was good. Very good.

"Name your price. I'm not leaving here without it," Cynthia crooned. She had to be at least seventy, and he was pretty sure in all of those years no one had ever turned her down.

"Sorry, that one isn't for sale. It's a painting I did of my fiancée. It belongs to her." He turned to Justus again, but she was looking down. She probably thought he was upset. And okay, he was. But no one was making fun of his art; in fact, everyone loved it.

That was more than he could have ever hoped for . . . and she'd made it happen.

"You painted it?" Cynthia's voice tended to carry . . . like to the next town over. "Rowdy, you're the artist?"

It seemed like the whole room turned to him.

Cynthia banged on her wineglass with one of her many diamond rings. "Attention, everyone: I know that we've all been wondering about the artist. It's Rowdy."

"Yes, my initials are HR." Rowdy took a deep breath and let the world see who he really was. The urge to run out the door and never come back was almost too strong to resist. "I'm an artist who makes wine."

Applause erupted from the everyone in the tasting room. Not only was his wine a hit, but it seemed that his artwork was too.

Maybe Texas Rose Ranch was ready for Burner Rowdy.

"Thank you all very much." He grinned at Justus and went to her. "But this wonderful launch party wouldn't have been possible without the help of my fiancée, Justus Jacobi." He stood beside her.

He wasn't all Burner or all Rose Ranch—he was a little bit of both, and that was okay. The authentic Rowdy loved designer clothes, reality TV, yoga, and painting.

"Wait, you're the woman in all of the paintings," a man from the back of the crowd called out.

"Yes, I am. Just this morning, we got engaged." Justus grinned at the crowd. "I think we should celebrate."

"We all know that the Riesling is fantastic, so now let's have some Hill Country Sparkling Wine." She nodded to Rosie, who directed the servers to start popping bottles of wine. "After you get your glass, please make your way out the front door. We have a hayride set up for you, followed by a barbecue. Enjoy your time at the Texas Rose Ranch, and please let us know if you need anything."

He liked seeing Justus in hostess mode. Rowdy hadn't even known that she had a hostess mode.

He squatted down so that he was eye level with her. "I didn't know you had this in you." He nodded in the general direction of the tasting room. "Thank you for believing in my art. Believing in me. Painting had always been a way for me to express myself on canvas that I didn't feel comfortable doing in real life, but thanks to you, I feel braver about sharing it with the world."

She kissed him lightly on the mouth. "I just want you to know that you never have to hide any part of yourself from the world. I wanted people to see the artist and man I fell in love with. Now everyone knows what I know."

This was turning out to be the best day ever.

Then Stan Goldberg walked into the tasting room with Katarina Smythe-Herringdale on his arm.

Holy crap.

# CHAPTER 32

Justus could feel the mood change in the room. Gone was the joviality, only to be replaced by a nervous tension. She turned her wheelchair around to see what had caused the drastic change and nearly ran into the mosaic birdbath.

The guy from *The Rich Housewives of Beverly Hills* reunion show, Stan Goldberg, and Katarina Smythe-Herringdale stood by the door, looking around. Her egg donor looked particularly anxious as she scanned each face, no doubt looking for her daughter. Justus was amused at the thought that her egg donor had no idea what she looked like as an adult. Justus couldn't think of a situation where she would ever not be able to recognize her son.

Stan looked her way and smiled. He walked toward her, but his eyes were on Rowdy. Stan stuck out a hand. "You must be Rowdy Rose. I apologize for crashing your party, but we were in the neighborhood and thought we'd stop by."

Neighborhood? So what, they were out roaming the Texas Hill Country? It's not like the ranch was near anything.

She glanced up at Rowdy, whose face reflected a combination of shock and dismay. He shook Stan's hand. "You're welcome here anytime."

Really, what else could he say?

Rowdy held up his right index finger. "If you'll excuse me, I need to make sure that my guests all get to the right place, and then we can talk." He looked down at her. "Give me a hand?"

He pushed her so fast out the front door she almost fell out of the wheelchair. When they were around the corner and out of earshot, Rowdy squatted down next to her. "Know how you forced me to deal with my family and my art?"

"Yes." It was all of thirty minutes ago. She'd broken her leg, not hit her head. Actually, she had hit her head, but she'd recovered.

"Well, um . . . I might have done the same for you." He took a deep breath and let it out slowly. "I called Stan Goldberg—"

"You did what?" Her voice was high and squeaky. If looks could kill, Rowdy would have exploded. Her worst nightmare had just stepped into her perfect little life.

She looked around. Was Hugh still with the twins? She didn't want him to see what a bitch his bio grandma was. She had to protect him. She tried to turn around and head to the bunkhouse, but Rowdy grabbed the right wheel.

"I can explain." But then he didn't. Nothing but silence. It was like he was preparing his defense. "I wanted to do something to help you deal with—"

"What? The fact that my egg donor is a bitch? How could you do this to me?" All she wanted to do was get away from here. She wheeled harder, but she couldn't shake off his hand. Damn wheelchair. She'd give anything to be able to stomp off in indignation, but getting up and hopping off wouldn't have the same effect.

"You need to deal with her," he said lamely. "I mean, I don't want you to hurt anymore because of her."

"So you invited her here? What was your plan? That we'd sit down and have a heart-to-heart, and everything would be forgiven and we'd be besties?" Justus hadn't seen this coming.

"No, I just, well . . ." He finger-combed his hair. "I thought if I got the two of you together, you could finally tell her what you really think of her. I didn't know they were coming. I only left Stan a message."

Justus shook her head. "I don't know what I did to you to make you hate me so much, but I am so sorry. Whatever it is, we could have just talked about it. You didn't have to get back at me. I thought you were better than that."

His face fell. She felt like a total bitch.

"Meeting my mother should have been my choice. Now you're forcing me to do something I don't want to do. And at a time when I'm not prepared to handle it." Kind of like when she hung his paintings in the tasting room. That wasn't the same. Those were paintings and this was her biological mother. Both dealt with family issues. God, she hated the logical side of her brain. Why couldn't she be one of those self-involved dreamer types whose head was always in the clouds?

Right now, her only choices were to go back inside and speak with her bio mom or to run away and sulk. She rolled her eyes. She wasn't a coward, but she was a world-class sulker. If she was going to do this, she'd do it alone.

"Fine." She tried to roll herself back around the corner, but he grabbed the handles and pushed her. "You stay outside." Her heart rate skyrocketed and the old feelings of inadequacy started to seep into her soul.

"Nope, sorry. We're a team, which means we handle all evil bitches together. I understand that you're mad at me, and we can talk about that some more later, but I'm going with you. It's nonnegotiable." Calmly he pushed her around the corner. "And I'm willing to bet that CanDee, my mom, my father, and Cinco are all in there waiting for you to come back. Here's something that you taught me about my family: they love me unconditionally, and they love you unconditionally. When push comes to shove, my family rallies and circles the wagons. You are family, and they won't let anything hurt you . . . ever." He leaned down and his breath kissed her ear. The hair on the back of her neck stood to atten-tion and saluted the zing of desire that went straight to her heart. "FYI: my mother is the one to watch. When she goes into protective mode, grizzly bear mommas could learn a thing or two. Her face goes all hard and her voice turns quiet. As children, we used to run and hide when we saw that look on her face. To this day, it still gives me goose bumps." He held out his arm so she could see the tiny raised hair follicles.

Some of the anxiety she was feeling subsided. While she didn't want anyone else to see how much her mother hated her, it was nice to know that there was a room full of people who loved her enough to help her face down her worst nightmare. That meant something. These people wanted her around because they loved her. She wasn't a mistake. She was perfect just the way she was. Her mother was the one with the problem. It was so clear to her.

So why did she feel nauseated? This was exactly how she'd felt right before she'd bungee jumped (for the first and last time), only at this moment, she really didn't want to take the leap. In fact, give her a bridge and she'd jump off it instead of meeting with her bio mom.

She and Rowdy would talk more about this later, but for right now, she had her reinforcements at the ready, and she was going into battle. With a glance toward the hayride where everyone seemed to be settling onto the large flatbeds piled with hay bales, she smoothed the wrinkles out of the light blue cotton sundress and fixed a smile on her face.

This would either be a new beginning or a wonderful ending to a terrible relationship. Either way, the page was turning on her mother, and it was up to her whether she wanted to include the woman in her future life story.

Rowdy rolled her through the open doorway, and what she saw set her soul aglow. CanDee, flanked by Bear and Cinco, was the second line of defense. Lucy, eyes mean, and Lefty stood in front of them. Lefty had a very sharp buck knife out and appeared to be cleaning his fingernails.

"Just so we have an understanding, if Justus so much as frowns or sighs deeply, I'll throw you into the wood chipper and feed your body to the pigs." Lucy's voice was scary as hell.

"Now, let's slow down here." Lefty paused in mid-knife intimidation. "I think the chipper is too quick. I vote we tie all of her limbs to four different trucks and then snap her apart like a wishbone."

Lucy nodded. "Great idea. I'll throw in some really nasty and painful flesh-eating bacteria. So the order is flesh-eating bacteria, snap like a wishbone, wood chipper, and then pigs. That sounds about right."

Katarina's face was turning a lovely shade of dirty-dishwater gray.

All of a sudden the seriousness and intricacy of the death sentence was hilarious. Justus threw back her head and laughed until her eyes watered. All of the years of trying to figure why her mother hated her so much seemed like wasted time. She already had all of the family that she'd ever need.

She wiped the tears off her cheeks and smiled up at her fierce protectors. "Thank you all for standing up for me. I have never felt so loved as I do in this moment." She turned to Katarina. "Now, I'm willing to hear what you have to say."

"You're her daughter?" Stan looked from Justus to Katarina and back again. "I thought your daughter was sixteen."

"I'm thirty and she's pushing fifty." Watching Stan glare at Katarina was wonderful. "And she's about as British as you are. She's from Longview, Texas."

Stan turned on her. "So what . . . exactly is true about you?"

"Well . . . um . . . there are lots of things." Katarina continued the accent even though it wasn't necessary and it sounded stupid. Everyone waited in rapt silence for her to list the "lots of things," but clearly she couldn't think of one.

She walked over to Justus and reached out her arms—stiff and clunky—as if she'd learned to hug from Frankenstein's monster. Her mother's body must have known sincerity wasn't in her DNA, so it pulled back and did its best not to touch Justus unnecessarily in case sincerity was watching.

Justus was so shocked she couldn't make her muscles hug back. She was getting tired of waiting. "Did you come here to say something to me, or did you just think, 'hey, I should stop by and visit the daughter whose name I once said should have been Abortion Jacobi'?"

It was a wonder that the collective intake of breath didn't suck all of the oxygen out of the room. Out of the corner of her eye, she saw Bear reach forward and hold his wife back. Lucy looked like she was ready to kill Katarina with her bare hands.

"Well, we're waiting." Stan was losing his patience. The look of disgust dawning on his face seemed to frighten Katarina more than the death threats.

"I am . . . um . . . sorry about the way that I treated you." Katarina sounded more scared than sorry.

"So you're sorry about the Rolex watch I scraped together the money to buy for you only to have it returned so you could take the cash value?" Justus was just getting started. "And are you sorry for sending back all of the birthday cards I made for you, along with a letter telling me to stop bothering you or you would take legal action? Or maybe you're sorry for stealing my college fund so you could get breast implants?"

"I was very young when I had you, and I didn't know what I wanted out of life. I made some mistakes." Katarina looked everywhere but at Justus.

Rowdy took a step forward. "Are you calling my fiancée a mistake?" He glanced over at his mother. "Dad, let Mom go. I want to watch her tear this bitch limb from limb."

"That is not what I meant. I mean that I've made mistakes when it came to Justus. I wish that I would have done things differently." Katarina bit her bottom lip so hard that tears pooled in her eyes.

Stan rolled his eyes. "Really, with the fake tears again? You begged me to bring you here because you felt so bad about what you'd done and wanted to make amends." His eyes narrowed. "I wanted to give you the benefit of the doubt, but I should have known better. I have a great BS meter, and your apology was lukewarm at best. I put up with your drama because it was good for ratings, but once the world learns just how toxic you really are, they're going to hate you." He rubbed his hands together in anticipation. "Your life expectancy as a trophy wife just ran out. You're fired. You can find your own way home."

Rowdy smiled at Stan. "Mr. Goldberg, you just earned yourself an invite to this weekend's party. We have one room left, and it's yours for the asking."

"I'd love to stay. I'm a huge fan of your wine."

"Oh, Stan, you'll be sorry. My fans won't put up with this. I make that show. You're going to regret this." Katarina stomped toward the door.

"Yeah, that's what Diana Metcalf said. Remember her?" Stan shook his head. "Yep, neither does anyone else."

"Wait," Justus called to her bio mother. "I just wanted you to know that I have a son. I'm telling you this because you will never see him. He's wonderful and charming and loved. I've spent my life trying to figure out why you hate me so much and it just hit me. You hate everyone . . . including yourself. There is no love in you. I didn't do anything wrong, but you will go on blaming me or your ex-husbands or"—Justus pointed to Stan—"the network for your troubles because you can't face who you are and what you've become. Your looks are fading, and once they're gone, there will be nothing left about you that the world finds remotely attractive. That's the saddest part. You will end up alone because you have nothing to offer anyone." Justus nodded to herself. "It's time for you to go. I'm done with you. I no longer need or want your love—I no longer want anything from you."

Lefty made to grab her arm, but Katarina pulled away.

"I'm going. Don't touch me. Don't you dare touch me." She stomped out the door.

"At least her fake accent is finally gone." Rowdy hugged Justus. "Wow, that's not how I thought that would go down." He walked behind the bar at the back of the room. "I don't know about y'all, but I could use a stiff drink." He pulled out two small bottles from below the bar. "How about some private-label port that I only make for family and friends?"

"That sounds perfect." Justus smiled at him. "I feel like the weight of the world has been lifted off of my shoulders. I can't believe that I've obsessed about her for so long."

She blew him a kiss. This was due to him and his family. She couldn't wait to tell her father and Maeve. Katarina had found ways to torture them enough over the years, so they'd get a big kick out of this. Not that a little humiliation made up for the missing child support or the nasty late-night ranting phone calls, but even little victories were victories.

"Can't wait." Stan bellied up to the bar. "Have you and your family considered doing a reality TV show?" He took a glass. "We could call it *Down on the Texas Rose*. It would be like *Duck Dynasty* meets *Dynasty*. I smell a hit."

Bear and Lucy shared a look. "Don't think so."

# EPILOGUE

*Burning Man—The first week of September, one year later.*

The wind kicked up on the Playa, tossing sand around in little dust devils. Rowdy stared up at the Burning Man Temple and felt at peace. It was sunrise, and only a few people dotted the landscape as the golds, yellows, pinks, and purples backlit the Temple. This year the intricate wooden structure was at least five stories tall. It was part gothic cathedral and part Egyptian pyramid and lovely in both its scope and delicacy.

The light was perfect.

He picked up his palette and combined three colors to match the top color of the sunrise.

Today was his wedding day, and he couldn't think of a better place to marry Justus or a better wedding present. He had tons of photos of the Temple, but the sunrise couldn't be captured digitally. He needed to paint it right now or lose it forever. As fast as he could, he added color and outlined. By the time the sun had risen, he was satisfied with the colors he'd gotten down on canvas. The watercolor wasn't close to being finished, but it would be in a couple of days.

"Fancy meeting you here," Justus said from behind him as she slid her arms around his waist. Her pronounced baby bump pressed against his lower back. "The Temple is so beautiful. I know burning it down is part of the tradition, but I will miss it."

He lifted her left hand and kissed her bare ring finger. "I know . . . me too. That's why I'm painting it, so we can have it forever."

Her arms slid away, and she came up beside him and looked at the painting. "The colors are amazing. I wish I had your talent."

"You have many talents of your own. Plants love you. All you do is walk by them and they perk up." If there was something worse than a black thumb, Rowdy was it. Two months ago, Justus had given him some sort of plant for his office. The poor thing had taken one look at him and promptly keeled over.

She leaned closer and traced the outline he'd made in the bottom left forefront of the canvas. He'd drawn more than just her standing outside the Temple. Rowdy had added himself to her right, and between them was Hugh. They were both holding their little boy's hands.

"It's perfect." She stood up on her tippy-toes and kissed him on the cheek.

Rowdy set the palette and brush down on the stool he'd brought with him. "I want to show you something."

"Okay. I can spare a couple more minutes, but Rosie has probably figured out that I snuck out by now. She'll have everyone searching for me." Justus sounded tired.

Rosie had planned the wedding of the century, Burning Man style. Everyone on the Playa was invited, so there was the possibility of feeding thousands. They were getting married in the Temple, surrounded by family and several thousand of their closest Burner friends. He was pretty sure Rosie could run the world with one arm tied behind her back.

Justus yawned.

"Up late last night?" Rowdy grinned. There was no better place to have a bachelor or bachelorette party than at Burning Man, which was one big party in itself.

"Your mom had a little too much tequila and kept jumping up on stage with Lindsey Buckingham. I had no idea she was such a fan of Fleetwood Mac. After the fifth time, they escorted her back to her RV. It takes a lot to get kicked out of a Burning Man event." Justus laced her fingers through his. "FYI—as loud as your parents were last night, you might have a little brother named Black Rock show up in nine months."

Rowdy made gagging noises. "Oh, God. Is that what I heard around three? I thought someone had run over a cat."

"I'm pretty sure that no cats were injured in last night's activities." She followed along beside him. "What did you want to show me?"

"See." He pointed to some writing on one of the beams in the Temple. "I know people come here to write messages to those they've lost, but, well . . . I did lose you, and then I found you again."

He read the message he'd written in bold, black Sharpie. "For Daisy, love of all of my lives—I will love you always."

She leaned up and kissed him on the mouth. "Great minds think alike."

She pulled him over to the center of the Temple and pointed to some writing.

She read, "For Houston, love of all of my lives—I will love you always."

"Damn, we're cute and not very original." Rowdy laughed to himself. He didn't know a person could be this happy. His father had told him that, every single day, he fell a little more in love with his mother. He hadn't truly understood that until now.

They had met in the Temple all those years ago, and later they would get married in front of their family and friends, but right now was their time, and he wanted to do this with just the two of them.

He turned to her and took her other hand. "I, Houston Harris Rose, take you, Justus Daisy Jacobi, to be my wife. I promise to laugh with you in good times and comfort you in bad times. You are my other half . . . my home. I will love you always."

"Wow, I didn't know we were going to do this here." She took a couple of deep breaths. "Sorry, I'm nervous. I just want to get this right." She took one more deep, cleansing breath and let it out slowly. "I, Justus Eleanor—aka Daisy—Jacobi choose to take you, Houston Harris Rose, as my husband. From the first moment I saw you, I knew that you were the life that I wanted. You are my other half, my heart, and my home. I will love you always."

Rowdy leaned down and kissed her. Over his left shoulder, he heard a camera click and reluctantly stepped back and turned around.

Lefty held up his smartphone and clicked several more pictures. "So glad I captured the happy moment. I just tweeted it out."

So much for privacy.

"Now I gotta go. Lots of people to see." Lefty shoved the phone in his back pocket. He'd become sort of a Burning Man cult hero. Two days ago when he'd showed up with the rest of the family, he'd walked out onto the Playa, set up an umbrella and two lawn chairs and a hand-made poster-board sign announcing him as Mr. Lefty—Life Coach and Cowboy Poet. Yesterday, the line to see him had to have been half a mile long.

"Um . . . Mr. Lefty, I know you're not set up yet, but I was wondering if you could help me."

Lefty put his arm around a dark-haired man in his twenties with so many facial piercings that he looked like he'd been attacked by a nail gun. The guy had to be at least a foot taller than him. "You certainly look like you could use my help. What's on your mind, son?"

"My girlfriend says I have commitment issues." The man shook his head. "I have no idea what's she's talking about."

"First thing, you need to get rid of them skinny jeans on account of they crunch up your doodads." He pointed to the dark-haired man's tight jeans. "A man can't even think straight when his doodads is all crunched up. And then we need to talk about all them piercings in your face. You look like a pincushion. Now, I'm not saying you need to change your identity, because who you is is who you is, I'm just wondering if you had a mouthful of water, would it leak out all them holes." Lefty patted him lightly. "See where I'm going with this?"

The man brightened. "It's a metaphor. All the holes in my face represent the holes in my soul."

"Well, that works too. I was just wondering how you got through the metal detector at the airport, but metaphors is good too." Lefty nodded as they walked away.

Justus smiled up at Rowdy. "So, I'll meet you back here in a few hours, and we'll do this all over again?"

He traced the daisy necklace around her neck. It turned out that Burning Man had a lost and found.

"Yes, ma'am. And next time you get a ring too." The gold wedding band in his pocket wasn't fancy, but it was very "Justus." The inscription had only one word . . .

"Always."

# ACKNOWLEDGMENTS

There are so many people who made this book a reality. First, a big thank-you to my fans—your kind words keep me going. Just when I'm ready to quit this whole writing game and be a checker at Costco or a barista at Starbucks, I get another letter of encouragement. Second, a gigantic thank-you to my fellow writers, Emily McKay, Tracy Wolff, Jane Myers Perrine, Catherine Arvil Morris, and Marlena Faulkner— I'm so glad none of us suffers from sanity. Third, thanks to Melody Guy for her invaluable insight. Woman, I don't know how you do it, but damn, you're good. And to Chris Werner, editor extraordinaire and possibly the most patient man I've ever met. When you told me that no question was stupid, I took that as a personal challenge. Finally, to my husband and daughter—I will love you both . . . always.

# ABOUT THE AUTHOR

 Katie Graykowski is an award-winning and bestselling author of four series: the Marilyns, the Lone Stars, PTO Murder Club, and Texas Rose Ranch. She likes sassy heroines, Mexican food, movies where lots of stuff gets blown up, and glitter nail polish. She lives on a hilltop outside Austin, Texas, where her home office has an excellent view of Texas Hill Country. When she's not writing, she's scuba diving.